Blood on the Book

The road to death is paved with good intentions

A Novel

By

Dan Remenyi

Blood on the Book
First edition, first print 2018
Copyright© 2018 the Author

Published by: ACPIL, Reading, RG4 9SJ, United Kingdom, info@academic-conferences.org

ISBN: 978-1-911218-29-6 (book)

ISBN: 978-1-911218-68-5 (Kindle)

978-1-911218-69-2 (ePub)

Available from a large number of 24/7 book shops and www.academic-bookshop.com

Contents

About the author

Dan Remenyi BSocSc, MBA, PhD. Born in Dublin and taken to South Africa by his family at the end of the 1950s, he is a prolific writer in the field of research methodology. He has also written four history books and one novel. Over the years he has worked as a Visiting Professor at more than a dozen universities and has taught  on research training programmes on all six continents. He lives in South Oxfordshire with his wife and her bees. As the children have left there is no longer a cat or any fish. And the foxes have taken the chickens and ducks. He is a regular speaker at conferences and other events.

Chapter One

Curiosity killed the cat

-Stop. I can't give you absolution for this.

-Why not? I'm a sinner and I need forgiveness. Don't I?

-The way this thing works is that you confess, then you are contrite, then I absolve you, and give you some penance to do. Now you told me your sorry story and the harm which followed, but you haven't given me the slightest indication that you're in any way sorry for what has happened. It seems to me that from your point of view this whole affair is simply water off a duck's back.

-Well Father, I am sort of sorry, but none of this was directly my fault really.

-Oh, really? You think so?

-What do you mean? What did I actually do that was all that wrong? I had absolutely nothing to do with the murder. And all my actions were well intentioned. Yes, I told a few lies. That's all.

-And, I say *what do you mean?* back to you. You have been recklessly involved in murder and fraud – even implicating Our Holy Mother the Church in it. You've come to confession because you know you messed up. Yes, indeed you have sinned, and not just a common or garden mortal sin. No. Your sin was one of the seven cardinal or deadly sins.

-What are you getting at Father? I had nothing to do with sloth. I hadn't any involvement that could be called gluttony or wrath. I wasn't envious of anyone. I wasn't...

-Well, let's come back to the number of lies you told to so many people. Your central sin was pride my son, which some would say is the most deadly sin of them all. After all, it was pride that brought Lucifer down. In your case it was your pride in the knowledge that you could identify a dodgy manuscript that started this sad story. It was pride that you knew how to solve the financial troubles of your friends struggling to make ends meet in their charitable work. It was pride in your belief that you could somehow square things with the crooks and the thug who came to find the instigators of the fraud which swindled their clients that caused so much harm. And as for telling a few lies, you lied through your teeth again and again. You even lied to those poor monks in Rome. You are a liar of Olympic proportions.

-I am sorry.

Deep down Finn was beginning to regret the idea of going to confession.

-And I don't necessarily feel that you have told me the whole story. You are clearly a well-educated man who can present his case in the best possible light and I feel that you have been doing that with me. I am not sure you have been truthful about this woman you met in Rome either.

-But Father, I did nothing. None of the things that happened were actioned by me. I did absolutely nothing so how can these sins be laid at my doorstep?

-Think again my son. You can't just air-brush out your involvement in murder and fraud like that. Think again.

Finn's mind began to wander back to where this whole business started.

Rome. It was in Rome, at the Café de Años in the Piazza della Napoli. That extravagant indulgence started all this. Such a beautiful place, so friendly and benign. Who would have thought that a chance meeting there would ultimately lead to a million-euro fraud, a murder or was it two, and now a hit man on the loose?

Finn had returned to Rome for the first time in 20 years. To him this had been a special city where he had been an undergraduate student at the Università di Roma. He had gone to Rome because he had always been fascinated by antiquity, and when he won the prize for being the best Latin scholar in his year at the national exams, he was awarded a sizeable scholarship. It was a generous sum of money which would pay all his educational expenses, tuition, living and other costs at any university he chose. Finn's family were not well-to-do and so the scholarship had been essential to him. He decided to learn Italian and experience something of what it might have been like to live in the Eternal City. He was a natural at languages, having a great ear, and he picked up Italian relatively quickly. Finn was accepted into the University with no problem and at the beginning of the academic year he settled comfortably into the way of life of an Italian student. He had often thought about returning to Rome but for one reason or another he just never got around to it. It was the intensity of his career, he told himself. Yes, his career had been satisfactory but it didn't give him much time to pursue the leisure-orientated things in life he would really enjoy. Now he had an assignment which took him to Rome and he would be able to mix work with a lot of pleasure.

Finn was really delighted to be back in Rome and he was determined to soak up as much of the *dolce vita* as possible while he was there. As a student, even with his scholarship he had to be careful with money and now he wanted to splash out a bit. This is what brought him to the famous and outrageously expensive Café de Años. He would treat himself to the best that Rome could offer. This restaurant was the sort of place where there were no prices on the menu. If you had to ask the price then you couldn't afford it. As he sat in the corner reading the enormous gilded menu and taking in all the glitzy decor of the restaurant with the waiters fussing about in their long white aprons, his mind began to wander back to his undergraduate days. How much fun they had had as students – those wonderful days; they will never be repeated. Well, the fun had been interspersed with a lot of hard work. But fun was his main memory from those distant days. And what friends he had made at that time with many other young people from all over Europe.

He began to survey the faces of the people in the restaurant. Across the room he could see a table where there was a party of about 20. Among them there was the face of a man that looked at first vaguely familiar. The waiters were fussing even more over this table than any of the others. A large number of bottles of champagne were being opened and large dishes of caviar were being placed on the table. Finn's memories began to focus. Could that face really be Antonio? Antonio Dameri had been a drinking pal in the good old days. He could just about hear some of the voices of the people around the table and he felt that there was a good chance that this man was his old pal from university days. Finn walked across the restaurant to the large table.

This man looked very much how Finn remembered Antonio, short, plump, with a great untidy head of jet-black hair. He was or was probably close to the right age. Antonio was always dressed too smart for the occasion as was this man in the restaurant.

-Am I mistaken or are you Antonio Dameri?

-Yes. Certainly, I am. And who are you, may I ask?

-Antonio, I am Finn Kelly. Don't you recognise my mop of flaming red hair? I am still as thin as a rake which you regularly reminded me of and said was not good for my social life. I hope you remember.

-My, oh my, Finn Kelly. How about that! Gee. Well, what an amazing surprise. I am not sure I would have recognised you in the street if you hadn't recognised me first. Time does leave its mark. Where have you been all these years? How wonderful to see you again. I am truly delighted.

-Antonio, what a lovely coincidence seeing you here.

-But look, as you can see I'm rather tied up now. This is a little celebration for my sister's daughter who is getting married and the close family are getting together tonight. So it is difficult...But how about meeting tomorrow? Why don't you come to my office? It is in the centre of the city. I'll be there all day. You may know that I work for the family business. We are in the big building with the family name plastered all over it in the Piazza Venezia. I will tell the reception people to bring you right up to my suite as soon as you arrive.

-Sure. See you tomorrow late morning.

Finn mused to himself that Antonio always had the busiest social life of all his acquaintances during his university days. He always had more parties to go to than anyone else. His popularity with the girls was legendary and maybe for that reason he never managed to keep a girlfriend for more than a few months. Finn wondered if Antonio had changed.

The following morning Finn was free. He had put aside his first whole day in Rome to take a stroll down memory lane and to visit the old haunts where he used to hang out with his pals. His favourite places were still all there. The coffee bars, the little restaurants, the quiet little squares tucked away down back alleys still all functioned like they did 20 years before. Yes, little had really changed, very little indeed. The streets were just as grimy as they had been and certainly no one had come with pots of paint to smarten up the old buildings. Away from the main piazza and boulevards of Rome the city hadn't been developed in a very long time. Despite general improvements in the Italian economy there was still a lot of poverty around, albeit out of sight to the general tourist. After a few hours of strolling around the centre of the city, he headed off for the Piazza Venezia. What a big building the Dameri Centre was! Finn had no idea that Antonio came from such a well-heeled family. It was going to be an interesting catch up with Antonio's experiences of the last couple of decades.

5

Entering through the large glass door at the front of the building, passing the smartly dressed security guards who nodded at him, Finn easily found the reception desk.

Antonio was as good as his word and the reception people quickly escorted him to the top floor where Finn was first greeted by Antonio's PA, and then escorted into the largest office suite he had ever been in. Finn thought to himself that the space was big enough to house 10 of his colleagues. Antonio came out from behind his desk to grab Finn by the shoulders and to repeat last night's salutations.

- Finn, what a wonderful surprise to have seen you last night. I have so little contact with friends from our university days that it is a real pleasure to bump into one every few years. Many of my friends went to America or moved north to take industrial jobs. I hope you're in Rome for some time. It will be great to see you and as you would say, chew the cud, as I have much to tell you and show you about this wonderful city which I remember you loved so much. For how long are you going to be here?

-I have an assignment I think will take several weeks, maybe even a month or two. But the work is going to be pretty intensive so I'm not going to have too much time on my hands. But it's great to see you again and it will be fun to catch up with your news.

-So what are you doing these days?

-I live in Dublin. I work at O'Connell College and I am here on an assignment with the Vatican.

-The Vatican! Do tell me more about the work you are actually doing? I recall that your undergraduate degree was in history as was mine, and I also recollect you were not terribly sure what you were going to do after you graduated. What did you end up doing? -When I returned to Dublin I found getting a job quite difficult. I wasn't that fussy about what sort of a job it was but there was a recession at that time. There had been lots of recessions in Ireland during those years.

Times were really tough for everyone in Ireland. But I had some international contacts and one thing led to another and resulted in my being offered an internship at the British Museum in London.

-That must have been favoloso, as we say in Italian.

A waiter dressed in a white uniform quietly entered the office.

-Gentlemen, coffee?

-Yes, Guido. My usual please.

-Finn, what would you like?

- I'll take a chance and have the same as you.

Finn continued.

-I spent three years there training as a curator. Yes. The three years were great. The work was fascinating but the conditions were tough. Juniors have to work hard to get established and the pay was awful. Living in London on low pay is not for sissies. But I was eventually offered a fulltime position and a couple of years later I won a scholarship to do a doctorate to study mediaeval art and literature at the Sorbonne in Paris.

-I can't remember if you spoke French? I remember helping you with your Italian, and by the time your degree was finished you were of course excellent. You spoke like a native Roman.

No, I didn't and that meant intensive language courses again. But it was a great career breakthrough. And what a beautiful city Paris is especially when one is a student, particularly a student of the arts.

-Wow! That is really fantastic, and then what did you do after that?

-Antonio, after Paris was finished I had some serious career decisions to make. I went back again to Dublin. I guess my roots are truly in Ireland. Conditions had changed there and having the doctorate from the Sorbonne was a great help and I was offered a position at O'Connell College.

-Hey. Wasn't that the atheist place? And aren't you a Catholic?

-Yes, indeed, to both your questions. When O'Connell College was set up there was a policy of no religious affiliation and the media took it to task. The press deliberately made up the atheist story. What actually happened was that the College especially wanted to avoid any chance of the Catholic Church interfering with its policies and practices, and 50 years ago when it was set up that was enough for it to be branded atheist. But in the past few decades the relationship between the College and the press has mellowed. That mudslinging episode is all history.

-So that's all history.

-Yes. It hasn't been mentioned for ages.

-Glad to hear that.

-O'Connell College offered many opportunities in my research field and five years later I found myself being offered the Fitzwilliam Chair of Mediaeval History.

-That really sounds…… as you say very POSH indeed.

-Yes it was, and I suppose it still is. Since then I've been associated with the University but I've also done a lot of applied research and some consultancy and that is why in I am Rome on a project for the Curia. I am sure you know them – the crowd that looks after administration for the Vatican. They are said to be the real power behind the throne of Saint Peter.

-Yes. They are well known to us Romans.

-So what about you Antonio? What have you been up to in the last … 20 years?

-But first Finn, what about marriage?

-I didn't do that. Far too busy or I didn't meet the right girl as some people would say. I have remained single to this day. There is no one on the horizon. Bachelorhood suits me perfectly.

Antonio reached for a cigarette from the solid silver box on the table but paused and thought better of it.

-My life has been definitely less exciting. When I finished my degree at the Università di Roma I went into the family business. Of course I was expected by my father to start at the bottom and he designed a special apprenticeship for me. It was tough working at the bottom. No allowances were made for me. I got little pay and plenty of tough jobs. Anyway after five years my father decided that I should get some specialised business education and he encouraged me to apply for an MBA at Harvard.

-Isn't it difficult to get into the Harvard MBA programme?

- Certainly. It wasn't a cinch to get in but I managed it and off I went to Boston for the two years. Boston is not an easy place in which to live. In the summer everyone swelters with the heat and the humidity is awful, and in winters it is as cold as ... I was going to say hell but maybe that is the wrong figure of speech.

-Yes. I know the climate in Boston. We have our share of American students at O'Connell.

-I am sure you know what I mean. That degree wasn't like our old days as undergraduates in Rome. We all had to, as our American friends would say, work our butts off seven days a week. But it was interesting and indeed, at the end of the degree there were many great job offers floating around if I'd had the freedom to take one. But alas I was required to come home and take an executive role in the family business. Not that I should complain but the family is always the family. Having Francesca with me was helpful. I met her in Boston and we married as soon as I had finished the degree. The

9

family would have preferred me to marry a homespun Italian girl, but an American Italian was, I guess, the second best.

-And any children?

-Now we have three gorgeous girls.

-And how did your return to the family firm go for you?

-Not so well at first. There are a lot of people who saw me as the boss's son who had been made into the Crown Prince and was just sitting around waiting to be promoted to the board of directors. Envy is a terrible thing. On top of this, there was a China crisis.

-What China crisis? Was there a China crisis?

-Yes. Indeed there was for us. I don't know if you remember but seven or eight years ago the Chinese government devalued their currency and changed their trading regulations which really affected our international business. Initially it hit us quite hard and we ended up having to close three factories.

-Not nice.

-It was decided I would be the man who would handle these closures and all the job redundancies associated with them. It wasn't pleasant work and I tried to get out of it but the family insisted. I got the nickname in the company of Antonio the Hatchet Man which was not only unfair but quite difficult to cope with. You know how affable I am and how I like to be liked by everyone. Anyway I felt I couldn't leave the family business so I just grinned and knuckled down and got on with it.

-Oh dear. That wasn't good. Of course it has changed by now has it not?

-Yes, indeed. You see my father and my uncle were killed in a tragic air crash a couple of years ago.

-Sorry to hear that.

-They had been flying themselves down to Sicily for an important meeting with some old Sicilian families about opening up new factories and the light aircraft they were flying in was caught in a terrible storm and crashed.

-I remember reading about that but I didn't associate the accident with you. It must have been a horrible shock to everyone in the family.

-I had been telling my papa for years that he shouldn't be flying himself around in a single engine aircraft. But he loved flying. He had thousands of hours on his licence and would not give it up. That day he and my uncle were really stupid in that they took a risk no professional aviator would take. The weather forecast was unclear but the prospect of an electric storm that time of the year over the Mediterranean was high. They were flying themselves and they were rather cocky.

-Oh dear.

-It was all over the Italian papers at the time. The media in general was pretty unkind to them saying it was irresponsible flying, and the truth is, that it probably was. And some crazy people in the media suggested that my family was somehow connected with the Mafia. It was just crazy.

-Wow.

-It caused a lot of upset.

-Sorry to hear that.

-So overnight I became the boss - the Il Supremo. It was ... professionally quite a shock. That is over and above the personal impact of losing a father in an avoidable accident and the adverse media that came with it. The next day I was dragged up to the top floor of the building. I got the office half the size of a tennis court. I was given two personal assistants. I was allocated the firm's poshest car with the uniformed chauffeur. I had a queue of people needing me to make decisions on all sorts of things that I had to become instantly familiar with. My father and uncle ran the business, at least made all the important decisions together with little help from anyone else, so it was a bit of a jig-saw puzzle at first.

-Clearly you coped?

-Yes indeed. But more than anything else, it is truly surprising how popular you become when you are the boss. Everyone was madly enthusiastic about my new vision for the business and about how I would lead it to higher and better levels of profitability.

-And did it?

-Again yes. Having my hand on the rudder was initially daunting but I must say I quickly grew to enjoy it very much and I found that running the business was much less taxing than I had anticipated. There is nothing terribly complex about our business. Our competitive advantage is related to a sustained market leadership over several decades and it really is difficult for anyone to shake us out of that position.

-Well, Antonio, I'm glad to hear that. What did you …

-And furthermore this business was much more profitable than I ever imagined. My family were careful to make sure that I didn't have much money during my university days. My father was secretive and he had stashed his money away in all sorts of old socks he kept well hidden under the bed and in Swiss bank accounts. I hadn't realised what it was going to be like to be seriously rich. I couldn't resist the new Ferrari and I bought the biggest Rolls-Royce I could find and a few other toys for boys. I decided that a villa in Capri, on the really ritzy side of the island, would be nice and I went ahead with that as well.

-I see it has become a really hard life for you! So many decisions about how to spend your money? If only we all had that problem!

Antonio couldn't help chuckling.

-But there's only so much of the stuff that you can spend money on before you get bored and then what is left? Well, for me it was art. I picked up a number of nice pieces I really enjoy, and I would be pleased to show you if you can find the time to spend a few hours with me at my home over the next few weeks? There is one piece in particular I think you will be thrilled with. It is a magnificent book. I live only a few kilometres out of the city.

Finn's mind returned to the confessional. That damned book he thought to himself. If he just hadn't been so bloody curious. Finn's grandmother used to always say that *curiosity killed the cat and information makes you fat*. He never really believed her. Boy oh boy, had he changed his mind.

Finn's thoughts drifted back to the Café de Años in Rome.

-Certainly, I would be delighted to do that. Is the art modern?

-Mostly. Although there are a couple of older pieces I also picked up. It is really quite an eclectic collection.

-Well I know about art during the mediaeval period but it would be fun to see what you have brought together. And I would be delighted to meet your wife and girls.

-So, Finn tell me about your project with the Holy Father at the Vatican?

-The Pope isn't involved. At least I hope not. I haven't met him and I have no wish to. I don't want anything to do with that end of the Vatican. As I mentioned to you, I not only research and teach at O'Connell College, I also do some consultancy work which has largely been to do with authenticating pieces of artwork that have recently been discovered. It's interesting how many so-called "lost pieces" have recently come to light, in Italy, the Balkans and even the Middle East. There have been discoveries all over the place.

-Yes Finn. I saw a documentary about that on the television.

-And, of course, there is a danger that some of these pieces could turn out not to be what they are first believed to be. In some cases there is even the possibility of fraud. So I specialise in identifying paintings from the mediaeval period. It's a great challenge. I find it really interesting. It is well paid. Of course it is difficult to be certain about some pieces that one sees, and there is a lot of responsibility associated with the decisions I have to make.

-I bet.

-This type of work is often quite secretive and I have signed a contract with the Vatican forbidding me to talk about the project I'm working on at present but it is not dissimilar to the work I've been doing in the consulting arena over the last decade. I was particularly pleased to take this job as it was going to take me back to Rome. It's really great to see you again as I really wanted to reconnect with my undergraduate days. I have often missed the flowing Chianti, not to mention the pasta and the gelato ... and of course the friends.

-That is a really interesting thing you're doing Finn, and I have to tell you that I have a direct connection to this world of rediscovered "lost art". You see a year or so ago after I had bought my first piece of art from the Gallery Garibaldi just across the piazza, I was called by the director and invited to attend a special showing of a piece of "lost art" that had recently been discovered by the monks in the hills behind Perugia.

-"Lost art"?

-Do you remember there was an earthquake that ran along part of the Apennines and shook the hell out of a number of villages and small towns leaving hundreds dead and several thousand people homeless?

Well, one of the casualties of that earthquake was an old monastery, which was severely damaged. In order to make it safe they had to tear down walls and behind one of the walls they found a trapdoor which led into a cellar that no one knew anything about. It was completely dark and surprisingly dry. They reckoned it had not been opened for several hundred years. In the cellar they found an old metal box which was full of books.

-Truly?

-These were illuminated manuscripts dated around 1320. According to the Director of the Gallery, this was the find of the century.

-I wholeheartedly agree.

-He was unforthcoming as to what precisely was in the box but he said that one book in particular had now been fully authenticated and that it was a work by monks which had been heavily influenced by Dante Alighieri's Divine Comedy.

-Dante Alighieri. Now there's a name to conjure with!

-This was considered a most important find. Now because the monks desperately needed money to rebuild the monastery they had decided to put this piece of art on the market provided it went into the hands of a connoisseur who would cherish it. The manuscript was absolutely unique. It gave a completely new view of the life and times of Dante and it provided a different perspective on his way of thinking. The Gallery identified me as an appropriate collector and as a prospective purchaser. And it turned out that they were asking a relatively modest sum for this masterpiece.

-And how much was that? I bet it didn't come cheap!

-Well, after a little negotiation they managed to let me have it for 1.5. Yes Euros 1.5 million. It was hard to negotiate because the money was going to the Church, after all. As far as I was concerned that makes it a really good cause. It's hard to negotiate with impoverished monks from a wrecked monastery in the mountains. I felt a bit of a swine trying to beat them down, but you know price negotiation is now deeply embedded in my DNA. So I did get a discount from the original asking price.

-My goodness. And nice to have that sort of money to spend on interesting things like that.

-Yes it is.

-And Antonio, I presume that the manuscript was authenticated by some scholarly authority.

-Yes.

-And who did the authentication?

-Professor…. Oh I can't remember his name now. He is a well-established figure at the University of Tontos which as you know is the most famous university in Italy, maybe the most famous university in the world. Their antiquarian scholars are amongst the most renowned in the world. I really would trust their opinion on any matter such as this.

-I would be delighted to see the book. Academically it is right down my street, so to speak. Just let me know what time would suit you and I'll make sure that I'm free.

-Why don't we do it next Friday? Come to my home at about 11 AM. Here is my personal card with my address and other details on it. And we will look at the book and then we can have lunch. Francesca and the girls won't be there then, but we still have a lot more catching up to do.

Back in the confessional, Finn again thought, but more strongly, Antonio's bloody book. Why had he become quite so involved?

In Rome the next few days rushed past Finn as he joined the many experts working for the Vatican. When he reported to the reception office he was greeted with a number of computerised forms to complete. He was impressed by this use of the technology as it saved him some time. He was then issued with an Identity Card, an email address and a number of passwords and codes enabling his entry to various buildings.

-Professor Kelly, please wear your Identity Card on your lapel whenever you are in any of our buildings. It will prevent you from being stopped and interrogated by our security people.

-Certainly.

-Also, while you are in Italy it is useful for you to keep the Vatican Identity Card on you at all times. If you need to establish your identity, having this card will give you special status in many institutions in Italy. Employees of the Vatican are generally considered to be special people in this country. It's as though you have diplomatic status within this country.

Finn was escorted to a large general office where he was introduced to three other members of the team with whom he would be working. There was an expert from Poland, Romania and Turkey. To his relief they all spoke perfect English and pretty good Italian. Finn was going to enjoy this project.

Finn instantly became fully absorbed in his work. The days of the week rushed by and when Friday arrived he half regretted that he had agreed to go and visit Antonio Dameri. But he had never been to a multi-millionaire's home before and had never visited the leafy suburbs in the hills behind Rome. So he decided to take a few hours off and indulge his curiosity as to what this previously "lost art" was really about.

Chapter Two

Antonio's book

The house was on an estate of maybe 20 hectares of immaculate lawns and collections of a series of different types of trees, all fitting into the perfectly planned landscape. It had clearly been designed and developed by an architect who had been given a free hand and a large cheque book. The taxi took Finn up the long drive to the front door. The house had been built in a classic Italianate style with its own Venetian tower and was big enough to be a private school or some similar institution. Security was clearly an important issue in this part of Rome, as there were tall walls all around as well as electric fencing on top of the walls. The driver had had to press a button at the large wrought iron gate to have it opened and so by the time they reached the front door Finn was greeted by what he would have described as The Butler who was immaculately dressed in an appropriate black suit and spoke impeccable English with no traceable accent. He definitely had been the recipient of elocution lessons.

-Yes, Professor Kelly. How nice of you to visit us. Welcome to the home of Signor Dameri. I trust your journey from the city has been pleasant. Signor Dameri is expecting you. Please follow me into the library.

No expense had been spared on this house. It was obvious that it had been decorated under the watchful eye of one of Italy's great artistic decorators. Finn knew this to be the sort of life he would never be able to aspire to, and he wouldn't want to either, but nonetheless, he enjoyed being a voyeur, even if only for a short time.

The library consisted of ceiling-high, wall-to-wall bookcases displaying all the great classics in the five languages of which Antonio Dameri was a fluent speaker. The floor was covered in expensive Persian carpets and rugs. Finn, who could never resist sticking his nose into other people's books, would have loved to have been left on his own to browse in the library for two or three hours; however, within a few minutes Antonio appeared with a big welcoming grin that showed how much he was about to enjoy showing his masterpiece to his old friend. He did not waste any time in getting down to the business of the visit.

-It is kept in a room which is climate-controlled. You do have to wear a special pair of gloves when you turn the pages and of course a surgical mask so you don't deposit too much carbon dioxide and water vapour on the pages. I'll give you all the gear when we enter the room below. Also I'd be grateful if you wouldn't stay too long looking at the book. I'm told that even with the controlled light, the book should not be subjected to brightness for more than about an hour at a time. Well, maybe an hour and a half would be a maximum.

-Oh, I'm well aware of all this sort of stuff. I am sure you realise this is not the first time I will have handled antiquarian books. It happens all the time in libraries around Europe where the more precious artefacts are stored. What will be your attitude to my taking a few photographs? It would be nice for me to have a few mementos to look at and think about while I'm in Rome.

-Well as you know if you don't use a flash it won't do the book any harm. So go ahead. By the way, the Gallery told me that the monks were not keen to have it known too widely that they had discovered these treasures. The monks appear to have thought that if the word gets out that they have a number of artistic treasures, too many people will come rushing to see them, thereby spoiling the peace and tranquillity they are accustomed to having in the monastery. So although I was not bound to secrecy, I was told that they would be grateful if I was discreet as to whom I told that I had acquired this long-lost treasure.

Finn had been well trained both during his years at the British Museum and again during his doctoral studies at the Sorbonne in

Paris. He knew how to handle precious artefacts from the mediaeval period and could detect the tell-tale signs of authenticity. He really enjoyed the challenge of reading the ancient script, and looking for secret messages in the wonderfully coloured illustrations. He spent a good hour pouring over the work, taking a number of photos which he assured Antonio were only for his own erudition and enjoyment and he would not spread them around. The piece of work now in front of him was simply magnificent. The craftsmanship was as good as Finn had ever seen. It was unfortunate that it had been lost to humanity for so many years and it was lucky that it had been preserved so well all these years, locked up in a box in a cellar. Finn was struck by how fortunate it was to still have access to this masterpiece.

Antonio had arranged for lunch to be served on the terrace next to the swimming pool where he and Finn relaxed, enjoying a glass of fine Italian wine while reminiscing about the old days. They once again reassured each other that the Università di Roma was a great place to have started their formal education and that the cultural exposure they had experienced was as important as the knowledge they had acquired.

-Finn, on the topic of cultural experiences, I was in Ireland a few years ago. The Italian trade ministry and the Irish equivalent organised a trip for leading industrialists and I was invited to participate. It was a great experience. We spent a week, mostly in Dublin but we also visited Cork and the Ring of Kerry and Connemara. Of course it rained a lot. But that didn't spoil the occasion. The Irish government wined and dined us extensively. They must have especially imported a lot of really good Italian wines, the sort of stuff you can't easily buy even in Italy. We saw a number of interesting historical sites.

And then we were taken to see the Book of Kells, at that other College in Dublin. You know it was the first time I had taken a proper look at an illuminated manuscript.

-It is a pity you didn't call on me. But of course you didn't know that I was in Dublin. I would have liked to have shown you around.

-Yes. It would have been great to have met up then. I was especially impressed by the Book of Kells. I guess it was having seen this magnificent piece of art that made me interested, when the Gallery Garibaldi approached me to buy the book which had been found in Montebello.

-But Antonio, the Book of Kells is the pride and joy of the Irish nation. You would never find it in a private collection.

-I know. And I am not trying to compare what I have to the Book of Kells. I am just saying that it was my visit to Dublin where I saw the great book that aroused my interest in the subject of illuminated manuscripts.

A couple of hours went by in a flash and Finn realised that he needed to get back to his day job at the Vatican. It was not necessary to call a taxi as Antonio's chauffeur was standing by to take Finn back to his office. This was Antonio's Rolls-Royce, a car of such elegance Finn had never been driven in before. This ritzy car and the even more ritzy house, looking like it had been especially developed for a billionaires' ideal homes exhibition and probably needing six or maybe more servants to maintain, made Finn wonder about the materialistic spirit that was central to Antonio's life. Finn wondered if his great wealth had actually brought him any real contentment. He had to admit it appeared to have done so.

On the way back Finn began to think about the manuscript he had just examined. It was indeed magnificent. But there was something about it that bothered him. During his studies at the Sorbonne, Finn had specialised in the period stretching from the 11th to the 14th century and he felt that he was fully familiar with all the books having any association with Dante. There had never been mention of a lost manuscript and what he had just examined did not entirely fit in to how Finn understood the body of work of the period, or how

Dante's ideas had influenced illuminated manuscripts. There was nothing suspicious about the book itself, except perhaps that it was so well preserved. And Finn knew that its good condition could have been the result of pure chance, or rather good fortune. Nonetheless Finn realised that he was going to think carefully about what he had just seen and he was going to make some enquiries.

Finn's work gave him access to the Vatican archives and as he did not need to work on Saturdays and was required to honour the Sabbath, he now had some time on his hands. He decided that he would spend a while exploring the databases within the Vatican systems on the subject of 14th century illuminated manuscripts and literature related to or influenced by Dante. The Vatican had been relatively slow to embrace computer technology. Initially it was thought to be too worldly to be put at the direct service of the Church, but over the years it had crept in slowly, until about five years ago when the new Pontiff decided that it was necessary to do some serious catching-up on the technology front. At that point, the Holy Father commanded his administrative officials in the Roman Curia to come of age and to employ modern technology wherever it would make the operation of the Church more efficient and effective. Leading edge systems were acquired for both administration and security purposes. It was rumoured to have cost hundreds of millions, but no one was ever allowed to speak about this. Money was, to all intents and purposes, a silent issue in the Vatican. Now Finn had all this technology at his disposal and he was thrilled to be able to use it.

It did not take long for Finn to reassure himself that there were no references whatsoever in any of the documents in the Vatican databases to special treasures being found in a monastery in the hills which had been wrecked by the earthquake, nor was there any suggestion that any lost treasures dating back to the 14th century had been recovered. This was no surprise to him. He wondered if this was because it was so recent, or was there a more complicated explanation? Finn knew the Catholic Church well enough to know that there were pockets of secrecy in various parts of the Church where special interests operated without the information necessarily being passed on to the authorities at the Vatican. The Church may look like a unitary hierarchical body from the outside, but there was some flexibility within it if one knew how to play the game. So, he would have to do a bit more snooping about.

Finn had another idea. He had used the inter-loan services of the Vatican library a number of times over the years and he knew the head of this service, Monsignor Henri Dubois. This man had previously worked at the Sorbonne where Finn had met him when he was a research student. Dubois, a small slightly-built man with thick horn-rimmed spectacles, who kept his head shaved at all times, was an excellent scholar and because of their mutual interest in mediaeval art they had stayed in contact over the years after Finn completed his doctorate. In fact a few years earlier they had collaborated on some research together. When Monsignor Dubois was appointed to the Vatican, Finn sometimes used these library services in both his research and consulting endeavours.

-Henri, I wonder if you could assist me. I am in need of some serious library searches and I think that you are just the person to help me with this. I'm interested in refreshing my knowledge on illuminated manuscripts and the more important elements of the body of work related to Dante Alighieri. I'm especially interested in what he wrote in the last years of his life and whether there was any suggestion that there may have been some incomplete works that had not been finalised and perhaps lost.

-What an interesting question Finn. I know that you specialised in that period during your doctoral studies and on this subject you probably know just about as much as anyone alive. Why do you want to look into this again?

Finn took a deep breath and lied, while crossing his fingers in his pocket.

-No special reason, Henri. You know what academics are like. Pure curiosity. I saw a copy of the Divina Commedia in a bookshop window the other day and it reminded me of how much I appreciated Dante's work and that led me to feel that I should spend a little time going over what he achieved in the last years of his life. I am also interested to find out if there is any new research published since I last looked at this topic. You know me, every now and again I get a crazy idea.

-Well, all the resources of this library are at your disposal on a 24/7 basis. I will send you all the necessary passwords and codes. And, of course, I will be happy to introduce you to anyone in my network whom you think might be able to provide any information that will facilitate your enquiries. Just let me know what I can do to assist you.

-Thank you.

-A pleasure, Finn.

-I appreciate your assistance very much.

For the rest of the weekend Finn brought himself up to date with all the issues related to both illuminated manuscripts and the work of Dante Alighieri. He read papers from all the leading scholars in the area, and then he read reviews of these papers and critiques of the reviews, until he felt that he really understood all the key issues involved.

Finn found a series of papers written by American academics who were concerned about how many discoveries there had been, over the past 10 years, of lost masterpieces. Work by several great masters including Leonardo da Vinci, Rembrandt and Van Gogh, which had not formerly been known, had recently been discovered. These academics were questioning the authenticity of some of these works and the vast sums of money they were fetching at auctions. Although Finn had been aware of these pieces of art he was a little surprised by the amount and the intensity of the criticism of the American academic and art critic establishment. If some of these are fakes, then they must be very good indeed.

Finn was amused by how much new work had been done on the topic of Dante Alighieri since his earlier studies in Paris, and now he was even more convinced that there was something not quite right with the artefact for which Antonio had paid €1.5 million.

Finn now realised that his next step in solving this puzzle would have to be making contact with Gallery Garibaldi to find out what they knew about the provenance of the work. He felt that at least they should be able to guide him towards the monastery where it was found and perhaps introduce him to the professor from the University of Tontos who had authenticated it.

Kneeling in the confessional Finn became somewhat surprised at how his reminiscences were becoming enjoyable and how they were helping him dilute the resentment which was building up in him towards the priest.

Chapter Three
The Gallery Garibaldi

In Finn's office in the Vatican the Director of Facilities was a lady called Maria Abano, who looked after visiting dignitaries and who it was said was acquainted with just about everything and everybody worth knowing in Rome. She was an attractive, charming, green eyed mature looking woman who was perhaps 40 years old, with a light olive complexion, and who had worked in the Vatican for many years. She always dressed impeccably in the latest styles produced by the fashion houses of Milan. She clearly stood out as the most elegant of the women employed in that Department. Having acquired a degree in mathematics, and teaching in a secondary school for a few years, she decided that a career in administration would be more interesting and rewarding to her.

Maria had joined the Curia as a junior. Her professional work ethic was perfect for the culture and she quickly moved from being a junior administrator to a more senior post and finally to being Head of Facilities. This was a most important job, as without the right services visiting experts would not be able to perform as well as expected. It was a job that required a high degree of diplomatic skill as well as insight as to who were the most influential and/or powerful people she had to deal with. She was in every way an overwhelming success and made personal friends of many senior officials, as well as the visitors to the Vatican.

Maria had taken an instant liking to Finn whom she thought to be handsome, softly spoken and clearly distinguished in his field. She helped him find suitable accommodation and had advised him on restaurants, the theatre, and other attractions he might be interested in.

So, Finn asked Maria if she could make some enquiries about the Gallery Garibaldi and make an appointment for him to see the

Director. This was easy as she knew the place well and was familiar with the Director, Mr Jeremy Williamson, whom she had met a couple of times at Vatican functions. He was an elderly American who had settled in Rome some 30 years before and had built up a substantial business catering to the eccentric artistic desires of the rich and the famous, not only in Rome but all over Italy. In fact, Gallery Garibaldi had a growing international client base with connections in London, Tokyo, Boston and Paris. The gallery regularly attracted media attention. It was certainly a place to be seen.

Three days later Finn found himself being welcomed to the Gallery Garibaldi, the biggest art emporium in central Rome. Gallery Garibaldi had what they called four salons, each of which specialised in a different period or type of art. There was the Roman salon where one could find some trinkets from the period of Claudius onwards. There was the mediaeval salon which was of most interest to Finn and he made a note to come back and have a closer look at the exhibits. Then there was an impressionist area and finally there was even some pop art. The management of the Gallery clearly wanted to satisfy all tastes.

Jeremy Williamson was an active-looking man, probably of some 70 years who sported a well-tailored suit from an overpriced Milanese fashion house and an oversized bow tie. He was certainly a suave man who exuded a high degree of confidence. His deeply lined face suggested a life full of experiences and over-exposure to intensive sunlight. He had a soft but clearly distinguishable Bostonian accent. He was waiting at the reception desk when Finn arrived. His steely eyes gave the impression of being entirely focused on whoever he spoke to.

-Welcome Professor Kelly to our Gallery and to Rome, although I believe that you know our city well.

-How did you know who I was?

-Maria Abano described you well and you look like a mediaevalist working for the Vatican, if you will forgive me for making such a personal observation. And of course, Maria is very astute in her observations.

-Thank you for the welcome to Rome and yes, I know Rome well enough. I spent my undergraduate years here and wonderful years they were......

-That's unusual. We get a fair share of foreign postgraduate students here but not that many undergraduates from abroad, although today with the EU and all that we really don't regard Ireland as being abroad.

-Well it's good to be back in the Eternal City again.

-So what can I do for you, Professor Kelly?

-Mr Williamson, twenty years ago one of my class mates at the Università di Roma was Antonio Dameri. I guess he is well known in Rome today.

-Yes. I imagine so.

-I visited Antonio the other day and was privileged to be shown his spectacular manuscript. I understand he purchased it from you.

-And?

-I wanted to know more about the piece you sold him.

-What do you mean?

-I am interested in old manuscripts, the type of artefact he bought from you. I am a mediaevalist and I found what Antonio had really quite fascinating. I had no idea that documents like that were available to any member of the public, even vastly rich ones like Antonio. -You are absolutely right. Artefacts like that do not become available often. We are fortunate enough to come across such manuscripts from time to time and it is our pleasure to be able to match them up with those individuals who appreciate this type of work. It is a splendid piece, is it not?

-Oh yes. Quite so. Do you have any others?

-Not at the moment, Professor.

-Well, I am interested in how the Dameri artefact was found and how it was authenticated?

Jeremy Williamson's attitude changed. He folded his arms and glared at Finn.

-Look. It is quite wrong of you to expect me to answer questions about this. The matters you speak of are private. The Gallery Garibaldi is only a conduit. We put our clients in touch with those who have remarkable things for which they want to find new owners. And by the way, we don't discuss the purchases our clients make with anyone ... not even academics. This Gallery's reputation is built on complete confidentiality and we guard our reputation quite jealously. A man of your experience and even reputation should surely have known this?

-Quite so. My curiosity, however, is purely academic. I am a university professor and teacher and mediaeval manuscripts are a special interest of mine.

-Then you should confine your interest to academic matters.

Finn was not quite sure what this comment actually meant but before he could say anything Williamson continued.

-If you like you may leave your contact details with the receptionist and if any other similar object comes to our attention as being on the market, we will let you know.

-Well, Mr Williamson, as an academic I am unlikely to be able to afford anything that Gallery Garibaldi would bring to the market. Anyway thank you for seeing me.

-Don't mention it, Professor.

What a disaster Finn thought to himself as he walked back to his office in the Vatican. He hadn't handled that well. Williamson's reaction was surprising. What might the suave American have to hide? If the art was legit why not talk to an academic about it? If it wasn't then it would be a different matter. Finn thought that this experience didn't bode well for Antonio's book.

It was now clear to Finn that if he wanted to pursue his interest in Antonio's mediaeval manuscript he would have to tackle the question from a different direction. Firstly, he would make some enquiries at the University of Tontos and after that he would visit the site where the manuscript was found. After being in Rome continuously for a few weeks Finn felt that a trip to the Italian countryside would be a nice diversion.

It was well known that the earthquake had been centred in the vicinity of the village of Montebello near the town of Perugia, and that the ancient abbey of the Order of Saint Francis Picallo had been heavily damaged. Because the Abbey was over 1000 years old it had been a major international news item. It was reported in the media that many exquisite murals on the walls had been destroyed. They were simply irreplaceable. On this occasion a number of countries had sent emergency aid to Italy to help relieve the suffering of the villagers.

Finn remembered that little was retrieved from the ruined monastery and at that time he had thought that rather surprising.

Montebello was a few hundred kilometres from Rome high in the Apennine Mountains and was not a place that Finn would have the time to rush off to easily. He was also quite familiar with the Department of Mediaeval Studies at the University of Tontos and he knew he would not have much difficulty in tracing the professor who had authenticated the manuscript. But for the immediate future Finn needed to focus on his own work with the Vatican that was turning out to be more interesting than he had thought, while at the same time being considerably more challenging.

Chapter Four

A little empirical research

By the end of the following week Finn had settled into his routine and was feeling more relaxed about his workload. There was in fact more work to do than was initially envisaged and the Curia had decided to extend the contract formerly agreed upon by Finn and O'Connell College and therefore he would be in a position to stay a little longer in Rome.

Finn decided to call his contact at University of Tontos - that great institution all Italians could be proud of. As he had envisaged it was easy to establish that Professor Max Ronanelli had done the authentication work for the manuscripts found at the Abbey in Montebello. Max had a worldwide reputation as an outstanding mediaevalist scholar. He had not only been published in many academic journals but he had also written a number of popular books on the subject and made some documentary films for Italian television. There was no doubt that he was a real authority in this field.

Professor Ronanelli's secretary appeared to want to be helpful but the work Finn was interested in had been done a few years ago and the Professor had since retired from the department. He had stayed on in the university beyond the usual retirement age but when at last he turned 75 the Dean of the faculty asked him to accept the university's retirement package. When he left he took all his records and files and no one in the department had any contact with the owner of this work.

Furthermore, it was sad to see that Ronanelli's health had not been all that good for the last few years and it was clear that he needed to be much less active. In fact, over the last few months he had become quite seriously ill. It was being whispered that dementia was beginning to set in.

Finn expressed how sad he was to hear this but wondered if he could have just a few minutes with the old man. But Finn was told quite firmly it was unlikely he would be able to speak to the Professor at this stage. A dead end, thought Finn.

So, Finn decided that he would have to take a few days off and go up the mountains to Montebello. This was not an unappealing prospect and it was just a matter of making sure that he had a couple of clear free days as he did not fancy the idea of making a return journey in one day.

However, before Finn had been able to finalise any of the necessary arrangements, a puzzling message was left for him at his office while he was out visiting some of the artworks he was assessing. He had received a call from the personal assistant of Cardinal Victor Baffasa inviting him to take afternoon tea with the Cardinal at his home. Finn was somewhat surprised as he had not met the Cardinal and had never before been invited to a Cardinal's home. Yes, he had bumped into a few Cardinals over the years due to his work, but Finn felt that this was going to be special. He wondered which aspect of the work he was doing with the Curia the Cardinal would be interested in, and perhaps the Cardinal might give him some more background to the works of art with which he was involved.

Finn was informed that the Cardinal would send a car for him later that afternoon. Even if he had been busy at that time, and he was not, this invitation was too interesting to decline. Finn decided to do a little research about Cardinal Victor Baffasa.

Finn's web search revealed a lot of bland information. The Cardinal worked in the Office of the Secretariat of State in the Roman Curia. He was born in Sicily of poor parents and had entered the church at an unusually early age. He had acquired a number of degrees in Canon Law at Catholic Universities. He was a polyglot, speaking 6 languages. There was no mention of what he was responsible for or anything about his current life. He was just another very important man dressed in a scarlet suit - or should one say, dress that would have been the envy of Santa Claus.

So, Finn turned to the lady who knew the members of the Curia.

-Maria, do you know, or do you know anything about, Cardinal Victor Baffasa?

-I have seen him at an occasional function I have had to attend but I know him mostly by reputation. The Cardinal has also had visiting experts here from time to time and I have looked after them. He is an unusual looking man. Why do you ask?

-I have been invited to tea with him this afternoon. He is sending a car for me.

-Lucky you. He must know that you are important.

-What can you tell me about him?

-He is one of the younger ones. He's in his late 60s. You know most of the members of the College of Cardinals are much older. There are over 200 Cardinals and most of them are in their 80s or 90s. Baffasa is said to be well connected in Italian society. His family has strong political connections, especially in the South of the country and of course in Sicily. He has been involved in trying to sort out some of the scandals which have plagued the Church in recent years. So, he is quite the warrior. Cardinal Baffasa is reputed to have the private ear of the Pope, that would make him very important, but one can never be too sure of the veracity of gossip like that. I wonder why he might want to see you. Have you any idea?

-No. Not really. The work I am doing does not report directly to anyone as high up in the hierarchy of the Curia as a Cardinal. Anyway I am sure that the experience will be interesting.

-Probably. But it could also be boring.

-Do you have any advice about dealing with Cardinals?

-Tread carefully. Cardinals are Princes of the Church and as such are important people. They can be touchy and it is never good to upset any of them. And Cardinal Baffasa is considered a powerful man.

At the appointed time, a large Vatican limousine arrived to pick up Finn and take him to the Cardinal's home. He was unaccustomed to be travelling in such a vehicle – big luxurious seats with such enormous legroom. He wondered if there was a secret cocktail cabinet built into the back panel behind the driver. If there was a secret compartment, Finn couldn't see it so he dismissed that idea as being unworthy of him. On the way Finn mused over what the home of a Cardinal should be called. As Maria had said Cardinals were regarded as Princes in the Catholic Church, therefore perhaps they lived in palaces?

On arrival Finn was ushered by two anxious-looking priests into the private study where the Cardinal was waiting for him behind his large antique desk. In his splendid crimson robes the Cardinal looked younger than the years ascribed to him by Maria. He was tall and slender with a pointed face and sunken eyes and dark hair meticulously combed which appeared to be kept in place by heavy hair cream. He wore a pince-nez, which contributed to the impression that the Cardinal was looking down his nose at the world as it passed by. It was clear that he was a man of considerable authority.

The Cardinal's study was a large cavernous room with the walls covered by exquisite paintings of scenes from both the New and the Old Testament. One could easily feel the characters from these paintings were gazing down at the occupants of the room with critical eyes. It occurred to Finn that this room deserved to be considered a museum in its own right. The Cardinal motioned him to sit down in an oversized armchair at the other side of the desk. Finn felt he was in the presence of an important man.

-Thank you for coming to see me Professor Kelly, and at such relatively short notice.

-Oh, please don't mention it, your Eminence. It was a pleasure to be invited. What a remarkable room in a remarkable house, or should I say palace?

-Thank you.

The Cardinal was not a man skilled in the art of small talk.

-How is your work going with the Curia? Are you enjoying being in Rome? It is a big and sometimes bewildering city. I have known some of our visiting dignitaries to feel lost while they are here in Rome. I hope that you have found a suitable place to live. I believe that your work keeps you in your office until late at night.

It was unclear to Finn which question he should answer first.

-The work is going well. Thank you for asking. I have always enjoyed being in Rome. It is such an elegant city. Among the cities of the world it is uniquely timeless. I have a small apartment that suits my needs perfectly. Yes, I have been working late, sometimes; but not always. I have been able to get around and enjoy some of the life in Rome.

-I am glad that you are enjoying being in Rome. If you were not it would not bode well for your work.

-Quite so, Your Eminence.

A young priest appeared at the door of the office with a large tray of tea. The Cardinal motioned him to put it on the table in the corner and asked him to pour two cups.

-I guess you are wondering, what is the real reason why I asked you to come out to visit me? Well I have heard that you have been making enquiries about one of the manuscripts found when the poor Abbey at Montebello was struck by the dreadful earthquake some three or four years ago, and I thought it might be useful to talk a little about that with you, Professor.

Finn had not seen this coming. He wondered how the Cardinal had known about his interest in the manuscript. Finn knew that the grapevine in the Vatican was a highly honed affair, but he hadn't really spoken to anyone about his interest in this subject.

-Your Eminence, I'm not sure how you know about this but you are correct. The manuscript I saw was a truly brilliant piece of work. It is highly unusual and as a scholar in the field of mediaeval literature, I am really quite curious about its provenance. I am also interested to learn as much as possible about the conditions of storage as it does not seem to have deteriorated much over the hundreds of years it was locked up in a box.

-Well let me start off by telling you a little about the monastery itself and, of course, the Order of Saint Francis Picallo. Saint Francis's story is a classic of late vocation and giving up worldly endeavours to pursue a contemplative life. Francis Picallo was in his 40s when he decided to give up his life of luxury and cut himself off from family and friends. He was originally from a powerful family in Venice. So, he went to a remote part of Italy so that he could make a clean break with his former life.

-Brave of him.

-However, within a short time he had a number of devotees wanting to follow his example. It took a few years for this movement to be established and for the Church to grant them some minor status and then they had a broader base of acceptability. Ordinary people began coming to receive a blessing from Francis and slowly but surely, his reputation began to grow as a holy man who could really help with peoples' problems. There were even some cases of healing reported.

-Healing, Your Eminence?

-Yes, but it was only some years after the death of Francis that the Church granted the formal status of an Order to the group. Their objectives were defined as being contemplative and scholarly and they were to express this through artistic works they would undertake. This was the true beginning of the Order but another century would pass before Pope Urban XXI canonised Francis. The monastery was built quite slowly over many years. The Order never had much in the way of resources as Montebello was always a poor village and the people in the area could only give very modest support to the monks. Visitors who came for help from the monks sometimes gave them nice presents but they never really amounted to much.

-An interesting story Your Eminence. Francis Picallo was not known to me before.

-He is very much an Italian Saint.

-He wasn't weeded out by Pope Paul who dumped dozens of Saints from the Church Calendar?

-No. Although over 90 saints were removed from the Catholic Calendar by Pope Paul, Francis Picallo was saved from the Papal axe by a small but enthusiastic band of supporters in the Curia.

-Quality versus quantity? Or something like that.

Cardinal Baffasa got out of his seat and walked around the desk to be closer to Finn. The tone of his voice changed and he looked Finn directly in the eyes.

-Professor Kelly, on the question of the manuscript, you know in the Vatican we are now much more alert to the fact that there are many treasures out there in our community, especially in our monasteries and convents, of which we are not aware. Over the centuries many great gifts were given to our Holy Mother the Church and very often no proper record of these was ever made. Our previous Holy Father decided that some organisation was necessary. I'm sure you know that we spent a large sum of money on employing computers and systems throughout the community and the recordkeeping that followed has brought to light many interesting pieces of art and other artefacts. All over the world we have made discoveries.

-And some very interesting ones.

-Of course, the work you are speaking of came to our attention in quite a different way. From ancient times, Italy has been so prone to earthquakes. Some people would tell you that it was earthquakes that really brought the Roman Empire to its knees. It is surprising that we have so many fine buildings still standing from antiquity. Montebello was a particularly fine example of architecture from its period and we were extremely sorry over its loss. It was so wrecked that it was beyond normal restoration. A few temporary repairs have been done. But we have noted that when funds become available we will rebuild it. I am not sure what I could specifically tell you about the manuscript that you have seen in the hands of Signor Dameri?

-Your Eminence, what I was interested ....

-Before you go on any further Professor Kelly, let me say that we, in the Church are protective about her assets and about what we are prepared to tell people about them. I suppose it has always been the case that the Church was operated on the basis of "a need-to know", and I am not terribly sure what your need is in this case?

Finn realised that the Cardinal was preparing him for a rejection. He knew that the Cardinal was likely to beat him over the head with the word "need".

-Your Eminence I don't have any real need or for that matter specific questions as such, that I want to ask. As you know I'm an academic and therefore I have a fairly active level of curiosity and I was looking to talk to people who had been involved in this discovery and I also would like to know how the manuscript moved from Montebello to the gallery in Rome where it was sold. Perhaps I could go and speak to the Abbot and find out from him how this whole thing unfolded?

-Oh I'm afraid not Professor Kelly. The Abbot was an old man when the earthquake struck and witnessing the destruction of the monastery and its surrounds made him quite ill, and, alas he did not recover.

-Oh, I'm sorry to hear that Your Eminence. Then maybe I could speak to some of the other monks who were there at the time.

-After the tragedy, the community of monks was split up with some of them going to different monasteries around the country. So, it might really be quite difficult for you to locate who was involved at that time. When we eventually rebuild the monastery we will call the community back, and then you could speak to them if you wish. But, that is unlikely to happen in the next few years.

-That is a great pity, Your Eminence.

Professor Kelly, I am wondering how your interest in Montebello fits in with your work at the Roman Curia?

-There is no direct connection, Your Eminence.

-I am therefore wondering if you really have the time to pursue this interest of yours? It would be a pity if your project with the Curia were to run into difficulty or unnecessary delays. I am sure that you don't want to attract any criticism upon yourself?

-Of course not Your Eminence.

Finn took this to be an implied threat and was about to reply strongly when he remembered Maria's comment that Cardinals could be touchy, and that it was not a good idea to upset any of them. He also recalled Maria's comment about how powerful this man was.

-I am certain that it will not have a negative impact on any of my work. I am sure that you know that I am a well-established professional and that I well know how to prioritise my time. Have no fear about my work for the Curia.

-Good. Very good, Professor Kelly.

With these words Finn became more uncomfortable. He wondered if he was correct in feeling the threat level was increasing.

-Professor, I wish you all success for your work with the Roman Curia and I would be pleased to chat to you again about the treasures in the Vatican when I am not so hard pressed to complete my report to the Holy Father.

To signal that the conversation was really over, Cardinal Baffasa extended his hand to Finn to give him an opportunity of kissing his Bishop's ring. The Cardinal then walked Finn out of his office, through the cavernous corridors and across the splendid courtyard to the waiting Vatican limousine which took him back to his office.

Finn's reaction to the Cardinal's home was similar to what he felt about Antonio's. It was far too big for one man. It would even be too big for an enormous Italian extended family. The house had been a Roman merchant's country villa dating from the end of the 18th or early 19thcentury. It wasn't glitzy like Antonio's house but it nonetheless spoke loudly of the wealth of the organisation behind the man who lived in it. Finn wondered if this was in fact the way that the Catholic Church ought to be spending its money. But alas, this was too big an issue for Finn to spend too much time pondering and his thoughts returned to the question of the increasingly enigmatic manuscript.

Finn was deeply puzzled. How did the Cardinal get to know that Finn was making enquiries about the manuscript? Had someone in the Vatican archives or library services been talking about Finn's interest in mediaeval manuscripts? Had the Gallery Garibaldi been in touch with the Cardinal? Had something filtered back to the Cardinal from the University of Tontos? It could hardly have been Maria in Finn's office who had been talking. Why was the Cardinal so defensive? Was the Cardinal really threatening him? What was this business about a "need-to-know"?

So many questions and so few answers.

Back in the confessional in Dublin Finn wondered what it was that drove his interest in Antonio's book. Why did he care whether it was authentic? Finn wondered if deep down he was bored with his work at the Vatican and at O'Connell College and that he just wanted some intellectual adventure. Or was it something else?

Chapter Five

Montebello

Finn returned to his office to find Maria anxious to know how his meeting with the Cardinal went. As he was not feeling particularly positive about the encounter he didn't want to disclose it to anyone, and perhaps especially Maria.

-Well enough I suppose. I think it was mostly a social visit.

-Oh really Finn. Cardinals generally don't do social visits. There would have been an agenda somewhere.

-Well he was very polite. We certainly didn't have an argument. I am not really sure, Maria, why I was called to the Cardinal's Palace. But I am a little perplexed as to why he went to the trouble to do so?

-He wasn't just being friendly?

-No. There was more to it than that but I am not quite sure what. By the way his abode is ridiculous. It's an enormous mansion. It's big enough to house a couple of Irish football teams. And the decor - well it's a bit like a museum.

-Oh yes. It is well known that some of the Cardinals live in places like that. Not at all suitable for the 21st century.

-And the car or rather the limousine he sent for me ... well it's all a bit over the top. No. That's not right. It is completely over the top.

Finn decided not to tell her about his interest in Montebello and how the Cardinal had known about it. It wasn't that he didn't trust Maria but rather he felt his interest in the manuscript might be seen by her to be his looking for a silly adventure.

-I am not surprised that Baffasa wanted to see you. Rome is really a small town and someone in the Vatican takes an interest in everything that goes on in it. I wouldn't be surprised if someone in the Vatican knows what you habitually have for breakfast.

Reflecting on the meeting with Baffasa, Finn was more convinced than ever that if he really wanted to know more about the manuscript he should go to Montebello as soon as he possibly could, and so he made arrangements to rent a vehicle from a car hire company for the following weekend.

On a bright Saturday morning at 9 am, Finn was on the road to Montebello. It was great to be out of the city. Memories of student excursions into the countryside flooded back. But back then he was always worried about spending time away from his studies and about his tight budget and if he could afford the luxuries that the other students took for granted. He was free from all of that now and he enjoyed it.

Four hours after leaving Rome he was in the ruined village in the heart of the mountains. He had travelled over 150 kilometres on good highway before he turned off onto country roads. There were then 40 kilometres of busy secondary roads before his journey took him up into the hills. There the roads were little more than country tracks. By the time he reached Montebello he felt that he had really been on a long journey.

It was pitiful to see how little redevelopment had taken place. Many of the houses were completely ruined, while some of the others bore the scars of the earthquake with what Finn imagined to be some pride. There were a number of prefabricated buildings and tents that really looked out of place in this old village. No doubt they were necessary to keep everything going.

Finn found one small bar that was operating and he decided to start off his visit to Montebello with an injection of caffeine. While there he began talking to the patron - an elderly man who had lived in the village all his life.

-Is it possible for a visitor like me to get to see the old monastery?

-Well, most of the monastery is cordoned off. The Church and for that matter the State, has done little to restore what was once a magnificent example of early mediaeval architecture. But you can look at it from the outside if you wish?

-Is there really no chance of going into the grounds and having a proper look? Maybe there's somebody here who might take me around who knows what parts of it are safe?

-Oh yes, if you want to do that then I suggest you get hold of Alessandro. He is the oldest living inhabitant of the village, except perhaps for the old lady of the village, Signora Bayvey, but she now has Alzheimer's and can't tell one day from the next or one person from another. No, she would be no use to you. Alessandro's your man. He knows this place like the back of his hand and he'll take you around for a modest fee. But he talks too much, so you need a lot of time when you go around the village with him.

-Great. Please tell me where to get hold of Alessandro?

Finn was directed to a tumbledown little house just up the street, that looked like its future was uncertain. When he knocked on the door Finn wondered whether that sort of motion might not cause the walls to tremble and perhaps even fall. The inside of the house was no better. It had clearly taken a heavy beating from the earthquake and it seemed to Finn that it was really on the border of being condemned, but on the other hand there was little doubt that living in this old building was better than being in a prefabricated box like those he had seen in other parts of the town.

Alessandro was an elderly man who had been in Montebello all his life and he was quite pleased to have an assignment to show a stranger around the village. Finn could not work out his age and he thought that it would be impolite to ask. But Alessandro seemed to be on the wrong side of 80. Nonetheless his mobility was good and he walked straight upright and reasonably quickly. He knew everyone in the village and even a lot of people who lived in nearby villages. Alessandro's parents and even grandparents had all come from this village. It was a very closed society and Finn acquired a distinct feeling which suggested to an outsider that there might be some in-breeding issues in this village.

The village of Montebello had not been well known to many people outside of the general area. However, the disaster had attracted a number of prying tourists in the early months after the earthquake; voyeurs they were, but by now the world had forgotten or at least had lost interest. There had been more recent catastrophes elsewhere. The old monastery was nothing more than a shell and even some of the outer walls had fallen down. Not much of the rubble had been taken away but some of it had. Where the rubble was cleared people were able to walk and marvel at the beautiful bits of architecture left. They just didn't make buildings like this anymore. There were also some murals still visible on the walls.

Alessandro had great stories to tell about how different parts of the monastery were built during different periods and different murals were associated with the work of different artists. Over the centuries, the monastery had been visited by several Popes. There had been a papal visit only 10 years ago and this had produced great excitement. It also appears that the monastery was often visited by Cardinals from Rome.

There was no doubt that the whole village had been intensely proud of their monastery and that its destruction in the earthquake had caused great despondency among many of the villagers.

As they were finishing the tour, Finn decided to ask Alessandro if he knew anything about the marvellous manuscripts that had been found as a result of the earthquake.

-Oh yes. Everyone in the village knows about them. They were discovered locked up in a big box in a hidden room no one knew anything about. It was a great surprise to everyone in the monastery, including the Abbot. I understand that some of them were 500 years old and they were valuable indeed. The monks were most pleased with this find and I believe they were allowed to sell some of them. That was unusual as the Church normally just keeps any treasure that turns up in any of its monasteries or convents. I understand that the money they received helped with some of the monk's relocation costs as the monastery didn't really have enough money for this sort of emergency. These days many monasteries are always run on a shoestring and this was definitely the case with Montebello.

-I wonder, Alessandro if you know who found the manuscripts?

-Oh yes. It was Brother ... mmm ... I can't seem to remember his name right now. I knew some of the monks better than the others and my memory of their names is beginning to slip. But I think it was Janus, and if I'm right, he was one of the few monks who did not leave Montebello. Yes. It was definitely Brother Janus. I now remember. Janus.

-Why didn't Brother Janus leave?

-A few of the monks said that they were too old to go to another religious house in another part of the country and as they had family in this area, they were given permission to stay and spend their old age with the relations. Yes, I'm pretty sure that Brother Janus now lives with his sister and her family a couple of kilometres north of the village.

-It would be really great if I could go and speak to him. If you give me his address and some decent directions, I'll go over there as soon as we have finished. I hope he'll be in today.

-The old men who live around here don't go far from home so it's quite likely that you will find him in even on the weekend, and if he isn't there his family will find him for you.

There was no difficulty in locating Brother Janus. His presence was well known by all his neighbours who were anxious to help Finn find him. Finn was brought in to his sister's home and offered coffee that he declined. It was a tiny house on a hillside surrounded by a few hundred square meters of land on which were kept a few goats and a dozen or so chickens. There was also an obviously active vegetable patch. Finn was struck by the contrast between this home and that of the Cardinal's and Antonio's in Rome.

Brother Janus was as elderly as Alessandro but not so mobile. He was somewhat bent over with arthritis or some similar ailment. He wore a highly unruly beard needing some trimming. He was dressed in the dark brown habit of his Order. His hands were large, and it was obvious that they used to be strong and hard. One had the impression that once upon a time he could have cracked walnuts in his palms.

-Brother Janus, I am working in the Vatican as an advisor to the Curia and I hope you won't mind talking to me a bit about the wonderful monastery in Montebello. I'm interested to know something about how it functioned and about what happened on the day of the great earthquake. I have been told that the monastery was really spectacular. I hope it won't bring back too many unpleasant memories for you, and if it does I'll understand and we can talk about something else.

-The monastery was a really wonderful place. There was nowhere else like it for hundreds of kilometres. I joined the Order straight from school when I was 16 and I spent the rest of my life there until the disaster. The earthquake was absolutely dreadful. It happened early in the morning just after we had all gathered in the church for morning mass. We were all together and we were able to get clear of the building quickly.

-Was anyone killed?

-No. Fortunately only one monk was hurt by falling masonry. None of us was killed. Some of our animals were badly hurt and had to be destroyed. And the building was wrecked. It is a great irony that God would visit such a catastrophe on such a holy a place as the monastery. There is little doubt that the earthquake set off the health

48

problems which now besiege the Abbot. But then, life is full of paradoxes, is it not? We are all subject to the mysterious will of God.

-Yes, indeed paradoxes seem to haunt us in all sorts of ways. So I understand that the monastery was quite substantial and that it had been there for a thousand years.

-The number of monks varied from time to time but there were always at least 50 of us, sometimes quite a few more. We needed everyone to keep the building in good order, and also we had a couple of hundred acres from which we fed ourselves and were also able to supply considerable amounts of the food for use in the village. People up here don't have much money. The relationship between the monastery and the village was always good.

-But, Brother Janus, as I understand it the main objective of the Order was a reflective one? Was not the monastery a refuge for those who wanted to distance themselves from the trials and tribulations of the world?

-Oh, yes, indeed it was.

-And I believe that you found the lost manuscripts in the box in the cellar?

-No. I didn't. You are mistaken. It must have been one of the other monks.

Finn was puzzled. Was Alessandro mistaken? Quite possibly. Or was the old man's memory playing tricks on him? Finn decided not to press the point but to carry on talking about the monastery.

-So the monastery was really a retreat from the world.

-But it was more than that. We were highly productive as well as being a refuge. We had a full scale scriptorium where we managed to produce manuscripts and books for special occasions in different parts of the Church. These were sent all over the world. That was considered special work and not everyone was adequately skilled to play a full role in the detailed work carried out there. But some of my brother monks were especially skilled at this. You really have to be an artist to be any good with a quill. I wasn't bad myself but there were several others who were much better than me.

-I did not know about the scriptorium. I thought that they were a thing of the past. Was it generally known that there was one in the monastery?

-Maybe not. The type of work is highly specialised and there was always a steady demand for some thing or another to be developed for a special occasion somewhere in the Church, sometimes overseas or some faraway part of the world. You know you have to be really dedicated to be able to produce illuminated manuscripts, and the way that we worked on them it was virtually impossible to be able to tell the difference between something we had produced and a piece of work produced in mediaeval times. We knew how to age the manuscripts and books so that they really looked like the, how do the French say, vrai de vrai. I myself was trained by the previous Abbot. He was a stickler for perfection.

-How long was the training?

-There was no formal period for this but no one was ever any good until he had worked alongside a master for at least 5 years. In some cases, it was longer.

-How interesting.

-But I wasn't anywhere near the best. Brother Phillipe was the most fantastic man when it came to illuminated manuscripts. And he could work so fast. He made all the rest of us look quite inadequate. There was a wide range of work done in the scriptorium - usually manuscripts that were in their own right fine pieces of art. They were normally created on the instructions of the Abbot who in turn had received an order from one of the high ups in Rome, a Cardinal I think. But over the years we had visits from many Cardinals.

-Do you know which Cardinals?

-No. I don't think that I ever heard any of their names but I was told that the last one was from the Office of the Secretariat of State from the Roman Curia. Cardinals are such important people. It was such a privilege that they visited us in person. We would never dream of referring to them by their name. We all bowed and scraped and call them Your Eminence.

-Of course.

-Occasionally the Abbot would get commissions directly from individuals who wanted this type of work done for themselves. When that happened, the monastery made some money out of the work and that was helpful, especially when it came to paying for the high level of maintenance that is necessary to keep a 1000-year-old building functioning in a reasonable way. We have never had any Parishioners give us money as such, although some of the villagers have been quite generous from time to time. By the way although the scriptorium was destroyed by the earthquake, the work being done there has not entirely ceased. You don't need a lot of equipment and, as I mentioned, Brother Philippe went, together with a few others, and resettled in a house owned by the Order not far from Rome itself.

Although he didn't show it in any way Finn was gobsmacked. He could hardly believe his ears. Was Brother Janus really telling him that the monks were producing manuscripts and passing them off as original mediaeval pieces of work? Could that really be true? Was Brother Janus so naïve that he did not realise that this could be a very difficult issue for the Church? Into Finn's mind came the image of himself now holding a hand grenade that could blow up but then he thought more and realised that he was actually handling a cruise missile.

But as a researcher Finn knew not to jump to conclusions. Maybe the old man was just confused? Maybe he wasn't remembering correctly? Finn reminded himself that old age has its consequences.

-Brother Janus I am a bit confused. Please tell me what use these beautiful illuminated manuscripts the monastery was producing were being put to?

-In some cases they were used for ceremonial purposes. In some cases, they were put in museums as examples of the type of work monasteries could do. In these cases, they were part of a display. Occasionally they were sold, I think. No, I am sure that some of them were sold.

-For how much would they be sold?

-That's a silly question to ask me.

Finn could see that this question had disturbed the old man.

-Why?

-I have no idea. None whatsoever. I had nothing to do with any of that. I'm just a scribe at heart. I have probably said enough, Professor Kelly. You should really put your questions to Brother Philippe who was at one time the assistant Abbot. He knows much more about this than I do. But I'm glad that you seem to like the work we were doing. It's always good to receive a little bit of appreciation. Yes. Brother Philippe would know much more about our work. As I said he is one of the monks who was relocated. They went to one of our houses near Rome. He is in the village of Castel del Dolfo. It is a spectacularly beautiful place.

-Would Brother Philippe be prepared to talk to me?

-You will have to ask him, but I think so, and he would know about the box of old manuscripts after the earthquake. As I said I think that he found them himself but I am not absolutely sure. He is a pleasant and easy-going man and I am sure that he would be pleased to tell you how the monastery functioned and he might even have some photos of our most beautiful pieces which were pure art. I heard recently that he and his team still work quite hard.

Finn took the hint and excused himself saying that it was time for him to go so he would not get back to Rome too late that night. Brother Janus gave Finn a blessing wishing him well for both the journey that evening and for his other work in the Vatican. Finn was struck by the simplicity of the life of this old man and how it contrasted so much with what he had seen in the home of his affluent friend Antonio and in the Palace of the Cardinal.

From the beginning Finn had felt there was something about Antonio's manuscript that didn't quite add up but he had not for a moment imagined that he would come across something like this. He knew that he had to be careful that he really understood what was being said to him, and that there was no chance there were misunderstandings creeping into the conversation. Was Antonio's manuscript produced in the scriptorium or was it found in the box in the cellar? Was this really a large scale fraud? Was that what was being explained to him? But how did this happen? Who could be responsible for passing off a modern piece of work as though it were an ancient original? Was it the Abbot? Was it the Gallery Garibaldi? What role did Professor Ronanelli have in this affair? How was the Cardinal involved? And perhaps most important of all, where was the money going to? If the price of Antonio's book was anything to go by there must have been a lot of money involved.

More questions and even fewer answers.

As he had planned, he spent the night in Perugia in a small hotel in the old town centre. He had a restless night dreaming about monks and scriptoria and bags of silver. The idea of bags of silver disturbed him. Finn's subconscious was notorious for regurgitating, while he slept, the events of the day and these dreams often gave him more insights into how he really felt about complex issues he had been involved with.

The following morning as Finn drove back to Rome he became more and more worried about the things that he had been told. He wondered if he had inadvertently stumbled on a nefarious trade involving a bunch of religious men, seemingly dedicated to following the rule of monastic life while at the same time putting into circulation fraudulent counterfeit pieces of mediaeval art in the form of illuminated manuscripts. Could the Holy Roman Catholic Church really be involved in such activities and if it was who was getting the benefit?

Finn couldn't help but remember the old aphorism attributed to the famous Roman orator Cicero, *Cui bono*? Cui bono or who benefits kept on repeating itself in Finn's mind.

Chapter Six

A little glass of wine

His newfound knowledge and suspicions presented Finn with the dilemma of whether or not to tell his friend Antonio. There was no doubt that Antonio would be devastated if it turned out that his manuscript was a fraud. Even if the €1.5 million did not mean all that much to him, Antonio's pride would be seriously damaged.

Finn decided that he should discuss the situation with someone who had an independent mind and might be able to see through the mist accumulating in his brain. The only person he knew in Rome who would fit this bill was Maria. So Finn decided to invite Maria to have a drink with him after work on the Monday evening. Work in the office normally finished before 6.30 PM and so there was plenty of time to have a drink before dinner.

-Maria, if you're free would you like to have a glass of wine with me after work this evening?

Maria was most pleased to receive this invitation. She dealt with many visitors to the Vatican every year but nearly all of them were either men of the cloth or were from a maturity point of view rather advanced. She had often thought that some of the people she looked after were not dissimilar to a well-ripened cheese. Finn was different. He was twenty-five years younger than average and with a sharp wit and a naughty twinkle in his eye he cut a quite different figure.

-Certainly Finn. What a nice idea, and I know just the right place, a small wine bar, not far from your apartment. Shall we meet at 7 o'clock?

-That would be great.

Finn sat restlessly at the bar sipping his glass of Chianti at 7 pm. Maria, as could have been anticipated, was a little late and arrived at

7.20 pm having changed into an eye-catching black crepe dress and a sparkling white shawl for their evening out. Finn was struck by how much more attractive Maria was when she was not in her usual working clothes.

-Finn, I was wondering when you were going to ask me out for a drink. I think this occasion is long overdue.

-Well, I can be a bit slow off the mark sometimes, but usually I get to the right place in the end. I am pleased that you think it is appropriate that we should spend an evening together. I wasn't sure what the protocol might be concerning Vatican employees socialising together.

-You're quite right Finn, it is not something that is encouraged but quite frankly, who cares?

-Well we have lots to talk about and it will certainly be nice to get to know you a bit better, but as someone who is so well-informed about what goes on in this city, I was hoping you would be able to give me some information about some issues that have been bothering me.

-Oh yes.

-As you know I was an undergraduate at the Università di Roma and one of my drinking pals was Antonio Dameri.

-What good or should I say POSH company you were keeping!

- I didn't know anything about his family at the time and of course he was just another student like the rest of us and he seemed to be on a relatively tight budget. He didn't drive a Ferrari or anything like that.

-And…

-I bumped into him the other day at the Cafe de Años.

-That must have been an expensive outing!

-Yes the restaurant is very pricy.

-But worth it ... I trust?

Finn realised that was a rhetorical question.

-As a result of this chance encounter, Antonio and I got together in his office and later in his home. What an amazing set-up he has. It's hard to believe there is so much wealth concentrated in such relatively young hands. I wonder if he is actually a billionaire?

-Oh yes. He could well be in the billionaire class. The family Dameri is regarded as one of the wealthiest families in Italy. They are probably Euro billionaires. It is an interesting family, because the grandfather started the business with very little. Some people say that grandpa Dameri took his life savings to Monte Carlo where he struck it lucky and that gave him the capital to get the business going. They say that by the time he handed the business over to his son it was well established at a national level but it was Antonio's father who moulded the business into the global organisation it is now. You never see anything written about Antonio's business acumen. It appears that he is an adequate administrator, but he doesn't have the business or financial flair of his father.

-That's interesting.

-Although there was never any formal complaint made against him, the media, on more than one occasion, suggested that Antonio's father had some dealings that were not quite as clean as he would like you to believe.

-What was really being said about Antonio's father's business dealings?

-The comments were always vague but it was remarkable just how quickly the business grew. The business was so diversified that it was hard to know precisely what they were doing and although it was suggested to him a few times that the business should be launched on the stock market, he always refused. There was also the fact that he had strong connections in the South of the country as well as in Sicily, an area known for some nefarious activities.

-Well there's no law against wanting to keep your business dealings private.

-Quite right.

-Antonio told me he had been buying art from the Gallery Garibaldi and, as you know, I went to see Jeremy Williamson. He wasn't a terribly friendly man and I didn't get far with him. I had a distinct feeling that he was somebody who had things to hide.

-The Gallery Garibaldi is fairly unique in Rome. It deals at the highest end of the art market. You won't find anything in there for much less than €1 million. So, Williamson is famous for being particular about whom he shows around his gallery and to whom he gives any information. I don't imagine that he had anything particular against you.

-I am glad to hear that. Do you have any ideas about where he would source the artworks he sells?

-He's been in business for a long time, and one of the principal drivers of a successful top end art gallery is to establish a network of sellers and buyers. There is nothing terribly mysterious about this but it is enormously difficult to break through and succeed in the art business. Williamson has a successful operation. I know this because I have heard from reliable sources he will buy first-class airline tickets to fly people in to see an item he has on sale. They will be put up in the best hotels. To do this he has to be confident that he will really do some good business, no doubt.

-He knows his market, then.

-Yes. But it is also worth mentioning that a few years ago when the museums in Baghdad were looted it is said that many of the treasures stolen ended up coming to Europe through Rome. These were priceless artefacts sold to unscrupulous collectors for large sums of money. There was a suggestion at the time that perhaps some of these artefacts had come through the Gallery Garibaldi. But no evidence was found that would stand up in court. I know about this because a cousin of mine is an officer in the Carabinieri. He is a very useful contact for hearing about some of the real scandals which go on in Rome. This city is truly full of gossip.

Finn wanted to tell Maria about the illuminated manuscript but he felt she was so confident about her knowledge of the Dameri family and the Gallery Garibaldi that his suspicions might seem silly, and anyway he was really enjoying her company and he felt that it would be good to have a pleasant evening with her. So he decided to order another bottle of the house's best Chianti and after they had finished those drinks they then proceeded to dinner in a nearby cosy restaurant.

The evening was spent with Finn telling Maria about his background in Dublin. He entertained her with stories of his childhood, his schooldays and his being awarded the Latin prize, and the subsequent scholarship that took him to Rome.

-By the time I left school I really wanted to get away from Dublin or rather Ireland. My father was a civil servant and my mother was a primary school teacher. In those days I had thought that they were the most boring people in the world and I was scared that I would become the same. Of course I no longer see it that way. As an island Ireland is, in a way, quite culturally limited and I wanted to experience the greater world. Rome seemed to me to be one of the most fabulous cities in the world and I was delighted with the opportunities I received here. Italian student life was simply magnificent. I learnt to appreciate Chianti. Admittedly it was the cheap variety. Some of my rich and rather snobby acquaintances would say that the grapes used in this cheap wine should only be fed to pigs but I didn't mind. I will always be most grateful for the education I received in Italy.

Finn went on to recount how he had struggled in London as an intern with the British Museum.

-The British Museum was the most magnificent place to work but it is absolutely no fun living in London on an intern's salary. The accommodation I was able to afford was simply grim and after Rome many of the things I wanted to do just seem to be so expensive. But of course I met some great people and made some fantastic contacts and that was what I needed in order to obtain a place in Paris to study at the Sorbonne. Living in Paris was great fun especially on the Left Bank where I was able to meet many from the artistic set. But alas there was no way in which I was going to obtain a permanent position in France so I returned to Ireland.

-But isn't O'Connell College good?

-Oh yes, especially as I now hold a full Chair. Dublin is still a relatively limited and limiting place but the job at O'Connell is great. We attract some of the best students in the world to Dublin and it is a very uplifting experience to work with young people who really want to learn. And I do get opportunities to do some really fascinating consultancy work such as I am now doing for the Vatican.

Maria recalled for Finn her early days as a pupil in a convent in Naples. She hadn't liked the discipline imposed by the nuns. She was continually in trouble with the Mother Superior and was glad when her school days were over.

-What bothered me the most about that convent was the fact that it was being run with the same rules that had been in place since it was established nearly 200 years ago. The nuns had no idea that they were in the 20th century, and towards the end of it as well. Everything was run by the bell and when we weren't being taught or eating we were praying. We were in bed with lights out every night at nine o'clock. We had very little contact with the rest of the city and this really wasn't good for any child growing up at the time.

-So you used to break the rules Maria?

-Yes whenever I could. But unfortunately I was caught more often than not.

Maria had come from a well-to-do family. Her father was a doctor and her mother an architect and they had insisted that she take a degree in mathematics at the University of Tontos. Both parents had argued that a mathematics degree gave one the most flexibility when it came to a career choice.

-I had no idea what I wanted to do when I left school. My exam results were good enough to allow me to get into any university I wanted to, and being equally talented in both scientific subjects and the humanities it made it very difficult for me to know what to do. In the end the pressure from my parents was too much and I went off to study mathematics. Although I was fairly good at it I didn't think the subject itself terribly much fun.

Maria's parents were Italians who did not have much time for the dogma of the Catholic Church. They were not atheists or anything like that, but they were weary of the hierarchy.

-My parents never managed mass on Sundays. There was just too much to do in preparing Sunday lunch and in any case Papa just didn't like the local Parish priest. Italy might have the Vatican and the maybe hundreds of thousands of clergy in this country but many of us are really quite disinterested and would rather get on with our own lives on our own.

While Maria had really enjoyed her university days and finishing her degree, looking for a job was a culture shock. Initially she took a post as a teacher in a private school. But she was looking for something more challenging.

-In the end my work as a teacher made me feel that I had never really left school and so I decided I had to get out of it and do something really quite different.

Maria decided that a career in administration might be the right thing for her. She did a Diploma in Business Studies in Rome and started looking for a job. It was purely fortuitous that a vacancy in the Roman Curia was advertised and although it was a junior post Maria could see the potential of working in the Vatican. Maybe in defiance of her family objections to her getting involved with the Church she applied and was subsequently offered the job. Despite the fact that the Curia is male dominated Maria did not find it difficult to make progress with her career and over the following few years she had been promoted several times and was now Director of the Facilities the Vatican offered its visiting dignitaries.

-I now manage a team of three people and we have somewhere between 20 and 50 guests of the Vatican to look after at any given point in time. It can be a very busy job and it certainly can have its ups and downs. Some of the guests have found themselves in difficulties. We had a couple of men from Australia who were actually mugged a few years back. We have had, on a number of occasions, individuals who have lost their briefcases with all their documentation including passport etc. We have seen over the years a couple of people who needed urgent hospitalisations due to a variety of illnesses including heart attacks, thromboses and other chronic ailments. We have had more than one guest who was caught in a police raid on a rather dodgy nightclub. When these things happen it's my job to sort them out. It's no surprise to me if the phone rings in the small hours of the morning.

-What a wonderful job you have, Maria! You must meet and deal with some amazing people.

-Well it certainly has its moments. And of course, these interesting crises normally have a way of happening at the most inconvenient times of day.

Like Finn, Maria had not married and was completely unattached. She also said that at the present time she was not in a hurry to have a man in her life. Being single was good for her now.

The evening flew by rapidly and at about 11.30 pm Finn finished the evening by giving Maria a hug and a perfunctory kiss on both cheeks before putting her in a taxi to go home.

From the point of view of discussing Antonio Dameri's €1.5 million manuscript Finn knew that the evening had not been a success as he had not been able to share his suspicions with Maria. But on the other hand he had found Maria's company more than diverting and he thought to himself that there might be some future in a relationship with her.

Finn was due to take a break from the Vatican project back in Dublin so he could catch up with some of his business at O'Connell College and also see his friends. So he decided to put the illuminated manuscript issue to the back of his mind until he returned to the Vatican in a week's time. Clearly there was no urgency to make any decisions right away and mulling these issues over in his mind should bring to him a greater degree of clarity than he was experiencing at the moment.

The following Friday evening Finn took the express train to the Leonardo da Vinci Airport to catch the non-stop flight from Rome to Dublin. As was often the case it was delayed, and he arrived in Dublin shortly before midnight and took a taxi home.

Chapter Seven

Is there ever enough money?

Returning to Dublin did not disappoint Finn. He walked out of the terminal to find the inevitable dark wet winter's night where it was raining cats and dogs. There was a chilling wind blowing off the Irish Sea and everyone who was out and about was buttoned up well. It did not take long to find a taxi and within 20 minutes Finn was in his apartment in Drumcondra on the North side of the city. After a small nightcap of Irish whiskey, he was soon asleep but up early the following morning to tackle the many chores he had to face during his week home.

Finn lived in a converted Georgian townhouse on one of the more opulent Georgian squares that had been built during the 19th century on that side of Dublin. It was indeed good to be back home, although he had to admit that he was already missing the wonderful sunshine he had grown to enjoy in Rome. But, bad weather does not deter Dubliners. Finn had a hectic schedule for the next week. He had to see several of his doctoral students in O'Connell College. He had a meeting of the trustees of the charity with which he was highly engaged and, as an amateur thespian, he had been invited to attend a planning meeting to discuss which play they would be producing in the New Year. One of the possible plays was Oscar Wilde's The Importance of Being Ernest, and Finn was really looking forward to the possibility of having a role in that event. But all of this was going to wait until next week. The weekend was going to be devoted to getting in touch with some friends with whom he had been exchanging emails over the past month.

Monday morning found Finn in his office at O'Connell College. Finn shared the services of Moira Flannigan who looked after the administrative support for 3 professors in his Department. She had been in regular contact with Finn while he was away and had kept him up to date with most of the developments in the Department. She also controlled his appointments diary.

Moira had booked his diary pretty comprehensively for the week. The first morning had been put aside for doctoral students. Word had got out that he was back and all his five doctoral students wanted to see him although none of these researchers had special problems needing Finn's attention. He was a well-organised supervisor and had set them on straight paths which would lead to them obtaining their degrees without too much difficulty. However, as they hadn't seen him for a month, they were all eager to be able to report back to him on their progress. These meetings were completed by lunchtime when Finn received a call from Kathleen Daly, the Director of the Ringsend Shelter for Abused Children, the charity for which Finn was one of the trustees, to confirm their meeting that afternoon.

Finn had been a trustee of this charity for the past three years. He had been asked to assist with organising its administrative and financial activities which, until Finn gave it some structure, was spectacularly badly organised. Like some other charities in Dublin this one was headed up by a talented and well-meaning Director who unfortunately had little head for organisation or for financial matters, and who found it difficult to implement the type of business controls needed to ensure the efficiency and effectiveness or the continuity of the organisation. By simply being a trustee and regularly attending the management meetings, Finn had brought some clarity to the organisation's objectives.

There was no doubt that Kathleen was an effective Director. Her combination of charm and determination, not to mention her striking good looks, had resulted in the charity more than doubling in size over the past five years. Finn was very proud of her and very pleased to have played a part in its success.

-It is good to see you back Finn. How have you been getting on in the Eternal City?

-Kathleen, I am working with an interesting group of colleagues and other experts from different countries in continental Europe. We are a highly eclectic team of mediaevalists from four different counties. We have quite different approaches to work but we seem to be able to hold our team together all right.

-That's interesting.

-It certainly is. We've made a lot of progress with our assignment but there is a lot of work to do. It is time-consuming work so I often have to stay late in the office, and I doubt that the work will be finalised by the time the contract originally specified. It's very easy to be unduly optimistic about how long this type of work takes.

-Will they extend the contract?

-I would imagine so. I would be pleased to have some more work which might also lead to a number of research opportunities. There are loads of things to do for the Church in understanding and managing its art collections.

-Otherwise what's it like living in Rome?

-Well, Rome is a truly beautiful city. Living there is great. I sometimes feel like pinching myself in case I am dreaming. And the work is interesting and the pay is good. Of course the weather is much better than Dublin. Otherwise I am definitely an outsider there and so I do occasionally miss not being at home. How have things been going here, in good old Dubs?

-I wish I could say that there wasn't much news, but there is, and it is not good. The past month has been particularly tough. You know before you left for Rome we heard that our government grant was to be cut next year. They said that they had to make savings across the board and that a 10% cut was being planned for the coming year. Well only last week we heard that their calculations were wrong and that the cut was going to have to be 20%. That would make a really big hole in our finances. And as though that was not enough bad news we were contacted by Gass Brothers, as you know one of our biggest donors, to be advised that next year they would not be able to keep up the level of their donations. They couldn't tell me by how much they would have to cut their contribution but I did get out of the fellow who phoned that it would probably be 25%. I think it is fair to say that next year we are going to be in dire straits.

-That's bloody awful. That will make a huge hole in our finances. What are we going to do? We don't have a lot of reserves. We'll have to revise the budgets for next year. That of course won't get us any more money but it will tell us where we are.

Finn could feel panic coming over him but he quickly realised that this would be unproductive and it might even make things much worse for Kathleen. He bit his tongue and told himself to keep his cool.

-Finn, I got Larry O'Neil to start that already. We will have to cancel our new projects and we may even have to do some cutting back. I hate the thought of making any redundancies. But, if we haven't the money …well we will just have to cut our cloth according to our …

- On the other hand Kathleen, don't jump to too many conclusions until we have done the figures, but you are right the news is awful. I'll put my thinking cap on and see if I can come up with any new ideas about possible sources of funding. But let's not panic. We have the funds to see this year through and if the worst comes to the worst there are enough reserves to see us through to the second half of next year. By then we will have come up with a plan.

-Jaysus, I hope you are right. I would hate to see all the work I have done over the past decade end up on the rubbish heap because this bloody government can't balance its budget. It's so unfair. Let them cut some of the Ministers salaries or expense accounts before they attack money going to the charity sector - and especially when it's for kids. What they do makes no bloody sense at all.

-OK. Let's keep our cool and see what we can do. There must be some money out there that we can find and tap into. I'll be back from Rome no later than the end of next month and in the meantime I will put the word out that we need new funding. I know some ritzy people who might be prepared to put some money our way.

The most important thing is to avoid panicking. We can indulge in a little of that later if we can't get out of this jam.

-I really hope you are right and we will be able to cope. Losing my job would be bloody awful but it would be far worse if the service we offer some of these children has to be withdrawn. It is such a ridiculously unfair world we live in.

Finn knew it would be difficult to find any more money during this period of economic crisis but he couldn't think of anything else to say to Kathleen at that moment. He was no fund-raiser which he knew was a highly skilled job, but wanted to try to be as positive as possible about the Shelter. Deep down he was quite depressed about these circumstances and really didn't have much of an idea whom he could approach. But deep down he felt there must be something he could do.

The next few days flew past with the normal routine of being in College. All his colleagues were preparing for the start of a new term and there was much talk about a new syllabus being introduced in his department. There was to be a greater emphasis on research- based scholarship, even at undergraduate level, and this required the redesign of a number of courses and modules.

In addition, there had recently been the appointment of a new Principal or Head of the College. This was a great surprise as the Court of Governors, who elects the Principal broke new ground by appointing a woman.

It had happened on this occasion that the majority of the senior members of College could not agree on any of the men who were prepared to stand for the post, so a woman was proposed as a compromise candidate and to the surprise of a number of the old male members of the College, she was successful. Now there was a lot of gossip going around about her and whether she could successfully do the job. It was the first time in the College's 40-odd year history that a woman had been elected to this prestigious post and there was much rejoicing among certain parts of the community.

On her first day the newcomer had decided to shake the place up by asking all senior professors to produce detailed plans of what they intended to achieve over the next three-years and Finn found himself spending many hours on the project in order to produce a balanced statement showing his interest in consulting as well as teaching and research. These documents are never easy to get right and Finn being academically ambitious wanted to make the right impression to the new principal.

Chapter Eight

O'Connell amateur dramatics

When Thursday evening arrived, Finn was pleased to be able to forget about all these issues and go to the meeting of the O'Connell College Amateur Dramatic Society of which he was an active member. Twice a year the society put on a play written by an Irish playwright at the College. The performance of these plays was considered an important cultural event in Dublin and they were always booked out long in advance. This evening it would be announced which play they would do next. There had been quite a lot of discussion about which play to choose and two plays had been shortlisted. The first was Oscar Wilde's The Importance of Being Ernest, and the other was Brenan Behan's The Quare Fellow. Both of these plays had enthusiastic support and it was not certain as to which one would be chosen. However, after an hour's debate and a close vote it was decided on the basis of its popular appeal to go with the Oscar Wilde. Sean O'Toole, who was also a member of staff at O'Connell College and had been a lifelong friend of Finn in that they had known each other since primary school, was now the Chair of the Society and as such he had to use his casting vote, as the rest of the Society was split down the middle about which play to put on.

-Sean, I guess you have just demonstrated the great advantage of being in the Chair of the Society. You got to make the decision and you are going to be in one of your favourite plays. As I will be away for some of the rehearsal time I can't play too big a role but I would be grateful if you would still keep me in mind for one of the minor characters. -Certainly

-You know Finn I really do like Wilde but it is a pity that he left us such a small body of work.

-Sean, I guess he wasn't planning to go to jail or to die so young.

-Yes. You must be right, but it makes it difficult to teach him at university level, or to keep his presence in the contemporary theatre. It's a pity that he did not live and work for another 20 or even 30 years.

-If wishes were horses, beggars would ride!

-Quite so.

-But maybe his genius was tied up in the extravagances leading to his downfall. Perhaps his brilliant wit fed on the extraordinary chances he took and so his downfall was inevitable?

-Finn, I am not sure about that. I know Wilde's work so well that I can easily imitate his style and I don't go about flaunting anti-establishment sexual sympathies. Of course even if I had them I wouldn't ... and I hasten to add I don't.

Finn reflected on how conservative Sean O'Toole had always been. At school he was a smallish lad who was recruited as an altar-boy from an early age. He was as straight as a die, not participating in any of the growing-up pranks which the other boy delighted in. Sean O'Toole was definitely not going to be caught smoking fags - or anything else for that matter - behind the bicycle sheds, or climbing over the back walls of his neighbours' houses to steal their apples after dark.

-Yes. But you are not actually Wilde.

-True, but I can imitate Wilde's style, vocabulary and wit so well that even an expert would not be able to tell the difference. You know Finn, this type of imitation is being done regularly now. Just think of how the film industry has continued to produce new Bond films which have been written by Ian Fleming imitators. If the industry wanted to they could have pretended they had found more original books. No-one but special members of the literati would have known any different.

-Can something like that really be done for the writing of someone like Oscar Wilde?

-For sure.

-After all, he was a complicated man and he had such an unusual turn of phrase. I don't think that it is fair to compare Oscar Wilde's work with Bond movie scripts. However, come to think of it I suppose, there is a relatively constant theme running through his theatrical works.

-Finn, I am working on a book we are going to call The Soul of the Author. It will be co-authored with a colleague, Paddy Walsh who was a former student of mine – one of the most brilliant students I ever had - in which we are exploring what the underpinning characteristics of a given author are, and how we can understand how to write like such an individual. This is the first book to deeply investigate the psyche of different authors, looking at their motivation, their socio-political-economic circumstances, and putting together a model of how their minds actually worked.

-Can you do that?

-Yes.

-I am not a psychologist, but this sounds a bit off the wall. Are you sure?

-Finn I know nothing like this has ever been done before. We have been working on it for several years now. It has been a truly fascinating project. We haven't really told anyone about it until recently as we were not terribly sure how well our idea for this book would work out in practice. We will complete the work next month and we think we know who might be prepared to publish such a book as this, although we acknowledge it might turn out to be quite a challenge as our ideas are, to say the least, quite unusual.

-That sounds like it will make some interesting reading. Do keep me in mind for an early copy of the book.

-And, by the way, I have nearly finished writing a play in the style of Wilde and if you promise not to tell anyone I will show you my draft and you can give me your opinion. The play is to be called "Being Excellent", and it is set in O'Connell College in the early 1870s when Wilde was a student here. By the way, I have already worked out the plots for three more plays I estimate I could write within one year, if I could afford to take sabbatical from the College. But, as you know, the College rules for this type of leave are quite difficult and end up being expensive.

-Oh yes. I would love to see your new Wilde play. How long is it?

-It's a short one. About 180 pages. I have it here on a memory stick and if you promise not to copy it and just read it on your computer screen you can take it with you tonight. As we are having lunch at the club tomorrow, you can give it back to me then.

-Certainly. I won't copy or print it. Many thanks for this opportunity. I am really looking forward to reading this. A new Oscar Wilde – there's a thought.

When Finn arrived home he poured himself a double whiskey and made directly for his computer. He loaded the text of Being Excellent and started into it with considerable energy. Before he knew where he was, he had consumed several more double whiskeys and he was two thirds of the way through the book. Sean was right. He was able to write in such a way that one could be convinced that it was written by Wilde himself. It was a play of manners appropriate to a young man of means setting out for a university education in the middle of the 19th century. Wilde's wit was ever present with remarks never seen before. As expected, the young man in the story got into many jams, but in the usual way, all things turned out well in the end. It was a masterpiece.

Finn knew that Sean was a highly talented and creative academic and that he was the leading authority on Wilde in Ireland, but he hadn't realised that Sean could produce material like this. It was now going on for midnight and Finn decided to call it a day and seek some rest.

During the night, Finn was plagued with several restless dreams about the Ringsend Shelter for Abused Children and about Oscar Wilde. They were mostly vague dreams, only partially remembered when he woke up. But in one of the dreams Oscar Wilde came to visit the Shelter and was delighted to be asked to help save the charity. Of course Finn did not register if, in his dream, Wilde did save the Shelter and, if so, how he did it.

Finn woke up the following morning feeling like he had been hit by a 10-ton truck. This was partly due to the inadequate sleep he had. It was compounded by the fact that he had consumed nearly half a bottle of whiskey. He was also troubled by a thought that was beginning to formulate in his mind about how Oscar Wilde might be able to help the Shelter. Finn was not really an adventurous man and so the idea that was coming together in his mind to combine the charity and Wilde was somewhat disturbing. But the more he thought about it the more compelling it seemed to him. It was an archetypal example of an idea slowly but steadily growing on him.

The Faculty Club at O'Connell College regularly frequented by Finn and Sean is a posh haven of tranquillity for senior academics and a few administrators. Decorated with paintings of former Principals and other Dublin dignitaries from previous years, it exudes the dignity of being part of the College history, although in truth O'Connell College is not all that old. They met there at 12.30 when they both took the traditional glass of extra dry sherry and stood in front of the fire while waiting to be called to their table.

Finn handed the memory stick back to Sean.

-Here you are Sean. I haven't copied it and it hasn't been printed.

-So Finn, what do you think about Being Excellent?

-Mmm … I don't quite know how to put it. I have to say that I think it is … outstanding. You have really captured the spirit of Oscar Wilde in a most elegant way. I doubt that there are many people alive who would argue that this wasn't written by the man himself. I never realised you had that sort of talent as I have always taken you for being just another dreary academic, like myself. In my view your creativity score has just rocketed through the ceiling.

-Don't talk nonsense, most academics have a reasonable streak of creativity and all it needs is a challenge to bring it out of them.

-You've certainly done that.

-Do you think it will be easy to find a publisher? You think I should write under a pseudonym, maybe Oscar Wilde the Second? Or what? I am very naive about the possibilities of making something out of this manuscript. It would be nice to have a bestseller and to make some money out of my writing, at last.

-Money is important.

-Yes, indeed it is and as you know I have wished I could write that best seller but it has always eluded me. Mind you, it's not quite ready yet. I still want to spend about a week or so on it before I will regard it as being completely finished.

This was Finn's opportunity to verbalise the ideas that had been developing in his head since he woke up that morning.

-Well, I have a proposition I want to make to you, but before I do so, I need you to assure me you will be able to keep it most secret. Knowing you, this might be difficult but you really have to with this one. Do you remember when we were children and we shared a secret with someone, we asked them to cross their heart and swear to die if they didn't keep the secret? Well I'm going to ask you to double cross your heart and double swear to die. What I'm going to tell you could be dangerous, but, on the other hand, you could really help me and many others.

-My goodness. What can the secret be?

-You swear to die?

Sean resisted the temptation to laugh. Was Finn being serious? He hadn't heard anyone talk like this since childhood.

-Yes, of course.

-When I was in Rome I encountered an old friend of mine from university days who came into a lot of money. He used some of his new wealth to buy a most beautiful artefact that was sold to him as an ancient illuminated manuscript based on a number of events in the life and work of Dante Alighieri. Well, there was something about this document that sparked my curiosity and I....

Twenty minutes later Finn had told Sean the whole story.

-So Finn, you think that you have encountered a well-established group of monks who are producing ancient manuscripts that are really modern productions. What shall we call them, counterfeit?

-Yes. I am pretty sure that is the case.

-And your university friend paid €1.5 million for such a document.

-Yes. That's impressive, isn't it?

-And you think that they are still carrying on with this work?

-Yes. Without any doubt; I established that.

-And you think that these are being distributed through one of the most famous Art Galleries in Rome?

-Yes.

-So, what do you propose to do about it?

-I was initially really concerned about this as I wasn't sure what responsibility I had to uncover these nefarious activities. I worried about telling my old university friend. It then occurred to me that I would be spoiling the belief he has in his truly wonderful artefact. Why should I do that? I am quite clear that Antonio would not thank me for such a revelation. I think that he is the type that would have shot the messenger. It isn't as though he spent money he didn't have or that his purchase has led to some hardship. So, after a certain amount of mental anguish, I decided that I should remain silent. It is not up to me to be a snitch.

-So why are you telling me the story? You have something in mind?

-Yes. I do.

-Well, spit it out.

-I had a dream last night about how Oscar Wilde might be able to help the Ringsend Shelter for Abused Children. I am sure that this was my subconscious suggesting to me that what I found out about monks and manuscripts in Rome might be of use to some of the more vulnerable and underprivileged people in Dublin. It seems to me that we might be able to use these monks in Italy to help the Ringsend Society for Abused Children out of their present financial crisis.

-Oh, really. Where is the connection?

-I know this is going to sound crazy to you, so please do hear me through to the end. If we take Being Excellent and ask the monks to, I don't know what I should call it, maybe transcribe, or reformat, or redevelop the text, in such a way that it appears we have found a "lost" manuscript of Oscar Wilde, we could have a document that would sell for a large sum of money. I have no idea how much we would get but I suspect that it would be several hundred thousands of euros. It might even be a million. My cause is such a good one that I think the monks might have difficulty in refusing to do this for me. And the Director of the Gallery, Jeremy Williamson appears to me like a man who is sufficiently enterprising, or should I say greedy, that he would not be able to resist the offer of making another bundle of money.

-Mmm.

-Williamson might even be able to claim that the manuscript has been stolen and therefore the new owner would have to agree to keep his or her possession of it secret. I would not expect you to do this for nothing. If we do this I think that you could end up with a lot more money than any publishing contract you might be offered. I think it would be fair to offer you, let's say 10 or even 20% of what we get. That would give you enough money to take a sabbatical and I could keep my favourite charity going for quite some time.

-What an idea! You are right it is crazy. I would never have thought it of you.

-What do you say to my proposition?

-Wow. You are ... you're quite right. This is the craziest idea I've heard for a very long time. I don't know what to say. I will have to think about it carefully.

-But please give me your initial reaction.

-First of all, I'm flattered that you think my work is good enough to be passed off as a "lost" original, but, at the same time, I am worried that you have come up with such a hare-brained scheme. Isn't it fraught with all sorts of dangers? And isn't it criminal?

-Yes, I guess that it is criminal. But it's a little crime, to help so many kids. And whoever buys this book will be loaded. The money won't mean a damn thing to him or her. As far as dangers are concerned, I think we can do this in such a way as to minimise, if not eliminate, any danger.

-But won't the monks tell?

- I think not. There is a lot of secrecy about the activities deep within the Catholic Church. I don't think that the scriptorium was known about by many people. Going by Antonio's document their work is truly excellent. Whoever buys Being Excellent will be thrilled with it, and we can tell him or her that it is important that their ownership of the document is kept quiet, otherwise the successors of the Wilde family will want it back. That should keep his or her mouth shut, tightly.

-I guess so.

-Sean, I think that I can manage a project like this so there would be a good result for all of us. And being perfectly honest, these are desperate times and I'm sickened at the thought of what will happen to these kids we look after if we have to close. The more I think of it the more I feel the risks are not great. I am sure I can manage this to the benefit of both our interests. The way I could set this up, the College will never know. It'll be good for you to have the money to get away from the College and do the writing you want to do. Maybe these shenanigans in Rome will turn out to be a godsend to both of us.

-I'll have to think about this carefully. The idea does sound quite attractive. I could certainly use the money. As you know I have never been quite able to adjust my tastes to an academic salary.

Finn was amused by Sean's odd moments of honesty.

-If this can be done in such a way that it will not be traced back to me, then I think I might be prepared to go along with it. I'll let you know tomorrow. In the meantime, let's focus on lunch.

Chapter Nine
Bringing it together

Sean O'Toole phoned early the following morning and agreed to go along with Finn's proposed scheme. He made a big point of saying that he wasn't doing it for the money alone, but of course, the money would be helpful. Sean wanted a few days to put some final touches to his manuscript. When this was done he would then send Being Excellent to Finn in Rome by courier. He also confirmed that his name would not appear on any part of the document or be involved in any of the processes that Finn was planning to subject the document to. To ensure maximum security a courier would be used to send the manuscript to Rome because it would not be safe to transmit such a document electronically, as electronic transmissions could always be traced.

That afternoon Moira Flannigan, Finn's departmental assistant, received a call from the Principal's office to say that if Professor Kelly was available, the Principal would like him to call on her at home at 6 pm. Finn was really surprised to receive such an invitation.

-Moira, what could the Principal want with me?

-I wasn't told and I didn't think it was my place to ask.

-And where am I to meet her?

-At her Official Residence.

-You're kidding?

-No I am not.

-But that is most unusual.

Few people were invited to the Principal's Official Residence. The Principal's Official home was regarded as quite private. It was a prestigious place where important College entertainment took place. Some people said it was completely over the top and so Finn saw this as a complement. Or, Finn wondered, was it?

Finn arrived as the clock struck 6.

-Professor Kelly ... may I call you Finn? Titles are so formal.

-Certainly, Principal.

-I invited you today to congratulate you and to tell you how pleased I and my senior colleagues are at your being invited to advise the Vatican. This has just been drawn to our attention and we know how prestigious it is to be asked to work alongside their experts. This is a great credit to you and it will bring considerable kudos and even prestige to the College as well. As you know O'Connell has had a number of outstanding scholars over the years who have won many prizes including a Nobel Prize, but we haven't had enough recognition in other fields and your work is helping in this respect.

-I am glad you see it that way, Principal.

-We will be issuing a press release next week; that is if you have no objection.

-Of course not, Principal. But please note that my work in the Vatican is actually classified as confidential.

-Finn, we do not expect to make any comment on the nature of your work.

-Just as well.

-As you know Finn, we are always concerned that our Faculty do not spend too much time on outside work but, in this case, we are pleased with what you are doing. Your reputation as a caring supervisor is well known in the college and so I imagine you have made adequate arrangements for the supervision of your research students.

-Yes. Indeed. I absolutely have.

-Good. I am glad to hear that from you.

-We have regular email exchanges and we talk frequently by video conference, Principal.

-We are also pleased because, as I imagine you are aware, there are still a few people who see O'Connell College as a very radical place; we were once referred to as the atheist's college, and being invited to assist the Vatican will help put an end to that nonsense. It can be so difficult to put that kind of history firmly behind one.

-I certainly never gave any credence to any of that type of thinking. Although, out of the dozen or so Principals we have had over the years, only the last few haven't been well known for their atheistic or socialistic opinions. Over the years the College has had some pretty wild Principals.

-That's all history. Anyway, thank you again for being such a good ambassador for the College. By the way I have heard some of my colleagues talk about proposing you for an honorary doctorate.

-That would be grand.

-For honorary doctorates, there is a certain amount of formality to go through first. There are a couple of committees who have a say in these matters and as you know they tend to move slowly. I can't be seen to be pushing them.

-Of course.

After a few glasses of the College's finest wine from its extensive cellars, Finn went home and packed for his return journey to Rome.

It had not occurred to him before that his work with the Vatican could have such a direct and positive affect on his career in the College. He was pleased indeed with this turn of events. Having the personal approval of the Principal could mean other sorts of promotions and opportunities could come his way in the future.

The following morning Finn flew back to Rome as planned. His Aer Lingus flight was delayed and he waited a long time for his luggage at the airport in Rome before taking the bus into the centre of the city. This time he was not so delighted to be back in the eternal city. What he intended to do weighed on him quite heavily. He was determined to finish the work at the Vatican as soon as possible and at the same time he would also put together the arrangements discussed with Sean O'Toole in Dublin.

The next morning when Finn saw Maria Abano in the office she cheerfully asked him about his trip to Dublin.

-It was a great trip. I hadn't realised that I was missing Dublin as much as I really was. It was good to see my students and some old friends. But I also had some pretty disappointing news. A charity that is important to me and of which I am a trustee looks like having its funding badly cut, and may well be in considerable financial difficulty next year. That was a bolt out of the blue.

-That's sad. I hope that something can be done about it.

-I do hope that's so. It would cause a lot of hardship to quite vulnerable people if it closed. The State social system in Ireland is not all that wonderful. Anyway in the meantime I need to get on with my consulting assignment here and get back to Dublin to help the Shelter if I can.

That afternoon Finn asked Maria if she might be able to help him find Brother Philippe whom he had been told was now living in the village of Castel del Dolfo. Maria knew about the Order of Saint Francis Picallo and it didn't take her long to get the address of the Order's house in the village. It was 50-odd kilometres from the centre of Rome and there was a regular bus to the village taking about an hour and a half, as it stopped many times to pick up and drop off local passengers on the way. Finn decided that he would venture out there on the first Saturday he was free.

It turned out to be an unseasonably warm day for that time of year. Travelling by local bus in Italy is a great experience, which Finn would normally have enjoyed very much, but on this occasion he had too many other things on his mind. The bus was packed with noisy passengers, including screaming children, making the journey even less pleasant than it would normally have been on a hot day.

When eventually he got to the bus station in Castel del Dolfo, Finn made some enquiries and was directed to the religious Order's house which was about a kilometre from the bus station. It was a large building on a substantial piece of land with some religious emblems on the gate and over the building's front door. Many would not have called it a monastery. Finn was admitted by a monk who asked how he could be helpful and when Finn said he was looking for Brother Philippe he was asked for his name and then he was directed to a substantial waiting room where he took a seat. This room was full of statues and pictures of the saints which Finn found somewhat oppressive.

About 15 minutes later Brother Philippe appeared. He was a much younger man than Brother Janus. He was tall, slim and clean shaven. Although he was dressed in a brown habit, he looked more like a technocrat in a large corporation than a monk. He was quietly spoken with almost accentless English and he exhibited a thoroughly urbane manner.

-Professor Kelly, how nice to meet you. I was wondering if, or rather, when you were going to pay me a visit. I heard from Brother Janus that you had visited Montebello and that you were interested in our poor monastery that took such a terrible beating during the earthquake.

-Yes, it certainly did.

-And, of course it remains in ruins.

-I am sorry.

-Don't worry. We know our importance or the lack of it to the Italian State. Our politicians can spend money like water on prestigious projects when the mood takes them, but not on rebuilding a monastery. What governments spend their citizen's money on can be a mystery.

-Indeed.

-Brother Janus also mentioned that you had a particular interest in our scriptorium. So how can I help you?

-First of all I should say that I'm a mediaevalist at O'Connell College in Dublin. I am currently engaged as a consultant by the Vatican, working on a project related to establishing the authenticity of a number of art treasures which have been found in various churches and monasteries, mostly in what we used to refer to as Eastern Europe. You may already know all of this as the grapevine seems to work brilliantly in Rome. Anyway, I have come to see you entirely on private business having nothing to do with either my work at O'Connell College or the Vatican. I need to emphasise that and I would like our conversation to be treated in the most confidential way possible.

-Certainly. As you wish.

-I have an active interest in a wide variety of subjects dating back to mediaeval times. My doctoral research I did at the Sorbonne was on the subject of literature during the 14th century. Although I had heard of the Montebello earthquake, I hadn't realised that old manuscripts had been found there. I am especially interested in learning about how the earthquake affected the monastery buildings, and how the Order of Saint Francis Picallo coped with the devastation that this brought about. Both Alessandro and Brother Janus were able to give me interesting perspectives on the earthquake. -I am sure they were.

-I was also interested in learning something about the illuminated manuscript which was found locked up in a box in the room discovered when some walls were taken down to make the remains of the monastery safe. And, by the way, another issue was raised. In my discussion with Brother Janus it was mentioned that the scriptorium sometimes produced replicas of ancient documents and I am interested in learning more about this type of work.

-You certainly want to talk about a lot of different things.

-I hope you don't mind.

-The details of the dreadful earthquake and the series of events that followed have been reported by a number of different individuals, some of whom have given rather confused accounts. As you know second-hand information is often quite dangerous. I was in the thick of things at that time. The Abbot was old and I was effectively deputising for him. The fact of the matter is that the monastery was destroyed. As you have no doubt seen it was completely ruined. Fortunately, none of the monks lost their lives. A few were hurt and all of us were badly traumatised. After the event, it was necessary to clear the site of a lot of fallen debris and this work took several months. In clearing out one part of the ruined monastery, we found a trapdoor leading to a cellar where we discovered several large boxes, one of which contained a number of important documents. We were delighted to find these and sent them off to the Vatican to the appropriate authorities.

-Brother Philippe, it was a blessing, if not a miracle, that none of the monks were hurt.

-A great blessing indeed, Professor Kelly.

-Did you not see the documents again?

-No. Professor Kelly, concerning the scriptorium you have been hearing about. Before discussing the replica work, I should say that after the earthquake we felt rather abandoned by the hierarchy in the

Church. We had always believed that the monastery at Montebello was an important part of the fabric of the Church in Italy, but it seems that resources were not going to be made available for its restoration for quite some time. That is a great sadness to all of us who spent our lives in that monastery.

-I am sure that must be the case, and it is indeed a pity that the Order of Saint Francis Picallo has been spread about in other parts of the country. That must have had a dreadful impact on the community.

-Our community is now very splintered.

-Sorry to hear that.

-Concerning the scriptorium, our scriptorium was not big. Not many of my brother monks had either the talent or the inclination to do the fine work required in producing illuminated manuscripts. It is both a gift and a calling to be involved in this type of work. But, on the other hand we didn't want the skills to die out and so we were prepared to undertake assignments offered to us, normally by high dignitaries in Rome. Over the past 20 years, we have normally produced a few, in fact quite a few pieces of work for them. And we did one or two private commissions when we were asked. We never saw these as moneymaking opportunities, but we did accept donations for the upkeep of the monastery. As you know, it is expensive to maintain a 1000-year-old building.

-Indeed. And where did most of your output go to?

-To cathedrals or other religious institutions around the world. We were never sure where their final destinations would be. It didn't really matter to us. We knew that handing the work over to the Church meant that it would be really well appreciated wherever it ended up.

-How have you gone about ageing these documents so that they appear to be authentically mediaeval?

-I don't think that it is appropriate for me to discuss that with you.

-But it must have been a central issue for you, making documents look old.

-All I am prepared to say is that we don't do that as such. We used the same techniques and materials that had been employed in the monastery for hundreds of years. In some cases we are using the same instruments. We source materials in the same way as the monastery always did. All of this makes for a fine product when completed.

Finn was not entirely satisfied with this answer. It was clear that Brother Philippe was avoiding this question. But he felt that he couldn't press him for any more detail at this stage. Perhaps he should regard the answer to this question as the monks' trade secret.

-Brother Philippe, did you know that the manuscript you produced referring to the thinking of Dante Alighieri was sold through the Gallery Garibaldi? It was reported to be an ancient manuscript and was sold for a large sum of money.

-I am not sure if I recall the document you are referring to but let me assure you that none of us here have any knowledge of any of the commercial transactions that may have resulted from a work we have produced. Money and finance are of no concern to us at all.

Finn felt he had reached the point where he could put his secret proposition to the monk.

-Well Brother, I wonder if you could help me with a possible project that would be dear to my heart. I am a trustee of a charity in Dublin offering a range of services to abused children. This charity provides services to at least 50 different families every day and has come under severe financial pressure due to both government and private individuals having trouble with their budgets during the current austerity.

-Sorry to hear that.

-The charity is in danger of having to close down if we cannot find more funding in the near future.

Finn crossed his fingers again in anticipation of the lie he was about to tell.

-We have come across a document that is a "lost" play of the famous Irish author, Oscar Wilde. Oscar Wilde died at the end of the 19th century and this play that has been found was written somewhere in the early 1870s. We know that it will not easily be accepted as genuine, because Oscar Wilde died early and did not leave a significant body of work behind him. We would like this to be transcribed, or maybe I should say reproduced, in such a way that it would encourage a belief in its authenticity.

-I see.

-This would not be done for the financial gain of any individual but rather to save the charity from having to massively reduce the services it offers these abused children. I wonder if you would be prepared to take on a private commission such as this? It would be a great service to some of the less fortunate children of Dublin.

-What an interesting idea. A proposition like this has never been put to me before. Mmm ... Well, I would have to discuss this with my brother monks, but it does appear that you have a good cause and that maybe we should be active in trying to help you under these circumstances. Why don't you give me a couple of days, or maybe you could come out and see me again in a week's time? I'll talk it over and maybe we can find a way of helping you.

-Thank you very much Brother Philippe. I am happy with that suggestion. So, at the same time next week, I will be here.

-Yes, Professor Kelly, that would be good.

Finn caught the bus back to Rome feeling that he had achieved the main objective of his visit to Castel del Dolfo. He felt that Brother Philippe had probably been disingenuous about the issue of ageing the documents and he regretted that he felt he had to lie to the monk about the true nature of the document he had asked him to work on. But he felt that it was probably all right if both sides pretended that they didn't really know what was going on. What was important to Finn was that he had been completely genuine about the reason for producing this document and that the money he might be able to make from it would go to a good cause. By the time the bus arrived at the bus station in Rome, Finn had convinced himself that there was no harm in what he was doing. If they were able to sell such a book for a large sum of money it would probably be to a wealthy individual who did not need the money, and thus he would be perfectly justified to use it for charity.

Finn kept on saying to himself "What harm would be done to the buyer? Only a multi-millionaire would buy such a thing. A person like that would be completely indifferent to what would be for them a small amount of money, just like his friend Antonio was. Yes, his friend Antonio didn't give a jot about the money. And so much good would be done for the kids in Dublin". Deep down Finn was becoming aware that this was the way he was going to have to manage his conscience.

The manuscript from Sean O'Toole arrived as promised. Sean had not made many changes to it, but he had slightly tightened the plot of the play. Finn thought this would make a really fine addition to the library of someone with more money than sense. Now Finn began thinking about how he could sell the book with relatively little publicity. He knew he could hardly take an advertisement in The Times. So, the question became whom did he know who was really wealthy and would be happy to hand over serious money?

He did have one or two ideas, but he also wondered whether he should go back to the Gallery Garibaldi and talk to Jeremy Williamson. He was pretty sure that Williamson, with his suave manner, was the right man for this job and that he would be able to sell the book at a high price. He realised that if he went along this route Williamson would need a substantial cut, but then he thought that instead of obtaining a few hundred thousand euros for the book, he might be able to get a lot more. Anyway, he didn't have to make a decision at this time and he would just allow random ideas to float by him for the moment.

On the following Saturday, Finn retraced steps back to Castel del Dolfo. He was nervous that Brother Philippe might not accept his proposition and he was worried about what he might be able to do under those circumstances.

-Professor Kelly, I and my fellow brothers have decided that your cause is just and we will accept your commission. It won't be an easy assignment but we have an active network of very accomplished people in the Church. We do not expect to make any money out of this, but we will accept a donation from you of a few thousand euros that will cover the cost of our materials. This can be paid to us when the work is complete. We cannot be certain how long this task will take but it will be at least three months, maybe a little longer, and we will get in contact with you when it is done and you can come back here and pick it up. Make sure we have a postal address for you as we would like to communicate with you by letter. In the meantime, I assume you have the text with you and I will be pleased to accept it now.

Delighted, Finn could think of nothing to say. He handed over the parcel he had received from Sean O'Toole by courier.

-This is not the original document found in the Dublin attic. It is a transcript. The original is very tattered and hardly legible. It too difficult to work with.

-I see. Are you sure of the authenticity of the manuscript?

Finn crossed his fingers and lied.

-Yes. Certainly.

Finn then thanked the monk profusely and made sure that Brother Philippe had his address in Dublin.

Back in his office in the Vatican, Maria asked Finn how he got on with his trip to Castel del Dolfo. Not wanting to speak about this within earshot of any of his colleagues, Finn invited Maria for another drink that evening, which she cheerfully accepted.

They met again at the same wine bar as before and at the same time. On this occasion, Maria wearing a short red dress with a rainbow scarf cut a stunning figure. Finn was coming to realise just how impressive his newfound friend really was. Clearly she was dressing to impress Finn and Finn was becoming increasingly impressed.

-So how did you know that I've made a visit to Castel del Dolfo?

-I saw you looking up the bus timetable on your computer the other day.

-Wow! You are perceptive. Not much gets past you, does it?

-That's probably the reason that I am Director of Facilities!

-I was told about the order of Saint Francis Picallo by Cardinal Baffasa; you know, the friendly man dressed in the scarlet frock who invited me to tea in his palace about a month ago.

-Oh, yes. That one.

-He told me that the Order had a house in Castel del Dolfo where they were doing some interesting work related to the scriptorium they used to have in the monastery at Montebello. I went down there to visit and see the type of work they were producing and, indeed, it is impressive. Some of it is so good that I could hardly tell the difference between what they are producing today and what they were doing hundreds of years ago. It's a real credit to them that they have such skilled craftsmen in their Order.

-I knew about the Order of Saint Francis Picallo, I guess all Italians do. Saint Francis is a well-loved Saint. But I had no idea of the type of work you are now describing. I thought that scriptoria were things of the past.

-So did I. But, in fact, it appears they are alive and well and quite active, at least in the Order of Saint Francis Picallo.

-What type of work are they producing and what is it being used for?

Finn wasn't sure how he should answer this question as he didn't quite know how much Maria would have known about the involvement of the Church in these activities and whether he could trust her with his suspicions.

-I am not entirely sure how to describe it. They make beautiful pieces of art and they send them all over the world, from what I can make out. I would have to say that much of the work is ornamental and that it is being used for ceremonial purposes by the Church. Having looked at it now, it doesn't really fall within my orbit of interest.

But that was enough business chat for the evening. Finn found Maria's company most engaging and they spent a pleasant evening together, initially discussing both his and her work in the Curia. As Maria worked for the Curia, Finn felt there was no harm in telling her about some of the extraordinary pieces of art that he had been examining over the last few months. On her part, Maria was quite open about the challenges her job offered and how the different individuals in the Curia work together, or in some cases how the personalities clashed and their behaviour was somewhat dysfunctional.

After they finished their bottle of wine Finn proposed dinner and Maria suggested the perfect little trattoria, off the beaten track and owned by a distant cousin of hers. Finn became aware of his need to show some affection and took Maria's hand in what was quite a clumsy way. Maria graciously responded with what Finn regarded as a little encouragement.

-Maria, the way you have helped me on a number of occasions has really been great and I do really want you to know that I would have had a lot of trouble without your help and guidance.

-I haven't done much and everything I have done has been a pleasure.

-I have been a visitor at a number of universities in recent years and the interest shown in helping guests varies enormously. Sometime visitors are all but ignored and they have to fend for themselves.

-Of course, Finn, some visitors don't want any help and find what I offer to do an intrusion, but you seemed to me to be much more open and approachable and maybe we could be friends.

-Yes. I felt the same.

-So did I.

-Maria, is it not a lucky coincidence that neither of us have significant others in our lives right now?

Smiling at Finn in an enigmatic way Maria replied.

-Maybe.

-When you said that there was not a man in your life and that you weren't looking for one you gave me the impression that you had probably been badly hurt by someone. Would you like to tell me about it?

-I had a long standing relationship which ended very abruptly.

-How come?

-Giorgio had a dreadful motor bike accident.

-Oh my goodness.

-It was absolutely catastrophic; and so completely unexpected.

-What happened?

-I don't really like to talk too much about it. In any event the details are hardly important.

-That must have been terrible.

-I then met Alfonso. We were very fond of each other. But he was married.

Finn was puzzled.

-I knew he was married. He was separated from his wife. Our relationship became very complicated. I think he wanted to marry me but his wife wouldn't give him a divorce. Although divorce has been legal in Italy since 1970 it is not all that socially acceptable.

-Just like in Ireland.

-So about a year ago we decided to go our separate ways.

-That seems sad.

-Yes. It was, but you never know how relationships will turn out. It was for the best. I am now well over it and maybe my feelings about not being interested in another relationship are … one might say, on the wane.

-I am pleased to hear that.

Smiling widely at Finn, Maria decided it was time for him to tell all.

-So Finn, now that you know about me, do tell why you are unattached?

-I don't have a tragedy in my history like you do. My story is much more mundane. When I was here as an undergraduate I met a wonderful girl. She was from Milan. She too was studying history and we fell in love. We had a wonderful couple of years. She was from a well-established industrial family and they had quite specific plans for her. Those plans did not include an Irish man and if the truth was told a rather impecunious boyfriend. It just wasn't going to work.

- I can well imagine.

-When I got back to Ireland I felt very unsettled, and then going to live in London and Paris I didn't meet anyone with whom I wanted a long term relationship. I found plenty of short term great fun affairs and that has been good enough for me up until now.

-So?

-Well time marches on and perhaps I am now changing. I am not entirely sure but it seems to me that there may be some special advantages to a longer term involvement now.

-How carefully you chose your words, Finn.

-One never knows how the affairs of the heart are going to work out. Sometimes the more one thinks about them the more confused one gets. Sometimes the only way is to blindly follow one's instinct. Some people say let the chemistry take over.

-Maybe they are right.

The waiter interrupted the conversation with a request that they order some food.

Then another magnificent bottle of wine arrived and the conversation continued on a much less intensely personal basis.

The evening again ended with Finn putting Maria in a taxi. This time they enjoyed a longer good night hug. Finn was of the definite impression that if he had wanted to, they could spend more time together, perhaps over a nightcap in her apartment. It was becoming clear to Finn that Maria was more interested in him than he in her. He was not a man to take advantage of this as he did not yet feel that developing a more intimate relationship with her was really in either of their interests. His assignment would come to an end and he would move back to Dublin. But nonetheless, Maria was good company and he wondered if there might be some future with her.

Finn's work continued for another six weeks. He was busy during the days, but he began to see Maria on a reasonably regular basis in the evenings. It did not take too long for their friendship to develop into a more amorous level. They found that they had much in common and had similar expectations for the future. Soon Maria began to frequent Finn's apartment with the inevitable consequences of two consenting adults enjoying each other's company. However, both stayed far away from any form of real commitment.

-Maria, what is the Vatican policy on relationships between employees?

-It is highly frowned upon. If they knew about us, I am sure that I would be dismissed and your contract would be terminated.

-Oh really.

-Without doubt.

And you are prepared to take that chance?

-I told you that I didn't like the Mother Superior's bullying attitude in the convent. It's the same thing here.

-Well they had better not find out.

-I wholeheartedly agree.

-Do you think that after my work finishes and I return to Dublin it will be feasible for us to see each other from time to time?

-I don't know, why not? Distance isn't what it used to be. And with video conferencing, we are in a much better position to stay in touch than anyone was before.

-Right. Let's see how we feel about all of that when the time comes.

In due course, Finn finished his assignment. The officials of the Curia were pleased with his work and asked him if they could call upon him again from time to time when new discoveries were made - which were, in fact, more frequently than most people realised. Finn was pleased to agree to this, subject to his availability, as his duties back in Dublin were of great importance to him. Of course, an occasional trip back to Rome to see Maria would be most welcome.

So, Finn returned to O'Connell College. He met with the director of the Ringsend Shelter for Abused Children, Kathleen Daly and told her that he had cast some bread on the water in the hope he might be able to land a sizeable donation for the charity within the next few months. He emphasised that these types of activities take a long time and that she should not expect to hear one way the other for at least six months. Of course she knew this already. In the meantime, he advised her to continue her best efforts in raising funds from her own network.

Two months later a letter arrived from Brother Philippe stating that the project was more challenging than he had first thought and that more research on his part was necessary. The letter went on to say that the Brothers were still hopeful that they could complete the project as promised, but that it would take a little longer. At first Finn was disappointed but then he realised that it was a big step from working with mediaeval scripts to creating a 19th century document. The monks had agreed to work outside their natural comfort zone. And he knew well enough that this type of work could not be rushed.

Finn's work at the College was hectic so time did not appear to drag on and three months later he received a letter with a postmark from Rome inviting him to visit Brother Philippe in Castel del Dolfo the following Saturday afternoon. He was delighted and booked his flight to Rome immediately to arrive Friday night so there would be little chance of missing his appointment with the monk. He also arranged to spend a couple of extra days in Rome to have some time to spend with Maria. In due course, Finn presented himself at the house of the Order of Saint Francis Picallo where he was warmly greeted by Brother Philippe and was handed a box he assumed was the finished product.

-Professor Kelly, I am sorry that this job took longer than we had originally envisaged. We had to find our way in a literary milieu that we were not that familiar with or accustomed to. Fortunately, some of the Brothers here are amongst the best historical researchers in the world and of course, our calligraphy is ... magnificent. We then had some issues related to the sourcing of the appropriate materials to match the age of the document. We are now all pleased with the quality of this work.

-And how did you get over all those challenges?

-You don't need to know the details but everything turned out alright in the end.

-I am so pleased to hear that.

-I am confident you will find the work satisfactory and that whoever ends up owning this beautiful manuscript will get much pleasure from it. There will be no record here of our involvement with this and I would highly recommend you keep silent about our association.

-Indeed Brother Philippe, and this envelope should cover the Order's expenses. I did add some extra because of the additional work. If it isn't enough please let me know.

Brother Philippe nodded with approval.

-Good luck with whatever you do with the document, Professor.

-Thank you and goodbye.

Finn retraced his steps back to Rome and immediately went to his hotel where he opened the box. What a wonderful job the monks had done for him. It was perfect. He was so thrilled. He marvelled at the craftsmanship that had gone into producing this artefact. Now he had to find someone who really wanted to personally own an original "lost" play of Oscar Wilde, Being Excellent.

Was this going to be easy? He wondered.

Chapter Ten

Selling to Williamson

Finn thought he knew someone who would like to own the play but he also realised that Sean O'Toole, being one of the world's leading experts on Oscar Wilde, would also be well placed to find a purchaser. His and Sean's contacts were entirely in Ireland. But, would Ireland have a big enough community of wealthy individuals to ensure that a really good price was obtained? Finn thought probably not. Finn believed that a more international market needed to be accessed. It occurred to Finn that Jeremy Williamson, being American, would have a much greater network than he or Sean could ever hope to reach on their own. Maybe he should make an approach to Williamson to find out what he might be able to do for him. He knew he would have to be quite careful about this if for no other reason than that his last meeting with Williamson had not been terribly comfortable. So, he called Williamson's office and made an appointment to meet him on the Monday morning.

In the meantime, he had arranged to meet Maria and his Oscar Wilde book would be safely stored away until Monday.

Finn suggested that they meet in the Piazza Navona at the Fontana dei Quattro Fiumi which is one of the best known and popular landmarks in Rome. It was midday and the piazza was abuzz with not only Romans, but people from all over the world. Both Finn and Maria were delighted to be with one another and to be within a crowd that exuded the vibrant buzz of this ancient city. They strolled around the piazza for a while before taking off for the Pantheon and then the Trevi Fountain when they began to look for a suitable restaurant for lunch, which they eventually found down one of the many side streets.

-Back in Rome again, Finn.

-Yes and wonderful to be here, especially with you.

-But you didn't come back to see me?

-Well Maria, not only you. I have a few things to tidy up related to my work at the Vatican.

- I hadn't heard about that.

-I guess you don't know all the secrets of the Vatican.

-Oh, a secret mission then?

-No, of course not. I was just using a turn of phrase. My work is often confidential but never secret.

-I am glad you have come. Keeping up by exchanging email is not very satisfactory.

-And the occasional video calls?

-It's all rather flat, Finn, don't you think?

-Would you really like to come and spend some time with me in Dublin?

-Why not?

-A somewhat ambiguous answer. But I take it that it was meant in a positive way?

-Of course.

Much of the rest of the afternoon was spent over a much extended lunch with a number of different types of libations followed by digestives. Finn and Maria teased each other about their work, future expectations and their distant friendship. Finn felt that Maria had become, for him, a special person but he was not yet ready to see her play a larger role in his life.

Maria had commitments with her family that evening and so with a great hug and a longer than usual farewell kiss they parted company.

On Monday morning the Gallery Garibaldi was quite busy when
Finn arrived. There was a large Vatican limousine parked outside
with a patient chauffer guarding it against any traffic police. The
vehicle was exactly the same as the one in which he had been driven
to and from Cardinal Baffasa's palace. Finn was told that Mr
Williamson was in a meeting and that he would be available shortly.
After 15 minutes he was ushered into Williamson's office.

-The Gallery is having a busy day?

-Yes, indeed. But most days are busy.

-I see a Cardinal's limousine parked outside. It looks like the one that
took me to visit the distinguished Cardinal Baffasa recently.

-All those cars look the same. I don't have much spare time today so
if you don't mind, may we please get right down to business.

Finn was aware that his comment had just been brushed off and he
didn't like that much, but he was more concerned with his business
objective than any social small talk.

-Certainly. What I came here to tell you is that I have been working
with a group of people in Dublin who have come across a piece of
artistic work we think, sorry I mean they think, might have some
considerable value. It is quite a long story but they have discovered
an unknown or should I say 'lost play' written by Oscar Wilde back
in the 1870s while he was a student at O'Connell College. It was
found in the belongings of the great-grandson of an old retainer who
worked for the Wilde family in Dublin from the middle of the 19th
century for some 30 years. It seems that when Oscar was leaving
O'Connell College to go to Oxford University some of his
possessions were shoved together in a trunk, left in the attic of his
parents' home and forgotten about. Some thirty years later, when the
house was being sold and the old family retainer was being
pensioned off, it appears he was given the old trunk and he added his
own belongings to it before taking it away.

-Interesting.

-No one noticed that there was a manuscript at the bottom of the old trunk. Once again it went into storage and has only recently been re-opened. To the great surprise of everyone concerned they found a manuscript of what is Oscar Wilde's first drama written in 1870 or 1871. My associates in Dublin feel this might be worth a substantial amount of money and it occurred to me that you might be interested in handling the sale of this document for them. Does this sound like something you would be prepared to do?

-I would certainly have to know a bit more about it before I could make a decision, but, in principle, this appears to be a project that could interest me. You know the Gallery Garibaldi has extensive connections with artistic interests in the USA and finds such as you have described could well be of interest to well-placed Irish Americans who like to invest in culturally rich assets. Let me think about this and get back to you.

-I actually have the document with me. Would you like to have a quick look at it?

-Most certainly, Professor Kelly. But I am really pressed for time this morning.

-I think that in just a few minutes you will get a clear impression of what this manuscript is all about.

-You're right.

Finn placed his brief case on Williamson's desk and extracted the box containing the manuscript. Williamson had a pair of white cotton gloves on his desk which he put on and came round to stand by Finn's side. Although completely silent Finn could detect that Williamson was clearly impressed with what he was looking at.

After three or four minutes Williamson rekindled the conversation.

-Very interesting, Professor.

-Mr Williamson, I am only in Rome for another couple of days. Would you be able to let me know tomorrow if you are interested in taking on this project? I can come by your office again at the same time?

-Yes. That should be fine. I'll see you then tomorrow morning.

Under the watchful eye of Williamson Finn carefully packed up the book back into its box and into the briefcase.

Finn left the Gallery Garibaldi with the distinct impression that Jeremy Williamson would take on this assignment. This seemed to Finn to be the preferred way of handling its sale as he would therefore not have to get involved in the detail of looking for a purchaser. Presumably, he concluded, he could hand the book over to Williamson and just collect a cheque in due course.

The following morning Finn was in Williamson's office at the appointed time.

-Professor Kelly, we normally don't deal with middlemen, especially academic middlemen. We always like to really get to know the source of the works which we promote. It reduces the amount of potential confusion which can arise in these sorts of deals. However, in your case I think that I can make an exception.

-Thank you.

-Your connections to the Vatican suggest to me that you are going to be highly reliable and that you also will understand the importance of our code of silence. Our business is built on confidentiality, or rather absolute confidentiality.

-I understand that; I am glad you think I am trustworthy.

-After consideration my associates and I should say, especially our Boston partners have said, that if we can examine the book in detail and we come to the conclusion that it is genuine, we will take on this project for you. I presume you are prepared to leave it with us.

Finn did not like the idea of leaving his precious book with Williamson but he bit his lip as he realised that he would have to do this.

-Oh yes. Of course.

-It will take us a week or so to study the manuscript thoroughly and assess it and make a final decision but all being well you will know by the end of the month.

-And what do you think a piece of work like this might be worth?

-I can't say until I have studied the manuscript carefully but I'm sure that you're looking at seven figures. We might put it up for auction or we might place it privately. We will take a commission of one third of the net receipts for handling this for you.

Finn, who of course, knew nothing about the art world and absolutely zero about how such deals were structured thought this commission was rather steep but then if the book could be sold for €1 million and with all the work being done by Williamson, this was an easy solution to the problems of the charity for the next couple of years.

Finn handed over the box containing the book, received a receipt, and took himself back to his hotel. He had one more thing he had to do in Rome before he could return to Dublin. When he was a student Finn had a bank account with the Banco del Santa Paulo del Spirito Santo and he went there to see if his old account could be revived. He was impressed with the computer system that brought up his old records. He told the bank officials that he was now a consultant to the Vatican and dropped the names of some of the officials he had met there in recent months. The bank officials were impressed and, with relatively little fuss, Finn's account was resuscitated. He would now have somewhere to lodge the money he hoped to receive in due course from Williamson. He made arrangements for internet banking so that all the transactions related to his current project could be completed on-line without needing to visit the bank again.

Once again Finn and Maria met up briefly in what had now become their favourite wine bar. Finn was very distracted by the success he had had with Williamson but he did not feel that he could share this with Maria. So the conversation was about his busy day and about how he was not looking forward to his flight home to the dismal weather in Dublin. He felt saying goodbye to Maria was not easy. It was now time to suggest that Maria came to visit him in Dublin at O'Connell College. The following month or so was going to be difficult due to pressure of work and other commitments so they selected dates a couple of months ahead and he offered to buy the tickets. The time flashed by and Finn rushed to catch a taxi to the airport from where he flew back again on the late flight to Dublin.

Finn had always been a man with considerable confidence in himself and in whatever plans he thought up. He had never been prone to self-doubt or to anxiety-related problems. But now he was beginning to feel a certain level of anxiousness, and he began to wonder how easy or difficult it was going to be to accomplish his objective. Was Williamson going to take on this commission? Would Williamson treat him fairly? Would a big sum of money really arrive? Finn was not all that sure. He was clearly in uncharted waters.

Chapter Eleven

Success?

On the last day of the month, another letter arrived with a Roman postmark. Finn opened it anxiously and pulled out the expensive letterhead. The message was brief, simply stating that Williamson and his associates would be pleased to accept this project and they estimated the value of the item to be approximately €1.5 million. The letter also said that the process of finding an appropriate owner for the treasure would take 3 to 6 months. Finally, it closed by saying that it was necessary for Finn to send an appropriate bank account number where the results of the sale could be lodged. Finn had expected to have to produce some certification as to the provenance of the work but in the end this was not asked for.

Finn was really staggered by the alleged value. It had never occurred to him that this work would be worth so much money. Such a sum would really help the embattled charity. Moments later, he realised that one third of this would have to go to Williamson. But, even then, it would be a handsome figure. He then recalled that he had promised a percentage to Sean O'Toole. He remembered saying something to the effect that Sean could have 10 to 20% but now he wondered whether that percentage was of the gross or the net and he wondered what Sean would actually settle for. He knew Sean was always short of money.

Initially Finn had thought the book would only be worth a few hundred thousand euros, but now it appeared that he had substantially underestimated what it might fetch. Every cent he could give to the charity would be useful to them. It also occurred to Finn that it was far too early to get involved in these thoughts as there was a long journey between putting something up for sale and having money in the bank that could be shared. So, he decided to try to forget about these issues for the time being and wait and see what was going to happen.

On the following Tuesday Finn attended the monthly meeting with Kathleen Daly and the other trustees at the offices of the Ringsend Shelter for Abused Children. The mood of the meeting was quite sombre. After formally opening the meeting, Kathleen began.

-Ladies and gentlemen, I don't have any good news to report. The revised budgets show that we will have to do some serious reductions in programmes next year as we will have a hole in the budget of at least a quarter of a million euros. I think we will have to cut back on at least two programmes and we may have to make a few redundancies. Finn when we last met you told me you were going to do some thinking about how we might be able to raise some new money. Have you come up with anything?

-Before I go into that have you been back to see the Government Grants Department, Kathleen? And what have they said to you about how the Shelter's grant will be affected next year?

-Yes. I have. And I got nowhere. They cannot tell me anything except that there will be major cuts. The level will only be formally announced early next year. We will only be given six months' notice and they are saying that we had better make arrangements to cut our cloth according to our means. I am astounded at the cheek of these people. They are pulling the plug on some of the poorest and most vulnerable individuals in the community and they don't seem to give a damn. So, Finn, what have you been able to do?

-I put a few feelers out among some substantial benefactors. I haven't had any commitments yet, but, on the other hand I have some sympathetic ears listening to me and I am hopeful that we will receive a substantial amount in the next few months. But let's make sure we don't count our chickens before they are hatched.

-Can't you tell us who you've been talking to, or just give us some sort of clue?

-No. Sorry I can't. My discussions have been entirely confidential. It would kill any hope of funds if it got out that I was talking and breaking any confidences.

-Is it likely to be European or American money?

-Sorry. Can't say. Won't say.

Finn realised that it was getting easier and easier for him to lie and that he was almost enjoying it. He wondered where that was going to lead him.

The next few months passed relatively quickly for Finn. He was busy with his research students, who continued to need fairly constant attention. He had a little bit of teaching to do which he did not find a chore. He had a couple of local consulting assignments and of course, he had a major research paper he had been working on for some time. For his academic career a major research paper was a really important event, and he knew that he had to give it a hundred and twenty per cent of his attention. This, he was finding difficult to do.

Eventually towards the middle of spring details arrived from his Italian bank that he had received €1.1 million. The bank statement didn't say anything else and there was no indication as to who had deposited the money. He stared at the bank statement for ages. He could hardly believe he was seeing a figure like this in his own personal bank account. He did a quick calculation. Williamson must have received over a million and a half for the book. This was about 10 years' gross salary.

Finn knew a little about money laundering laws and he wondered why his bank was not querying this receipt. It occurred to him that Williamson must have made the necessary arrangements to avoid this and that it would be better if he knew nothing about what Williamson did. Deniability was a concept that Finn had heard of.

He knew what had to be done and this involved the challenge of deciding how much to offer Sean O'Toole. He decided to act quickly. He would give Sean about 10%, actually €100,000 of the net receipts and transfer the balance of the money immediately into the bank account of the charity. He would take nothing for his own costs. Doing this would settle this matter and would no longer distract him from his academic duties.

Finn phoned Kathleen and arranged to meet in her office.

-Kathleen, when you next look at the Shelter's bank statement you will notice an additional sum has been deposited. You will find a transfer of €1 million into the account this morning.

-You said what?

-You heard me quite correctly, €1 million was deposited into the Shelter's account this morning. Do you remember I told you a few months ago that I had put out some feelers to some substantial benefactors asking whether they would support the Shelter? Well, they decided to do so, and the money came through this morning. I decided not to delay transferring the money directly, so you will have use of it in the next couple of days after your bank has cleared the transaction.

-My goodness gracious me. How fantastic. Did you say €1 million? What a fabulous sum of money. I can hardly believe it. How did you manage to pull this off?

-Never mind about that. It was just a lucky break. And don't expect me to be able to do this again. But it should be helpful in a number of different ways.

-You're absolutely right, we can get back to our original plans.

-Kathleen I wouldn't do that. I would treat this money as a reserve you should have in case there are any other reductions in government grants or if some of your more established donors run into problems and are unable to keep up their contributions. Times are tough in the financial world and I think we must be careful about how we continue to manage the Shelter.

Finn met up with Sean that afternoon and they both went together to one of the better and more expensive pubs of Grafton Street not generally frequented by O'Connell College people.

-Sean, I had better tell you exactly how much I got for Being Excellent. In all I received €1.1 million and I gave a round million to the Shelter and I deposited €100,000 in your account this morning. I know we didn't discuss exactly how much you were going to get from the sale of Being Excellent but I think that €100,000 is much more than either of us had originally thought would come your way. I hope you will consider that amount to be reasonable compensation for the work you did.

-That's not even 10% Finn. Didn't we talk about something like 10, or maybe even 20%. What happened?

-I know. But we originally thought that the book would only be worth a few hundred thousand euros and it turned out to be worth more than 1 million and anyway you told me you were not doing this for the money.

-That's right but even so I think you might have consulted me before you distributed the money. I think that perhaps my efforts were worth a little more. After all it is said that charity does begin at home.

-Come on Sean, the money has gone to a real charity! Let's not make a big thing of this? We're lifelong pals aren't we? I am not taking a penny for myself.

Finn became aware that the money was more important to Sean than he had originally thought. He felt vaguely annoyed with himself that he had not seen this side of Sean before.

-The €100,000 will certainly be useful but my luck with the gee-gee has not been great lately and whatever moneys I can get my hands on will be very useful to keep the bookies at bay. Are you sure there is not a bit more you can put my way?

-No, Sean. I have nothing left from the money I received. I apologise if my actions were a bit precipitous but you can at least feel comforted by the fact that the money has gone to a really good cause. I have taken nothing for myself and I haven't tried to recover any of my own personal expenses.

In the end Kathleen Daly was delighted with the funds she received but Sean O'Toole was not as enthusiastic about his share. Nonetheless they both congratulated Finn on his fundraising abilities.

Sean would now be able to take sabbatical leave and do some of the writing that he wanted to, and the future of Kathleen's charity was not as bleak as it had looked the day before. Also she knew that she would have to take a different attitude towards fundraising by using a small part of the money she had just received to appoint a professional fundraising officer.

Finn knew he had to control a certain sense of guilt which he was beginning to feel about having redirected resources from the wealthy to help the poor. Whenever a moment of guilt raised its head he would tell himself that this whole caper had been a good thing. With his Irish Catholic education, he was aware of how destructive guilt could be, so he was determined to put such feelings behind him and to now focus on his research and his other duties in the College. He was determined to concentrate on ensuring that Being Excellent was deeply in his past.

Finn continued to keep contact with Maria. They spoke through video conferencing a couple of times a week. Her trip to Dublin would be coming up soon and that was something he was looking forward to. Finn was anxious to make his caper with the book ancient history.

Chapter Twelve

Bloody murder at O'Connell College

Early one morning, a few weeks later, when Finn arrived at the front entrance of O'Connell College there were two police cars and a strip of police tape reading *Crime Scene, Don't Enter,* preventing faculty and students from entering the College grounds. Everyone who wanted to go into O'Connell College was told to walk around to the Dooley Street entrance. Finn's office was in the Social Science Block, easily accessible from the other entrance, so it didn't bother him much to take the slightly longer walk around the college. However, he was curious about what was going on so he strolled over to the main quadrangle where there was an ambulance and a number of other cars parked. There were several men and a woman standing around, some of whom had a variety of professional-looking cameras in their hands. Finn approached one of these men.

-What has been going on?

-It appears that someone was murdered in his office yesterday evening. There hasn't been an official statement made yet, but we understand that it was the bursar, Mr Frank Mullally. We don't know much more about it at the moment, but I'm sure it will be broadcast on the media any minute now. I understand that it's the first time anything like this has happened in O'Connell College. I think we are in for a piece of really juicy scandalous news. Anyway, O'Connell College always makes great headlines, especially if it's sensational! This will turn out to be a humdinger.

Finn was more than a little puzzled by this turn of events and he decided not to wait around. He was better off going directly to his office. No doubt he would hear the full story in due course.

By late morning the main headline on the television in the RTE news was *Bursar Murdered in O'Connell College -Bullet to the Brain in Execution type killing.* It appeared that the cleaners found the body of

Frank Mullally when they arrived this morning slumped over his desk in a pool of blood in his office located over the front gate. Mullally appears to have been shot at close range with a small calibre gun. The time of death was yet to be confirmed but initial indications were that he was shot early evening the day before. No one has reported having heard a shot so it is assumed a silencer was used with the gun. Nothing appears to have been removed from his office or from the person of the deceased. There were, as yet, no clues as to the motive for this tragedy. Mr Mullally's personal assistant said that it was quite common for him to work late and that he often had appointments after hours in his office. The role of Bursar at O'Connell College was a hectic one, especially since financial cutbacks at the College had resulted in a number of administrative staff being made redundant.

By late afternoon the news programme had been expanded and various individuals had been interviewed who gave testimonials attesting to what a fine colleague Frank Mullally had been. The Principal even made an appearance expressing condolences to the Mullally family and asking anyone who had any information of any kind that might help the Gardaí in their enquiries to come forward. But there was still no clue as to why this murder had taken place.

The inspection of the crime scene is always a slow business and the Gardaí spent the whole of that day in the College. Fingertip searches were performed in various parts of the college grounds in the hope of finding some clue which might help them understand what had happened the night before. Various members of faculty were questioned as well as a number of administrative staff. But no one had any ideas helpful to the investigation. Notices were put up around the College and in the adjacent streets asking the public to come forward with any information they might have.

A couple of days later the gossip in the common room ran wild. Finn arrived to find two of his colleagues deeply involved in idle gossip and speculation. The deputy bursar led the gossip mill.

-Terry, it's indeed absolutely shocking. The whole College is upset like I have never seen before. Shocked to the core we are.

-Rosemary, you know I don't know what Mullally could have been up to. He wasn't political. And I'm pretty sure he wasn't into any form of criminality. He was really a modest and docile sort of man. I wonder if there could have been something in his personal life. Was he misbehaving with the wrong sort of women? I wonder.

-I can't imagine that.

-I believe Mullally's office was a terrible mess. Blood and papers everywhere.

-I hope our poor cleaners didn't have to sort the mess out in the office. I am sure that the Gardaí won't go near it.

-I imagine that outside contractors were brought in.

-I did see some strange-looking people going in and coming out of his office in recent weeks. And I wondered what was going on.

-I'm sure you're just imagining that. I didn't see anyone around the college who looked out of place. You must be careful about what you say. Of course, there are always some unusual looking tourists who come in to see the Antiquarian Museum. But for goodness sake, they had nothing to do with Frank Mullally.

-You know you can never tell. They say still waters run deep. And Mullally was certainly in the category of still waters.

-Don't be absurd. Mullally was nothing like that. He was just a decent man … like the rest of us, I'm sure.

-On the other hand, I heard that Mullally had been rough on the number of overseas students whose registrations he had terminated. It appears they were not taking their studies seriously and he decided they were hanging around the College in the hope they might eventually get residence papers in Ireland.

-That's also an outrageous suggestion. Students don't murder a senior member of the College because of being expelled. How did you come up with such a crazy idea?

-You can never tell, can you now?

-Let's face the elephant in the room. Mullally had a few very bitter rows with people at the College. Being nice to the man, and we all know the old saying *De mortuis nihil nisi bonum- don't speak badly of the dead*, he was an arch conservative. Being more "frank" and no pun intended, some of Frank Mullally's attitudes would have been more becoming of a dinosaur.

-You have rubbed that in enough. Now, let it rest. Remember we always write RIP on the tombstone.

-Yes. Rest-In-Peace, indeed. Some of Mullally's ideas and attitudes should have been laid to rest many years ago.

-There does not appear to have been a burglary. Could this have been a totally random event? Dublin isn't like that. Is it? I think that the city isn't big enough to have complete crackpots who go around murdering for its own sake. Okay, we've had some drug wars in the past, and of course we've always had political, or at least some would say quasi-political violence with the IRA and the like, but there is no suggestion of that in this case. There has to be something quite different behind this.

-Dublin is rapidly acquiring some of the bad habits of bigger cities. Maybe unmotivated and senseless murder is one of the prices one pays for modernisation or globalisation or whatever they call it. - Thank goodness it's not up to us to find out who did this terrible thing. I am sure the Gardaí will do a good job in due course.

-Well, I'm not so sure how smart our Gardaí really is, and I'll bet this is gonna turn out to be one hell of a big challenge for them.

-Yes, I can't recall their success rate in solving murders, if ever indeed I really knew it, but it is not particularly high.

Finn stayed far away from this type of gossip. There was clearly no point in any of the speculation. Time would no doubt lead to some of the mystery being unravelled.

That evening Finn received a phone call from Sean O'Toole. He hadn't seen Sean for a few weeks and he was still feeling a bit sensitive about how Sean had shown his disappointment over receiving only €100,000.

-Finn, I am staying down with my cousin in Wexford where I'm doing a bit of writing. I arranged to be away from College for a month to get a bit of breathing space. I am finishing off a book I have been working on for more than two years on WB Yates and his revolutionary poems and I am making good progress at last. I received a call on my mobile from a friend of mine when I was in Kilmuckridge yesterday. You know mobile reception is dodgy where I am staying. Sometimes you can reach me and sometimes the line is quite bad. Anyway he lives in the same block of flats in Dublin. He told me that I have been burgled and that my whole place had been ransacked.

-Really?

-Apparently it looked like someone was searching for something they were unable to find. My friend has reported it to the Gardaí who are looking into the matter. It's really strange as I don't have anything of material value that anyone would want to steal. I don't keep money in the flat and I don't have expensive personal accessories that could easily be sold.

-Sean, that's odd. I'm not sure what to say. I'm glad you called me. Is there anything I can do to help?

-I don't think so right now. I only wanted to talk to a friend. I'm on my own down here. That's what I wanted so I could get on with the work. But it is a bit lonely.

-To be sure.

-Finn, I'm not rushing back to Dublin as I'm really in a creative mood for writing and I don't want to interrupt that. But I am a little disturbed with the break-in of my apartment coming just after the murder in the College. I can't imagine that they could be connected in any way but I have a very uneasy feeling, a sort of a premonition that something is not right.

-No. I can't see there being any real connection but both of these crimes seem quite senseless. Let me think about it. Do please give me a call before you come back to Dublin and I'll arrange to be here when you get back. If you want you can come and spend a few nights with me here in Drumcondra while you get your flat sorted out.

-Thanks. Let's see how I feel when the time comes.

Finn was pleased to be able to make a helpful suggestion to his friend, and thought nothing more about the burglary. It was just a silly crime, demonstrating the difficulties of modern life in a city.

Chapter Thirteen
A voice from Boston

The following day Finn received a phone call in his office from a man with a heavy Boston accent.

-Professor, your name was suggested to me by Sean O'Toole after I heard him give a lecture about the book he has been writing with Paddy Walsh called the Soul of the Author. He said the book isn't a hundred per cent finalised yet, but that he was expecting it to be so within the next few weeks. O'Toole is a great lecturer.

-Yes. I have heard him teach a number of times.

-He really captured the attention of the audience on what I think is really a fairly esoteric topic. My name is Joe Murphy and I represent the US – Irish Cultural Cooperative Society. We are a body that promotes the appreciation of Irish culture especially among the young generation in the United States – in the Boston area, of course. One of the things we do is ask distinguished scholars from Ireland to come across to Boston to deliver talks on their specialities. The purpose of this programme is to promote US-Irish Relations, especially by showcasing Irish expertise.

-Oh, yes.

-Dr O'Toole highly recommended you as Ireland's leading mediaevalist.

-That was nice of him.

-I am now in Ireland looking to invite a number of speakers to come over to us in the next few months. We are a hospitable group and we look after our guests very well. I wonder if I could interest you in coming over to us and giving a few lectures on your subject to some interested individuals?

-How nice of you to invite me.

-I would be pleased to come and see you in your office and discuss in detail how these trips work. If you're busy during the day I could come and see you after hours.

-I am flattered by your invitation. Who else have you invited?

-No one else yet. I am thinking about asking someone from Cork and Belfast.

That answer sounded far too vague to Finn.

-Mr Murphy you have caught me at a rather busy time.

-Surely not too busy to think about a generous offer?

-And I wonder if your audience would really be interested in my subject. You clearly know from O'Toole that I specialise in mediaeval art and literature, and it does not seem to me, at least at first glance, that the young generation you have referred to would flock to hear a talk on that subject. Mediaeval art is rather dry to the uninitiated. Certainly in this country young people show very little interest in this field of study.

-Well, Professor, I'm trying to cast my net wide and your name was mentioned as a leading figure in O'Connell College. And that's good enough for me to invite you to Boston. By the way, I also heard Sean O'Toole speak on the subject of Oscar Wilde. O'Toole is an erudite individual, is he not?

-Yes, indeed he is.

-O'Toole was saying that he had done some original research about how to get inside the minds of authors and so be able to produce new works which were indistinguishable from the writings of early masters.

-Oh, really.

-Yes, he was really interesting on that subject. The audience was fascinated.

-I haven't heard him on the subject.

-After his presentation, Professor, in general conversation, he mentioned that he was a close acquaintance of yours and that your services as a speaker in your field were highly sought after. We would, of course, be prepared to pay a handsome fee and we would make a donation to O'Connell College. We are prepared to pay the fee in cash if that would be helpful.

-That's all very generous of you. The College is always in need of money. Let me think about this for a while. I need a little time. I have done a lot of travelling over the past few months and have a very tight schedule for the rest of this year. Give me a call in a few days' time and we will see what we can do.

-Okay Professor but you won't get an offer as generous as this again in a hurry.

Finn found this call quite disquieting. He couldn't see the value of his travelling to the USA to talk on mediaeval art and literature to the younger American generation. It didn't ring true that anyone would connect a donation to the College with taking him to Boston to give a lecture. But worse still he was worried about how his name was connected with Sean O'Toole's in this way. It was not Finn's experience that lecturers at O'Connell College recommended each other in this way. They were personal friends and did not share any direct professional interests. He wondered what Sean had been saying about him at this talk on Oscar Wilde. Finn decided he had better meet up with Sean.

That afternoon Finn phoned Sean at his retreat in county Wexford and made arrangements with him to meet the following evening in an old travellers' watering hole or pub he sometimes frequented in Brittas Bay. The pub was called the Cunning Stunt and it was reputed to have been a pirates', smugglers' and highwaymen's hangout dating back to the 17th century when it was used by stagecoaches travelling down to Rosslare to meet with the boats that plied the Irish Sea on the way to South Wales. The pub got its name from the so-called king of the smugglers, who was known as the *Three-eyed Riley,* and he was infamous for the cunning way he tricked the King's tax collectors who were regularly fooled by this old rogue. Three-eyed Riley's ghost was said to haunt the place especially whenever anyone from the Irish Revenue Commissioners stop by for a drink. The pub was approximately halfway between Dublin and where Sean was staying in Wexford. Various people were said to have been murdered there over the years and the pub had the reputation of being haunted.

It is about 40 miles from Dublin to Brittas Bay and this journey normally takes an hour and a half. For some reason the traffic that evening was worse than usual and Finn struggled through brutal queues of cars and trucks. Sean had been waiting for him for some time and he already had begun to sample the local beverages.

-Sean, I took a strange phone call yesterday from a man who called himself Joe Murphy and said he was the representative of the US – Irish Cultural Cooperative Society. He invited me to go to Boston to deliver some lectures on mediaeval art and literature. I think it was a bogus invitation as I certainly can't see any point in my trying to entertain what he called "the younger generation" with that subject. This Murphy fellow said that he had got my name from you. What is this about?

-I don't remember a Joe Murphy as such. I have been speaking to a lot of groups in the last few months about the Soul of the Author and about Oscar Wilde in general. As you know giving talks to groups of people is an important activity for me as it supplements my relatively meagre income from the College. Furthermore, it is an anniversary of Oscar Wilde's death and there is a lot of interest in his life and works. I probably mentioned that you and I have recently played roles in The Importance of Being Ernest for the O'Connell College Amateur Dramatic Society. But I'm sorry I can't be any more specific than that. I hope you don't mind my giving you some acknowledgement for your work as a mediaevalist.

-Sean, you didn't say anything about Being Excellent did you?

-Finn, no, of course, not.

-Was there any discussion about Oscar Wilde's body of work?

-I think the issue of the fact that there is such a small body of work available to the modern reader is often raised when Oscar Wilde is discussed, but I don't remember there being any specific issues surrounding that.

-You know, when you phoned me the other night and you said you had a bad feeling about the senseless murder of Frank Mullally and the burglary of your apartment I thought nothing of it. But now I'm beginning to wonder if there isn't a connection and if this Murphy fellow hasn't got something to do with it. I haven't the faintest idea how this might connect at this stage but it is not giving me a good feeling. Did you start writing another "lost" Oscar Wilde play?

-Finn, I had been working on something like that but it is taking me a lot more time to get my mind around it than I had thought it would so I haven't made much progress. What I am doing right now is completely different. As I mentioned I am currently working on a much more academic work, a book about WB Yeats which should be helpful in my getting promotion at the College.

-Sean, did you tell anyone you were writing "lost" Oscar Wilde plays?

-No, of course not. Mmm ... I really don't think so. But I don't see that as worthy of being classified as a big dark secret.

-Are you crazy? Of course it is. You are going to have to wait a long time before you will be able to publish other Oscar Wilde-esque plays. If new plays start popping up that could have been written by

Oscar Wilde, it will have a direct impact on the credibility of Being Excellent. Someone, somewhere has paid a huge amount of money for that manuscript and they're going to feel that they have been cheated, or at least that their investment will have been devalued. The money we received for Being Excellent is directly related to its scarcity value. Your flat may have been burgled and ransacked in order to find out if there were any other Oscar Wilde-esque manuscripts about. But of course, that doesn't explain the murder of Mullally. You may have inadvertently put us in a difficult position.

-Finn, do you really think so?

-I don't know but I'm inclined to think that you should prolong your stay in Wexford for a bit longer.

-I was planning on being here for at least another couple of weeks so I'm in no hurry to get back to Dublin.

-Good. Stay put.

-But Finn, if this Murphy fellow is genuine then there might be plenty of money to be made by doing a lecture tour of New England.

-Look, I can't put my finger on exactly why I think this man is sinister, but sinister he is. I just know it.

Finn returned to Dublin much more concerned than he had been before. He didn't think that Sean would lie to him directly but he had a growing concern that Sean had let slip the fact that he was writing new plays that he could have published as though they had been written by Oscar Wilde. He had intuitively understood that Sean should not do this for quite some time and he regretted not discussing this more thoroughly with him months ago, and impressing on him the need for absolute discretion about what they had been doing. He wondered how Sean could be so naïve.

A few days later Joe Murphy phoned again. The Bostonian accent reminded him of Williamson. And of course Murphy knew that

O'Toole had been talking about how to imitate great author's works. Due to pressure of work and previous commitments Finn graciously declined his offer to go to Boston. In the conversation Murphy asked if Finn had seen Sean recently as he was hoping to invite him to Boston too. Finn replied that Sean was out of the country on a teaching assignment for the College in the Far East, but that he would tell Sean about the invitation when he returned. Finn took Murphy's mobile phone number though he strongly suspected that Murphy was not exactly what he purported to be, and that he and Sean would have to take every precaution to avoid him.

Worry now set in to Finn's daily routine. He worried about what might happen to Sean, and even to himself. He also worried about how the murder of Mullally could be explained in this context. Mullally had no obvious connection with either himself or Sean so could there really be any link? Finn wondered. Did Murphy visit Mullally in the hope of obtaining Sean's home address? Did the meeting go badly? Was there a row? Did Murphy want to keep his enquiry about Sean's address secret? Almost certainly, he would. Would Murphy actually murder Mullally just to keep that fact quiet? Why? Why not? Isn't that what American gangsters do? On the other hand, Finn felt there must be some way he would be able to square this circle and convince whoever was behind Murphy that neither he nor Sean would be any sort of a threat to them. Finn's academic leaning made him believe that if the cards were put on the table honestly, logic and therefore reason would surely prevail.

Soon Finn realised that he would have to do something positive about the situation. Murphy could only be a hired hand and it was important to get to whoever it was that had hired him. But how could this be done? Who knew about the creation of Being Excellent? Firstly, there was Brother Philippe and the other monks in Castel del Dolfo. Secondly there was Jeremy Williamson. But Finn had never told either of these people that the book he had asked them to work on and then sell was a complete fake. The question that quickly came to mind was who else could have found out? Who else knew? Was

Cardinal Baffasa somehow involved? Maybe the Cardinal knew that the Dameri document was a fake and that he had been in cahoots with Williamson. Maybe the Cardinal was one of the cardinals which Brother Janus had mentioned used to visit the monastery in Montebello? Finn could feel that he could easily be swept away on a tsunami of conspiracy theories. He began to wonder how he might be able to make sense of any of this.

Finn decided he would have to go back to Rome and talk to these people. In any event, it would be useful for him to visit his contacts at the Vatican. He wanted to be able to obtain more work from them in the future. Also it would be great to see Maria again. He had begun to feel that the absence of this attractive lady left a gap in his life.

Chapter Fourteen

Retracing his steps

Finn flew out on the 6 am flight to Rome. He began to feel that the flight from Dublin to Rome was no more daunting, or for that matter exciting, than catching the No. 48A bus to Dun Laoghaire. From take-off in Dublin, he was in his hotel room in Rome in four hours. This was going to be a difficult journey with little prospect of any joy in it for Finn, other than seeing Maria. He had made arrangements to pay a courtesy call to his contacts in the Vatican in order to enquire how the work he had been involved in was being received, and the prospects of any further assignments being offered. The people at the Vatican were still pleased with the work he had done and suggested they would be looking to invite Finn back for an extended period in the next few months. Finn graciously accepted their compliments, saying that he would be delighted to work with them again. He wondered whether a move to Rome might not be good for his career – if not a permanent move then at least a sabbatical.

Early that evening Finn met Maria for a drink in their favourite restaurant. Maria was delighted to see Finn again and greeted him with a most enthusiastic hug. She clearly expected to spend the evening with him but he was largely distracted as he was worrying about how his business visits would go on the following day. They had a few drinks and then he excused himself saying truthfully that he had been up before 4 AM that morning and he had a busy day ahead of him tomorrow. They agreed to meet again before he returned to Dublin the day after tomorrow.

That night Finn slept little. He had a number of dreams in which he was in strange places where he was lost and he did not know what to do next. He was particularly disturbed by one dream in which he was on a lecture tour but he did not know where he was or what subject he was supposed to be speaking about.

When he woke up he realised that he was subconsciously struggling with what his best strategy would be in approaching both Brother Philippe and Jeremy Williamson. He came to the conclusion that he would have to be direct and completely honest with them and if there was any question that they thought he had acted in bad faith he would have to find a way of fixing that and fixing it quickly. Quite what he would do if they were to ask for the money back he didn't know but he did have a flat in Dublin worth more than he had received from Being Excellent, and if needs be, he would sell that to clear any debt they thought he might have to them.

The following morning, he was up bright and early to catch the bus to the house of the Order of Saint Francis Picallo in Castel del Dolfo. It was an old bus on this route and it was particularly crowded and stuffy. The traffic was especially heavy. As he was anxious to meet Brother Philippe the journey seemed interminable. People were struggling to get on and off the bus and to find and gather up all their belongings. However, in due course he rang the bell on the big door of the house.

It was answered by the same very obliging young monk he had met several times before.

-May I please see Brother Philippe? I know that I don't have an appointment, but I was hoping that Brother Philippe would spare me a few minutes. I have come all the way from Dublin to see him. What I have to say to him won't take long, I promise.

-Oh, I'm so sorry, but Brother Philippe isn't here. He left us a few months ago.

The young monks tone was rather sad and he had a clear frown upon his face.

-Sorry. What do you mean by he left us? Do you mean that he has died?

-Oh. No, no. Not at all. Brother Philippe isn't dead. At least as far as I know he's not. He wasn't when he left here. He decided to leave the Order. Quite suddenly. Would you believe, after 30 years? He decided the monastic lifestyle was too placid and that he wanted to become a missionary. He took a position with the group who were teaching in a remote area of Ethiopia. I have been told they are a strict group and they only tolerate a limited amount of contact with the outside world.

-Ethiopia? What a strange decision for him to make!

-I think it had something to do with his meeting an Ethiopian who described to him the atrocities committed by the Italians in their country in the 1930s and the 1940s. Brother Philippe said that he had no idea of just how horrible the Italians had been to the indigenous people. It seems he somehow wanted to try to make amends for the invasion of that country during the war.

-I am surprised. Is there some way of contacting him?

-I don't know, but I'm sure it won't be easy. If you would like to leave your details I will see if I can pass them on to the Head of our House who, I'm sure, will try to be helpful if he can. That's all I can suggest for now. I wouldn't expect that you will hear back from him soon.

Finn was simply gobsmacked. The story the young monk had told him did not entirely ring true to Finn. But he couldn't quite bring himself to believe that this explanation was a complete fabrication but, on the other hand he had great difficulty accepting that he would not be able to speak to Brother Philippe about what had become for Finn a pressing matter. He felt very cut off. His connection to Brother Philippe had been very important to Finn. There wasn't much else he could do at this stage except leave his visiting card in the hope that Brother Philippe would be encouraged to contact him as soon as possible.

Back in Rome Finn knew he had to visit the Gallery Garibaldi. He was not looking forward to this as he had not at all warmed to Jeremy Williamson. He didn't have much faith that Williamson would be straight with him. But there was nothing for it but to face the lion in his den, or as some would have it, grab the bull by the horns. Finn went directly from the bus station to the Gallery Garibaldi.

When Finn arrived at the Gallery, he was struck by the fact that the decor had changed. It was not looking quite as glitzy and as modern as it had been. New decorators had been in and had toned down the front of house which now looked much softer and a lot more expensive. Finn wondered why they had decided to change the image of the business.

He approached the receptionist.

-My name is Professor Kelly and I would like to see Mr Jeremy Williamson. I don't have an appointment, but I am an established client and I would really only need to take a few minutes of his time.

-Please take a seat and I will have someone attend to you.

-Certainly.

A young woman dressed in a tailored business suit arrived two minutes later.

-Professor Kelly, I am sorry to say that Mr Williamson is no longer here. He retired two months ago.

-Retired?

-Yes. It appears he was planning his retirement for quite some time and he sprang it on all of us as a great surprise. There was no celebration, as one might expect when the boss of a small business leaves for his retirement. He just packed up and went. There are new owners managing the Gallery now. We put an ad in the newspaper announcing that the Gallery Garibaldi was now under new management. You may have seen it as it was in the national newspapers for a whole week. Can any of the new people help you? They are awfully nice and knowledgeable about art.

Finn's mind was descending into a whirl. He couldn't contact Brother Philippe and now Williamson had disappeared as well. What was going on?

-I am really surprised about Mr Williamson. It seems like only yesterday that I was talking to him. He did a deal for me. I just wanted to…

-I am sure that there is someone here who can help you. Let me call down one of our consultants who can look after whatever queries you have?

-No. Thank you. I don't think so. Er … mmm ... but could you possibly give me the contact details for Mr Williamson? It is a personal matter between Mr Williamson and me.

-I am sorry, but he didn't leave any that I am can disclose to you. If you give me your contact details, I will see if they can't be passed on to Mr Williamson. Maybe one of the new owners knows how to contact him but none of the workers do. However, I should say that when he left here he said he was going to buy a beach cottage far away from the madding crowds in the hope that no one would ever want to get in touch with him from this business again. We were all rather surprised. That doesn't sound too encouraging does it? So, I don't hold out much hope for his getting in touch with you, or anyone else for that matter.

Worry and dismay now set in much more intensively than before. Finn began to feel a bit like Alice as she tumbled down the rabbit hole. What was really going on? What should he do next? Were all the people who had been involved in the Being Excellent play hiding from him? He couldn't really believe that, but now he felt desperately alone and with a man like Joe Murphy hanging around in Dublin, Finn was, for the first time, really becoming scared.

Finn then remembered the Cardinal What was his name again ... Cardinal Victor Baffasa it was. He was a Prince of the Church whose study looked like a mediaeval museum or art gallery. Could he really have been involved in the scam on Antonio Dameri, and again with the Being Excellent play?

For now, nothing seemed to be impossible. It would not be easy to locate the Cardinal, so Finn called Maria and asked her if she would make some enquiries and find a phone number for his office. Maria was, of course, most obliging and it did not take long for her to find the appropriate telephone number. But Maria now wanted to know what this trip was really all about and insisted on meeting Finn again that evening.

As Finn was half expecting, the Cardinal was away on Church business and was not expected back for three weeks. But at least the Cardinal had not disappeared like the other two. Finn realised he was not going to be able to get to the people behind Joe Murphy and that he would have to try to deal with Joe directly, and by himself.

Later when Finn and Maria met she got straight to the point.

-So Finn, tell me why have you really come back to Rome now?

-Maria, I had two reasons. One you know. I wanted to show my face and remind the members of the Curia that I am available to do more work for them and the other is a much more private one I can't discuss. You know the type of projects I get involved in are invariably confidential and that I can't discuss them...

-Even with me? I am an insider in the Vatican.

-This is a private matter and I have to remain silent for the moment.

-OK. Will you be able to tell me later?

-Perhaps.

-And of course I came back to Rome because I wanted to see you. Let's arrange for you to come and visit me in Dublin. Can you take some time off at the end of next month? That weekend includes St Patrick's Day and that's a great time to be in Dublin. Come for a long weekend? Let's make 3 days of it and maybe we can travel a bit out into the country as well.

-I would love that.

Finn was booked on the late night flight to Dublin so he had a few hours left before he had to head for the airport. Having said goodbye to Maria he decided to go to one of his favourite coffee shops on the Via Venezia where he could attend to his email. There were a number of messages from Moira Flannigan about relatively minor issues that had cropped up in the Department in the last 24 hours. But there was one email that initially puzzled him and after some reflection, it struck terror into Finn's soul. O'Connell College Dublin sent emails to all members of staff whenever a member of the College or a student passed away. In Finn's inbox there was a message to the effect that the College was sad to announce that, as a result of a tragic accident, Paddy Walsh had died. Walsh's body had been found floating face down in the Grand Canal. It appeared that he had fallen in while in a state of inebriation and had drowned. Finn did not immediately connect with the name but slowly he began to realise that he had heard the name Paddy Walsh from Sean O'Toole in connection with a book he had been working on called, The Soul of the Author.

Having finished his email there was nothing else left for Finn to do but call a taxi to take him to Leonardo da Vinci Airport and start his journey back to Dublin as soon as possible.

Now the question was whether Finn could deal with this situation by himself or whether he should involve the Gardaí? At first he was comforted by the thought of the Gardaí, but then he began to realise that involving them would lead to a whole series of complications. He was no lawyer but he was aware of there being a legal concept called passing off and he wondered if his involvement with Being Excellent constituted any sort of crime. He regretted not having considered all the implications of his actions much earlier. If Finn was involved in some sort of crime, then the kudos he had received by working at the Vatican would instantly turn sour. He wondered if the College would fire him. He did have tenure, but tenure could be broken if a member of staff was found guilty of gross moral turpitude. He wondered if his financial project involving the writing of a "lost" masterpiece by Oscar Wilde constituted such an act. If the College did fire him, there was no way he could stay in Ireland. He would be thoroughly disgraced and he would have to go and look for work abroad. He had a friend working in Germany who had told him that there were a number of opportunities there in his field. A dismissal from an institution like O'Connell College would follow him for the rest of his life.

But then it occurred to him that even if he had spent the time thinking through all the detail he probably would have taken the same course of action. The "lost" play of Oscar Wilde had rescued the charity from its immediate crisis and probably sometime into the future. Furthermore, neither did Finn have any proof that Joe Murphy had been involved in Mullally's death, nor for that matter did he have any proof that the American had burgled and ransacked Sean's apartment. Maybe he was just becoming paranoid. Perhaps he had seen too many gangster movies. If he went to the Gardaí, it would have to be on the grounds of his gut feeling and this, he felt, would probably make him look rather stupid. But what else could he do?

Chapter Fifteen

Detective Inspector Shamus Quinn

Arriving at his office early for a seminar, Finn was greeted by Moira who reminded him that he had a fairly full diary that day. Finn was anxious to learn anything he could about the death of Paddy Walsh.

-Moira did you see anything in the papers about how Paddy Walsh ended up in the Grand Canal?

-There was a short article in the Independent, but it wasn't reported in any of the other newspapers. Apparently there had been a big celebratory get-together due to the fact that Dr Walsh had just finished a book he'd been working on for some years. The article said that the party went on late, that the weather was cold and wet and Dr Walsh had a fairly long cycle home. It suggested that he just slipped off his bike and fell into the canal. Being so late there was no one around to see what happened and therefore no one helped him. It appears that he may have struck his head against something hard as he fell in. By the way a number of students from the English Department were apparently at the shindig. I can ask around for more information if you like?

-Yes. Please do. I would like to know more. And I wonder, maybe Paddy Walsh should have taken the pledge! But then I understand that he always looked like he had just had, or was in desperate need of, another few drinks.

Moira responded to this comment with a wry smile. Paddy's drinking was a scandal in the College.

Finn was comforted by the fact that it didn't seem to him that Paddy Walsh's death was anything other than a tragic accident.
Paddy had, in certain circles, a reputation of being brilliant but a thorough reprobate, and it had been whispered that he was the sort of fellow who would almost certainly come to a sticky end.

Having spent the weekend worrying about how he might approach the Gardaí, Finn was now surprised to discover that there was a message on his voicemail from Detective Inspector Seamus Quinn requesting him to return his phone call as soon as it was convenient. He was slightly alarmed by this unusual turn of events and could not immediately think what might be the cause of this type of contact. He wondered if any of his students were in trouble.

During a lull in Finn's workload mid-morning, he decided to call the inspector.

-Good morning. My name is Finn Kelly. I received a message on my voicemail this morning saying that you wish to speak to me. I've been away for a few days. How can I help you Inspector?

-Thank you very much Professor for calling me back and so promptly. We are looking to interview Dr Sean O'Toole and we have been unable to locate him. Our enquiries have informed us that you are a close friend of Dr O'Toole and therefore, you might be able to enlighten us as to his whereabouts. It's simply a routine matter. Dr O'Toole is not in any trouble, as far as we are aware.

-I haven't seen Sean for a couple of weeks. I remember him telling me that it was possible that he might be away for a while on a teaching assignment, but I don't recall the dates that he said.

-Did he tell you where this teaching assignment was going to be?

-I don't recall that either. He was rather vague about it. He is normally quite vague about his work. My association with Sean is a social one. We have been friends since childhood and we both have a great interest in the O'Connell College Amateur Dramatic Society. I mostly see him at Society meetings. So we don't often talk about the detail of our work. What is the matter? Why do you want to get hold of Sean?

-Well, as I said it's really rather routine and I'm not at liberty to mention any of the detail.

-I had heard that Sean's apartment had been broken into and I understand ransacked as well and I wondered if that was what you wanted to speak to him about?

-I think it might be worth our while having a meeting. Would you be available if I came over to your office this afternoon? I could be there by 1 o'clock?

-I have quite a busy schedule today but I can arrange to release 15 minutes if that would be enough?

-Certainly, that would be fine.

Finn wondered why the inspector had decided that it would be appropriate to call for a meeting with him. He began to feel that he had said something inappropriate. He wondered about his comment concerning Sean's apartment and began to feel that maybe he had given away the fact that he had clearly spoken to Sean since the apartment had been wrecked. That was a mistake.

Prompt to the minute Detective Inspector Seamus Quinn knocked on Finn's office door.

Quinn was an unusual member of the Garda Síochána. A tall, slim, rather nervous looking man with an unsmiling poker face, he appeared to be somewhat younger than he really was. He tended to dress more formally than his colleagues and this had led to his being given the nickname "Sloppy Shay", as Dubliners sometimes like to take the mickey out of people they are fond of. Unlike many in the Gardaí he came from a middle class family and had originally trained as an analytical chemist. He had a degree from O'Connell College.

However, he had found the practice of science rather dull and decided to find a profession offering him much more opportunity to deal directly with interesting people, along with the challenge of solving difficult puzzles and problems. He was well known for having the fastest promotion record of any individual in the force. He was a pragmatic man who was intensely interested in getting a good result for the force. Over the years, many had thought that he was too clever for his own good, and wondered how long he would stay in the Gardaí. But for now, he was there climbing the corporate ladder as quickly as possible.

-Good day. My name is Detective Inspector Seamus Quinn and I'm based in the Pearse Street Gardaí station just around the corner. I am sure you know it. It is a well-known landmark in Dublin.

-Inspector, I realised immediately after you asked me for this appointment what I had said to arouse your interest.

-And what do you think that was?

-I mentioned that Sean's flat had been burgled.

-Well, I'm pleased we have got that issue out of the way. And now tell me how did you know it was broken into as we had not released that information to the media?

-To tell the truth, Sean phoned and told me, and he said that the Gardaí were looking into the matter.

-And did he not tell you where he was?

-No, he didn't. And I didn't think to ask him. When his call came through I was in a meeting with one of my research students and I found the telephone call a distraction. The call was all over within a couple of minutes.

Quinn wasn't sure if he completely believed Finn but he decided to leave that point for the moment.

-Oh, that's a pity as we would really like to get to the bottom of this matter. But tell me was there any particular reason why Dr O'Toole decided to phone you about this matter?

-I don't think so, other than the fact that ... no I am not really sure why he called me. Maybe it was just because we are rather good friends and he felt the need to tell someone about the disturbing thing that had happened? He did seem a little rattled by the affair. By the way, the Pearse Street Gardaí station is nowhere near Sean's home, so how come you have been assigned to look into this crime?

-How perceptive of you. You're quite right, I would not normally be involved in a burglary in Blackrock where Dr O'Toole lives. I am from the murder squad based in Pearse Street and Dr O'Toole's burglary would normally fall completely outside my field of interest except for one thing.

-So do tell me what exactly is that?

-Before I mention it, may I please ask you another question?

-Certainly.

-What have you made of the murder of Frank Mullally?

Finn was puzzled as to why he was being asked this question. He wondered what it could have to do with him? But he decided to be polite.

-I was completely gobsmacked. I could not make any sense of it at all. I don't know -or should I say I didn't know - Frank Mullally particularly well. He was a quiet, unassuming man who seemed to be fully committed to his job at the College, and was always thought highly of by the people who worked with him. He was a great bridge player and an active member of the College's bridge club. He had won a number of prizes for his skill at this over the years. He was proud of his achievements with bridge. It was pure shock to think that he was murdered in his office in the College. It was most extraordinary. I could not get my mind around the implications of this catastrophe for the College, never mind for Mullally and his family.

-And what do your colleagues think of it?

-Are you asking me for the gossip from the common room?

-Yes, I guess I am.

-The chitchat in the common room about the Mullally murder has so far been limited and completely superficial. No one has had the slightest inkling as to any possible motivation for this senseless killing. What has been suggested has been pure fantasy. I have heard nothing worth repeating. I'm sorry but I can't really help you with this.

-Is there nothing at all you can tell me?

Finn thought that Quinn's trawling for gossip was a bit unusual.

-The conversation in the common room is much more to do with academic affairs and with how the College is responding to the government's attempt to transform the higher education funding model in this country. People are much more interested in what is going to happen to their Departments as the government turns the financial screws tighter and tighter. It is a great worry to most of my colleagues. Next to this concern, Mullally's death has not captured that much of our attention. You might be surprised, but academics can be quite inward looking people.

-Are there no theories flying around the college as to what possible motives there might have been for this murder?

-I haven't heard anything to which I could personally attribute the smallest amount of credibility. No one here knows anything. You know, few people here have contact with their colleagues outside of their immediate sphere of interest. There is a well-known saying in this institution that a university is constituted of a number of people whose only real common interest is to ensure that there are adequate free spaces in the car park. In short, academics often don't know each other all that well and at the end of the day we know the administrators even less.

-Of course, that situation does not apply to you and Sean O'Toole?

-You're right. Sean O'Toole and I are in an important way different. We were at school together, the Christian Brothers at Stillorgan, and we ended up joining the Faculty at O'Connell at different times and of course, in different Departments in College. Our current mutual interest in amateur dramatics has been responsible for our staying in touch over the years.

-The reason that I asked you about Mullally is that there is possibly a connection between the murder in the College and O'Toole's apartment being ransacked.

-How come?

-We did not release to the media any detail concerning the condition of Mullally's office. There had been some sort of struggle before Mullally was shot and, as well as a bullet piercing his skull, a bullet had been shot into his computer screen. The screen was shattered and knocked off his desk. When our forensic scientists examined Mullally's computer, it appears that the College's staff records were being accessed when the screen was destroyed. The record that was open and appeared on the computer screen at that time was that of Sean O'Toole.

-My goodness. What could that possibly mean?

-It might be a coincidence but, on the other hand, there might be some significance in this fact. As far as we are able to tell, we think that O'Toole's apartment was broken into a few hours after Mullally was murdered and we wonder if there is some sort of connection between the two events. Do you think there could be any connection between them?

-Inspector, I haven't the faintest idea.

-Do you think that Mullally and O'Toole knew each other?

-I can't say that I do. I am not aware that Mullally and O'Toole were friends. O'Toole never mentioned Mullally to me. Of course, we all shared the same common room and faculty club, and we chatted to each other from time to time, but I can't think of any other connection between the two. This could easily be pure chance, in fact I think it must be purely chance. What we are saying is rather a case of *Post hoc ergo propter hoc,* don't you think?

-Of course. That could be true, Professor. But coincidences have to be treated with real caution.

Finn really wanted to tell the inspector much more about the situation and about his suspicions regarding the phone call from the man with the Boston accent, but he was even more scared of the repercussions that might follow than he was of Joe Murphy at that time. He thought he'd better keep his mouth shut but at the same time, he was prepared to release a little information that might be helpful to the inspector.

-Inspector, as a general rule I don't believe in coincidence but on the other hand, it is often said, especially by those who are a bit superstitious, and as you know we Irish are very superstitious, that misfortune comes in threes. I expect you know about the tragic death of our English lecturer Dr Paddy Walsh. It has been in the newspapers the last couple of days.

-Yes indeed. He fell into the Grand Canal, having been out on a serious bender with a number of his colleagues. Most unfortunate. But as the advertisement on the buses goes one should always drink responsibly – a thought that not all Dubliners have yet bought into. I have heard it said that Paddy Walsh was a powerfully serious drinker and that he'd been solidly at it for at least four hours before he got on his bicycle on a cold and wet winter's evening and started to cycle home along the canal.

-Well you may not have realised it, Inspector, but Paddy Walsh was a close associate of Sean O'Toole's. I don't know whether Sean knows about his death yet but I am quite sure he will be very upset when he does. Losing both a close associate and the use of your apartment because it was trashed within a couple of days is no doubt a blow. So we have three misfortunes occurring at the College within the space of a week. I hope that will be the end of it and we won't see any more regrettable events.

-Yes, I can see why O'Toole is going to be upset. When you hear from O'Toole again, as undoubtedly you will, please have him give me a ring. You have my number but here is a copy of my card. We simply want to get a few facts straight. I can't even say that we want to eliminate him from our enquiries.

Finn bade farewell to the inspector and wondered again if there was a connection between these three extraordinary events that had occurred in the last week, or was Paddy Walsh's death just a mishap on a wet and cold night on the footpath along the canal?

Quinn returned to Pearse Street and called a meeting of his murder squad, who crammed into the small conference room. The Garda murder squad in Dublin is small and besides Quinn, there are his sergeant and three other detectives.

-Let's review what we know about this murder at O'Connell College.

-OK.; starting at the very beginning.

-Frank Mullally was shot in the head by a small calibre gun on Friday early evening. It made a real mess. No unusual noise was reported so the weapon must have had a silencer. There was no break in at the College so the murderer simply walked in. Mullally was working late because an urgent report had been requested by the Principal and she needed it by early on Monday morning. It was not unusual for Mullally to work late. He was by all accounts a dedicated College-man who did not have all that much else in his life. There was nothing in Mullally's diary about a late appointment so the murder was probably unexpected.

-No burglary?

-No, although some papers were scattered on the floor, there does not appear to have been anything removed from the office, except perhaps some papers.

-Mullally's computer had been switched on, but the screen was destroyed by a bullet.

-That's really odd, isn't it?

-I guess.

-The cleaners don't work over the weekend so the body was only discovered Monday morning. They were in quite a state of shock.

-The lads from forensics haven't come up with any fingerprints or any other helpful evidence.

-What do we know about Mullally?

-According to the College records Mullally was 59 years old. He had been at O'Connell College for nearly 20 years. He joined the finance department and had been promoted several times until he took over as Bursar 5 years ago. He had a personal assistant and three other people reporting directly to him. For his job he dealt with the Principal and the Finance Director on an almost daily basis. The Deans of Faculty and the Heads of School also had contact with him. He did not have much to do with students.

-How did he get on with people?

-According to his personal assistant he was generally well thought of by his colleagues, although he was regarded as stubborn and rather tight fisted, but then he was a Cork man.

-And his background?

-Mullally was a UCD graduate who went on to qualify as a chartered accountant. He spent nearly 20 years in the profession as an auditor before taking up a position at O'Connell College. There is nothing exceptional that we have found in his professional career.

-What about him personally? You have interviewed the wife?

-Yes. He was married. His wife is called Tara. She is a bit older than him and already retired from teaching. So she is a stay-at-home woman now. He had two adult children, one of whom is an accountant and the other is a veterinarian. Both of them live in other parts of Ireland. They have been at the same address for 35 years. They own the property. It is as regular a family as you can find in Ireland.

-According to the wife he had no enemies and she has no idea who might want to harm him. He had few outside interests except for bridge. He was regarded as a champion bridge player and went to play the game twice a week at the Purple Rock Bridge Club which is located near his home. And he and his wife were fairly enthusiastic about the theatre, being fans of the Gaiety.

-I wonder about his relationship with his wife. Was that solid?

-We will have to try to find out.

-We need to find out who benefits from his death; presumably his wife? Was there a life assurance policy? How much? Is there a will? Are there any estranged members in his greater or extended family? - We need to find out who the family solicitor was.

-We searched his desk at home and picked up some bank statements. He was financially well placed. No debt and a fair amount of dosh in the bank. But nothing that could be regarded as suspicious.

-No drink problem and no drugs that we can see.

-Was he involved with gambling?

-At this stage we can't tell. We will have to go through his computer with a fine-tooth comb. That will reveal if there was any online gambling.

-He was a Church of Ireland man but not one to have attended services regularly; a Christmas and Easter sort of person.

-Mullally and Tara were accustomed to taking holidays abroad twice a year, mostly going to France and Spain. He apparently spoke okay Spanish.

-And French?

-Don't know.

-That's a start. We have to interview his colleagues and we will have to do some house–to-house calling in his neighbourhood. Also we will need to interview the people at the bridge club, and see if anyone has anything to say about him from his Church. Let's check with the Revenue services about his tax situation. I am also going to ask my contacts among the more criminal community if there is any word on the street about this crime.

-Let's meet again in 24 hours.

Chapter Sixteen

Paddy Walsh and the bottle

Quinn returned to his office.

After lunch Moira told Finn that she had met two students from Paddy Walsh's course who were at the party and one of them had offered to come over shortly to tell Finn more about what happened the night Walsh died.

When he arrived Moira introduced the student who was not shy about telling all he knew about Paddy's party.

-Professor, the party started at the usual time, about half past six at the McGinty and Goat pub where we normally hang out. You know it is the pub where James Joyce used to occasionally have a few jars on his own when he was working out something for one of his books. There were maybe 25 of us from the English Department. It was a great craic. Paddy had finished the book he had been writing with Sean O'Toole which had been accepted by the publisher and he was expecting a sizeable cheque as an advance on his future royalties. Paddy was convinced that his book would make him rich.

-What was the book about?

-It was called something like ... you know I can't remember Professor Kelly. I think it had "soul" in the title. It didn't make any difference to our celebrations.

-Was it the Soul of the Author?

-Yes. That's right, Professor. Paddy said the book would revolutionise how we thought about the skill of the author and that it would help many more people to be creative and to write as well as the great authors of recent times such as Yeats, Shaw, O'Casey and Wilde.

-And you believed him?

-Why not Professor Kelly? Walsh and O'Toole are pretty smart cookies, aren't they? Why would they lie?

-They weren't lying. At least in their own minds they were not lying. They were grossly exaggerating. But go on about the evening in the pub.

-Well, 25 members and students from the College's English Department on free booze makes quite an impression on any pub and as you know, the McGinty and Goat is a small establishment. So we dominated the place for the first few hours.

-Was there no one else there then?

-Professor, as usual with that pub, there were a couple of courting couples in the alcoves as I remember it. Oh, and yes, there were a couple of tourists, Americans I think sitting at the bar chatting to the bar man. They had loud broad accents and you could hear it clearly when they laughed.

-And?

-Well, the party began to thin out at about half past eight. By ten o'clock there were only eight of us left. Dr O'Toole had left as he was staying out of town. Paddy was still very animated. He was clearly four sheets to the wind, but he didn't want to stop drinking. That man had capacity. The others started to encourage Paddy to go home. Eventually he went up to the barman and paid the bill. I bet it was the biggest amount that anyone from O'Connell College had spent in that pub for years, if not ever. Paddy was escorted to his bicycle and he cycled off promising everyone he would be especially careful. I went home and slept restlessly, waking up with the mother of all hangovers.

-Thanks for coming by. Your account of the evening is interesting.
Like some talented people, Paddy Walsh had his problems and it is a
pity his life was so dreadfully cut short for a stupid bicycle accident.

Later that afternoon Finn telephoned Sean O'Toole and arranged to
meet with him again at Brittas Bay that evening. Sean had been
working intensely and had not been reading his emails or the
newspapers so he had not heard the news about Paddy Walsh. He
was very distraught.

-My god. Paddy's dead. My god. My god. I can't believe it.
Drowned in the canal. I can hardly take that in. How could that be
possible? Are you really sure? How awful. Could he not swim?

-I hear he struck his head.

-Oh Jaysus. Poor man. I suppose he died quickly.

-If you had been reading your email you would have seen the
College notice. And it was mentioned in the newspapers too.

-But I saw him earlier that evening. I came up to Dublin for a few
hours for the book celebration. It was really great that the Soul of the
Author was finished and accepted by a publisher. It took us far too
much time to write that book. It was a long trip to Dublin for a few
drinks. But I just had to accept that invitation. It was quite a party.
Paddy was on great form. He had a lot of his old pals around for his
special knees up. Of course drinking far more than he should have
been, but that was his hallmark. It was said that he had started
drinking at the age of 12.

-What!

-Both his parents were hard drinkers and had at one time or another
been under treatment for it. But no one in Paddy's circle of friends
bothered too much. He wasn't driving. He had lost his driving
licence some time back and that was why he rode a bicycle. I hadn't
realised that he was on his bike that night. I thought that he was

catching a cab or walking home afterwards. I wouldn't have let him ride a bike, but then, I had gone home sometime before the shindig came to an end.

-Maybe you couldn't have stopped him. He was a man with a mind of his own, especially after he had consumed a few jars.

-I will certainly miss him. He was a great colleague and a remarkably creative thinker. But I suppose at the end of the day, he was a drunk. I have often been surprised that he managed to keep his job at the College. The Soul of the Author is a great book which should do really well. I wonder if I will get all the royalties now.

-I doubt it, Sean. Walsh's estate will want his share.

-I didn't ask you to come to Brittas Bay to tell you about Paddy Walsh. There's a much more serious development that I need to discuss with you. I had a Detective Inspector Seamus Quinn from the Pearse Street Gardaí station come and see me. They have been trying to interview you about the burglary in your flat. While he was with me he told me about a much more worrying matter for us. I'm sure you will recall that Frank Mullally was murdered in his office just over a week ago. Well it appears that he was murdered while he was looking at the screen on his computer and that on the screen at the time the bullet entered his head was your staff record. Inspector Quinn was not making too much of this, saying that it could simply have been a coincidence, but on the other hand it has registered with him that your apartment was burgled a few hours after Mullally was murdered and he thinks that there may be some connection between the two events.

-Finn, I hadn't realised that. But that is very far-fetched, isn't it. - Well, this has made me quite jittery especially as we know that this man with the Boston accent who calls himself Joe Murphy has been looking for you. It's entirely possible that Joe Murphy got your address from Frank Mullally and then, not wanting to leave any trail behind, decided it would be easier to put a bullet in Mullally's skull.

If that is the case then my worst fears look like they are becoming a reality.

-Bloody hell. Are you really serious?

-I know it is just conjecture.

-Isn't all this just in your imagination? You are allowing it to run wild. Yes, very wild. Forgive the pun, as none was intended.

-Maybe. But then again maybe not.

-What are we going to do? If Mullally was bumped off by this Joe Murphy then it makes Paddy Walsh's death a bizarre coincidence? Could that be tied into this affair as well?

-I just don't know. I thought maybe Joe Murphy had been sent over here to intimidate you so that you wouldn't write any more "lost" Oscar Wilde plays. I made a quick trip back to Rome in an attempt to reach my contacts and to reassure them that no other works would appear that could dilute the value of the book which we had supplied them with, or create a situation in which the authenticity of Being Excellent might be challenged. But I couldn't contact anyone.

-Where had they gone?

-The monk who had led the group who did the work has disappeared into darkest Africa. The elderly American who organised the sale has retired and is now to all intents and purposes hiding out somewhere in a seaside resort in America. I wasn't able to reach the Cardinal who I suspected had some sort of involvement in the arrangement. I am effectively left entirely on my own. What I'm now worried about is whether Joe Murphy is here to scare you off or maybe he's here to finish you off. You must have said something to somebody to make these people have an interest in you. Can you not remember what you said?

-I really can't think. Maybe I made a comment to Paddy Walsh but it would have been something regarding the context of writing the Soul of the Author. I am pretty sure that I did not make a direct reference to Being Excellent to anyone other than you. Finn, could you yourself have let something slip?

-I hardly think so and if I had then why have I not been the target of Joe Murphy and whoever is behind him?

-Finn, maybe you are? Maybe Murphy hasn't got around to you yet? He knows where to find you and he can get to you anytime. This is all quite concerning.

-What I am also having trouble with, Sean, is working out who is behind Murphy. You know I don't have any idea where the book was sold. Was it a collector like Dameri who bought it in Rome? Or was it taken to the USA? Or somewhere else in the world?

-I guess it could be anywhere?

-Has Murphy been sent by the person who purchased the book? Is it Williamson, or could it be someone in the Vatican itself? The Cardinal who tried to scare me off enquiring about Montebello could also have his finger in this pie.

-Finn, it could hardly be the Vatican people. There may be shady individuals in the Church but that thought is so over the top. I can't really get my mind to go to that topic. It is just ridiculous.

-Maybe, Sean, I think that we have to go to the Gardaí but I am quite worried about the implications of what we did and whether there will be any legal repercussions. And what the College are going to think about this if it comes out in public? When we set out on this track it never occurred to me for an instant that anything like this would happen and now we are on the brink of being in serious disgrace. This is going to be embarrassing for both of us but especially for me after the way the Principal made a fuss about the prestige of my being involved with the Vatican.

-But, Finn, we did this for charity.

-Up to a point. But you got a six figure sum out of it. Remember?

-It certainly won't do my academic career any good either.

-The College's PR Department released several press releases giving my work at the Vatican some prominence. Imagine what the media is going to make of me now. If they don't fire me from O'Connell College I will probably have to leave anyway. You go back to Wexford for the meantime and I'll get in touch with Inspector Quinn and I'll explore what might be the consequences of what we have done from a legal point of view. I'll then let you know the news and we can meet together in Dublin in the next few days or whenever you decide to come back. But don't take too long.

-OK.

-Sean, the man I recently met from the Guards, the fellow called Inspector Shamus Quinn who came to see me about trying to find you, seemed a very decent man and I made some enquiries about him from my legal friends who do some criminal work. They say he is very well thought of among the criminal justice people in Dublin. I was pleased to hear that he has a grand record of solving cases. He is one of our graduates and he had the record of the most solved crimes in the Dublin area. I think that he is the sort of man we could talk to and get an objective view about our situation. It would be better if you were around when I did that but if you are not I can start a conversation with him by myself.

-I need another week to finish the work that I'm doing in Wexford and so I'd rather not come up to Dublin right away. You can keep me informed by phone about these issues. I'll come back next week and we can pick things up from there. I don't think there's any great urgency about this matter, especially if I am out of circulation.

-I hope you're right.

Finn and Sean left the public house separately and headed back to their respective destinations. Finn began to feel that Sean had not yet appreciated all the potential ramifications of this matter. On the other hand, he was aware of his own potential to be overly concerned about matters that were not fully under his control. Deep down he hoped he was seriously over reacting but he could not quite convince himself of this.

Finn could not shake off the feeling of impending catastrophe. He required several whiskeys to get to sleep that night and he had a number of disturbing dreams. He dreamt he was lost in a strange part of the city. He was in Dublin but it seemed different and the peculiar map he had wasn't working. In one of his dreams there was a man who kept on saying to him, "You have the wrong book. Get the book with the pictures. It will show you how to get out of here". Finn didn't know what book the man was talking about and in the dream he went into a shop to buy an atlas but the one he found had no maps in it. This surrealistic situation startled Finn into waking and he suddenly sat upright in bed.

Finn woke with the realisation that he could become seriously disturbed by the current developments triggered by Being Excellent and that he had to do something more about it. But what else could he do?

Chapter Seventeen

A difficult admission

The following morning Finn arrived at the College late. He had fallen asleep again after his disturbing dream and when he woke up he began to wrestle with thoughts about what he should now do. Before he knew what happened it was 10 o'clock.

As Finn walked into his building the receptionist Theresa Fahey beckoned to him.

-Professor Kelly, may I have a moment please?

-Certainly, Theresa.

-You had a visitor this morning. An unusual looking man with a funny American accent. He wanted to know where your office was. I asked him if he had an appointment and he said no. He wasn't pleased at the suggestion that he needed an appointment. But I told him he should phone your personal assistant and make one. He said he had something for you and he would have it delivered to your home address if I would give the details to him. I told him that the College did not release home addresses.

- Theresa, thanks - you handled that well.

- Of course, that didn't please this fellow either, but when I pointed out that you had not arrived in College yet he reluctantly agreed to go.

Finn realised that he had to take immediate action so he called the Pearse Street Garda Station and asked for Inspector Quinn. He was told that the Inspector was unavailable but would probably be back in the station late that afternoon at about 5 o'clock, not long before Finn would typically begin to pack up at his office and think about heading home. At exactly 5 pm the phone rang.

-Hello. Seamus Quinn here. I believe you phoned me this morning.

-Yes I did, Inspector. I wonder if we could meet up again. I've had a few ideas about the murder and the burglary. I think you might find them interesting.

-I can be across with you in about half an hour's time. Would that suit you?

-Certainly. I will wait for you here in my office, Inspector.

It was a wet day in Dublin and when Quinn arrived he was drenched.

-Inspector, what have you been doing? Point duty on O'Connell's Bridge in the pouring rain or something like that?

-No, not likely. Those days are certainly over for me. But I am part of the team that has been out all day making door-to-door enquiries around about where Mullally lived in the hope of learning something interesting about him.

-That's a long shot, is it not?

-It certainly is. But we have nothing else to go on at this stage. There are no clues as to why Mullally was murdered in his office. And whoever did this job was a professional. There do not appear to have been any mistakes made by the murderer so we are completely in the dark. I have spoken to a number of his colleagues in the College and we have drawn a complete blank. It appears that Mullally must have been one of the most boring men in this entire country, even more boring than most of the bishops really are.

Finn smiled at Quinn's comment and he wondered whether it was a double entendre.

-Inspector, it's hard to imagine that.

-We are thinking of putting a psychological profiler on this case, but there is so little for him or her to go by.

Finn decided it was time to tell a story, so he told Quinn to take off his wet overcoat and to sit down and be prepared to hear some interesting facts and then he took a deep breath. It was clear that he was quite agitated if not actually fearful of the consequences of telling his story.

-Look Inspector, I need to ... I need to tell you a pretty complicated story and I'm not terribly sure where I should start. So I will begin at the beginning and this is not going to be easy for me and it is going to take a while. I hope you don't mind.

-Professor Kelly, as long as it is relevant to my enquiries I'm happy to spend the whole evening here.

-Well, about a year ago I was appointed as an expert consultant to the Vatican concerning the authentication of a number of works of art which had recently been found in a variety of churches and other religious institutions in different parts of Europe. This assignment required me to reside in Rome for a period where I'd been an undergraduate student. I was pleased to have the opportunity to do so and while I was there I met an old pal I hadn't seen for 20 years or more.

A full 30 minutes later Finn had explained his encounters with Antonio Dameri, the Cardinal, Jeremy Williamson, Brother Janus and Brother Philippe. Finn then went on to explain his association with the Ringsend Shelter for Abused Children and how Sean O'Toole had prepared the manuscript that could be passed off as a "lost" Oscar Wilde. Finally, he related the handing over of the manuscript to Jeremy Williamson and the receipt of the money in the bank account was detailed.

Finn felt remarkably relieved that his story was out.

There is no doubt that the Inspector was very impressed by the amount of money.

-My goodness. And you received €1.1 million for that document. Not bad I would say. You're not pulling my leg?

-No. Absolutely not. The money is in the bank and being used by the Shelter as we speak.

-I can see how tempting that situation was. If I were you I might have done the same.

-The temptation was overwhelming.

-And did you not give any thought to what might happen if the College found out?

-No. I never thought for a moment that they would. Why would they? The College has no connection with the sort of people I was dealing with. And it seemed to me that the book would be bought by a super-rich banker who would have nothing better to do with the money and that it might as well go to charity.

-And if they did find out?

-Phew ... that would be the end of my career here, Inspector. Even though I have tenure I don't think that I would survive that.

-And Finn that was easy money was it not? Doesn't easy money often have consequences?

Finn could not think of a reply to this remark. But he thought to himself how true, how very true.

-What an amazing story. Well, let me first of all say I don't know how many laws you have broken, but whatever you did in Rome falls outside of my personal jurisdiction. The Garda Síochána in its own right has no real interest in what you got up to in Italy. Of course, if a European extradition order arrives we would be required to execute it. But as it stands at present, I can't see how you could be said to have committed a criminal offence in the Republic of Ireland. So rest assured that I will not attempt to arrest you this evening. But I'm sure you have more to tell me about this affair.

-Indeed. If only the matter had ended there. A couple of weeks ago, just before Frank Mullally was murdered I received a call from a man who called himself Joe Murphy, inviting me to go to Boston on behalf of the US – Irish Cultural Cooperative Society. Murphy said that they are a body that promotes the appreciation of Irish culture especially among the young generation in the United States.

-He said he was from Boston?

-No. But he had a classic Boston accent, although it was so good that it did seem to me that he might have been working hard to make his voice sound Bostonian. It also seemed that inviting me to Boston was disingenuous in that my speciality really doesn't have much to offer to the young generation in the United States. I am focused on my topic, and to those who are not aficionados my subject can be as boring as hell. Also in the conversation, he asked me if I could help them get in touch with Sean O'Toole. When my conversation with Murphy ended I became suspicious of his motives for calling me.

-And then?

-After I heard of O'Toole's break-in I wondered if Murphy might have been responsible for this, but it was clear to me from my conversation a few days earlier that he didn't know where O'Toole lived. My mind always tries to make connections between events and so, I wondered if there was any connection between Mullally, who would have known O'Toole's address, and the burglary. I know it's a long shot but I couldn't help but feel that there might be some link. Anyway when I heard that Paddy Walsh had been killed under strange circumstances, I began to feel that there really might be something going on. I know that this might sound a bit weird to you, but I have this deep premonition that something bad is going to happen. The old expression usually used with children, *"this will end in tears"*, keeps coming into my mind.

-Come, Professor Kelly, the Gardaí can't take any action on premonitions.

-I also had a dream in which Mullally, with part of his head missing was pointing at a map of the world and when I got close to it Mullally's finger was on Boston.

-Dreams are even less acceptable to the Gardaí than premonitions. Next you will be telling me you went to a gypsy fortune teller. I have to say Professor Kelly that your suggestion seems far-fetched to me. Did this Murphy fellow raise his head again?

-Yes, he did call me a second time to enquire if I was prepared to accept his invitation to Boston and once again he asked me if I had seen Sean O'Toole.

-You know, we in the Gardaí have been trying to reach O'Toole as well. He seems to have taken himself completely out of circulation. Do you know where he is?

-Well, not precisely. He is down somewhere in Wexford staying in a cottage belonging to his cousin while finishing off a book he is writing about WB Yeats. I think that he will be back in Dublin next week. I'm sure he'll come to see you straightaway once he is home again.

-Well that'll be useful. We will be able to get a few more things sorted out.

-So what will you do about Murphy?

-I'll make some enquiries about Joe Murphy but it's pretty clear that we don't know if he has committed any crime since there is no direct evidence to associate him either with Mullally's murder or O'Toole's break-in, or for that matter, with the accidental death of Paddy Walsh in the Grand Canal.

-But Inspector, don't you think there might be some connection between all these events?

-There could indeed be. But what evidence do you have to suggest that there is?

-None.

-So relax. And don't try to read anything more into the situation with Murphy than you need to at present. I know Boston quite well and there are a lot of US – Irish cultural interests in that city. For the moment, please just keep your cool. Some of my family went to Boston twenty-five years ago. My father's brother emigrated there as a young man and was successful. I have been to Boston a number of times and I quite like the city. Don't make Murphy a bogeyman, at least not yet.

-Will my story about the book Being Excellent have to come out?

-As things stand at the moment, no. I suspect that you have been seriously over-reacting. But, of course, you never can tell and who knows how this story will develop in the next few weeks. You took a big gamble with your career getting involved with shady business like this. I hope it was worth it.

-I'm beginning to wonder too.

During his conversation with Finn, Quinn had been taking copious notes about the events that were described and who had been involved with them. He then slipped the notebook into his jacket pocket before putting on his overcoat and heading off again into the rain.

Chapter Eighteen

O'Connell College gossip

It was now past 6 o'clock and despite still being wet from the day's workout in the rain, Quinn returned to his office in Pearse Street Gardaí station. There he summoned Detective Sergeant Siobhan Cavanagh into his office. Siobhan Cavanagh was an attractive, slightly built 29-year-old brunette who joined the force out of school at the age of 18. She had worked her way up into a plainclothes position and then eventually into the murder squad. Through hard practical experience and dedication to the exams she had been promoted to the level of Sergeant. She had been working closely with Quinn for the last two years and was impressed by his ability to solve difficult cases.

-Siobhan, do I remember correctly that you have a younger brother who is a student at O'Connell College right now?

-Yes, that is correct.

-I wonder if you'd mind doing a little bit of research for me. Research is the polite way of putting it but you could also say, snooping around. Could you please spend a short time, maybe a few hours or a day perhaps, with your brother finding out as much as you can for me about some of the faculty members in O'Connell College? I am really after student and service staff gossip.

-Soft information?

-Yes. I'm interested in Professor Kelly who is a mediaevalist, Dr Sean O'Toole who is a senior lecturer in the English department and the late Dr Paddy Walsh. Paddy Walsh met his maker the other night. You may have heard that he achieved the status by going for an unscheduled swim in the Grand Canal last week, apparently completely ratted out of his mind. But any information you could get for me from the students about these three people could be quite helpful.

-Certainly Sir. Consider it done.

At the same time, Quinn initiated several other enquiries about Joe Murphy and Jeremy Williamson. This he did by calling the duty officer responsible for interfacing with Europol and the FBI.

-Could you please find out what you can for me about a man called Jeremy Williamson, who until recently was the proprietor of an art gallery in Rome called the Gallery Garibaldi. I understand that he may have recently sold it and moved back to North America. I don't have any more detail than that at present and any information you could find for me would be most appreciated. Also, I need to find out about a man called Joe Murphy who we think comes from Boston and who has recently been visiting Ireland? Murphy may work for the US – Irish Cultural Cooperative Society, but I don't really know what that institution is or where it is based. Any information you can find for me would be helpful. Please treat both of these enquiries with a reasonable amount of urgency.

Quinn had one other potential source of information to tap. The Gardaí had a number of acquaintances who were available to research issues within the criminal community for an occasional favour and or a small contribution to their immediate funds. They were not really in the position to grass on specific criminals but they were often the source of useful information. Quinn made an arrangement to meet with Mick Dooley for a chat in one of Quinn's least favourite pubs in the docks.

-Mick, you haven't come across a Joe Murphy in your travels recently.

-Can't say I have. Is he a culchie or a jackeen?

-Neither. He's a Yank. Strong Boston accent.

-There are not many Yanks around my territory.

-He's just a visitor.

-And what do you want this geezer for?

-You know better than to ask that. Let's say we have an interest in him?

-As you know a couple of the families have reasonable strong American connections but of course nothing like it was in the old days. Remember peace has descended upon us – thanks be to gad.

Finn smiled wryly at this phony reference to the almighty.

-Just as well we don't want the American criminal classes over here. We have enough problems of our own.

-And what's the dosh situation?

-Maybe, I could slip you a few bob, maybe a score or two, but no more.

-I'll make some enquiries for you.

-OK. The sooner I get something the better.

-Well enough. If there is anything going on wit yer man I will let you know. But don't be mean with the whiskey now.

Twenty-four hours later, Siobhan was back in Pearse Street Station reporting to Quinn. Getting the information required had not been quite as easy as Siobhan had thought it would be but by having her brother introduce her to various students and members of the service staff within the College she had picked up a considerable amount of what really was gossip about the three individuals she had been researching. Siobhan knew that most of this information was essentially unverifiable. But even so it was always useful to put people into context.

-Siobhan, what have you found out for me?

-Inspector, let me start by saying what an unusual place O'Connell College is. And I am not referring to the architecture. I have enjoyed this little undercover project.

-Go on sergeant.

-Once my brother had introduced me to some of his friends they talked freely and what a huge amount of gossip there was. First the easy one.

-OK.

-According to student gossip Paddy Walsh was much liked by his students but at the end of the day he was simply a drunk; a drunk with talent, of course. He mixed a lot with the students especially in the pubs on campus. He was known to have been drunk in the College regularly, even in front of a class that he was trying to lecture. There is a bar in the Senior Common Room that opens at lunchtime and Walsh was a regular feature there. He often stayed well into the afternoon.

-Did he teach in the afternoon?

-Sometimes. The students say that he was always affable and loquacious, especially when he had a few pints in him. It appears that Walsh was considered to be the most brilliant teacher in the Department of English and that seems to be why the College put up with him. But because of the drink, it was thought that it would be unlikely he would have made any further progress with his career in the College. It was known that he was a friend of O'Toole's and that he was working on a book with him.

-What was the book about?

-No one seemed to know, and they cared even less. Student interest didn't go that far.

-Interesting.

-Walsh had a serious girlfriend who would sometimes pick him up from events when he was too drunk to find his way home alone. On the night of his fatal accident, she was away at her mother's in Cork. There was no suggestion made by anyone that there was any connection between Walsh and Kelly or Walsh and Mullally. I couldn't find any other information relating to him or his activities.

-Siobhan, thank you very much. That is useful.

-With regards Sean O'Toole, well he was not particularly admired by his students. He was regarded as a mediocre lecturer who did not have much time for his undergraduates. He did teach a fair amount and always had a number of research students, but he does not seem to have been anybody's first choice of either a lecturer or supervisor. He did not have much contact with the students outside of formal sessions in the classroom or in research seminars. He was virtually, if not completely, a teetotaller. Behind Walsh's back he was known to have said some pretty awful things about his drinking problem.

-But he hadn't taken the pledge himself?

-No, it seems he hadn't or if he did he wasn't serious about it. It seems O'Toole had a reputation for being more than just careful with money. It seems that he spent a lot of time and energy searching for research grants and other ways of supplementing his income. He wrote a column in a number of magazines; one in Ireland, another in the USA, and the third one in New Zealand. He is known to be fond of the horses and it appears that his favourite racetrack is Fairyhouse where he can be encountered at most meetings. He is said to have mixed luck in his dealings with the gee-gees.

-A gambling man no less. I wonder if or maybe how much, he was indebted to the bookies.

-No comment was made about that.

-Mmm.

-O'Toole is also known for his interest in the amateur dramatic society and his friendship with Professor Kelly and their mutual interest in this society was mentioned. He had a reputation of being a competent academic but probably someone who would not go much further up the University hierarchy. He is formally separated but not divorced from his wife who lives with his teenage children in Galway. His wife is a schoolteacher. It had been rumoured for some time that he did not get on well with his Head of School and that he was looking for an appointment in another university out of the country but no one had any idea as to where he was looking for a job.

-Interesting indeed. Now what about Finn Kelly?

-Professor Kelly is quite different. He is a much more respected member of staff. He is considerably more scholarly than the other two and he has a solid record of academic research published in a number of the better journals in his field. He has also written an important textbook on the subject and he is reputed to earn an interesting income from the royalties associated with this book. He is thought to be fairly generous and takes his students for a drink in the College pub from time to time.

-So he has student friends?

-Yes. He seems to be popular with both the students and by other members of Faculty. It is said he is ambitious and that he is likely to go places in the university hierarchy. However, he no longer has anything to do with undergraduate students and only involves himself with the supervision of doctoral research. His recent consultancy with the Vatican attracted the attention of the Principal, who ensured that he received a number of accolades in the media. There was some talk of giving him an honorary degree but I understand that the suggestion did not get much support in the end. There were some other interesting comments made about his social life.

-Like what?

-He is unmarried and has no long-term girlfriend. There used to be some gossip about the possibility that he might be gay, but that died a death a few years back. However, there is a stronger view that he prefers the company of younger women. One might be forgiven for saying the company of girls. There is no suggestion that he has any inclination towards paedophilia, but it does seem that he has a reputation for dating young students. Clearly they will all be well beyond the age of consent, but they would also be more than 20 years younger than him. The College is not at all pleased about such liaisons and I understand that his Head of Department had to speak to him about it at one point. I was told that this might be the reason why he no longer teaches undergraduates and that his talents are reserved for working with the older students doing senior research. Of course this might just be malicious rumours. It's the sort of thing that is really just about impossible to verify.

-Siobhan that is really great work. You have been busy indeed. Thank you so much. Is there anything else you have to tell me about any of these three people?

-I guess I could go on quite a bit about Kelly. He has a much higher visibility both in the College and in the country, than the other two. He is popular, probably one of the most popular lecturers in the entire College. He is known for the fact he's involved with an important charity in Ringsend. He is regarded as being determined to achieve its objectives and that he has a genuine loyalty and affection for the College. It is generally thought that he will probably end up by being Dean of the Faculty and, maybe one day he might even be in a position to run for Principal. He is definitely a man to watch.

-I suggest that his reaching high office like that is subject to him not doing anything stupid or reckless with his reputation and career. In summary, all three of these people have or had significant issues. For Walsh it was alcohol, and that seems to have been his undoing. For O'Toole it seems to be money, and that must be quite an important issue for an academic as there are significant ceilings to the amount of money that academics can earn. For Kelly it looks like it might be women.

Quinn and Cavanagh's conversation was interrupted by a phone call from Sean O'Toole.

-Inspector Quinn, I understand that you have been talking to Professor Kelly and that you have expressed interest in interviewing me concerning the burglary of my flat last week.

-Yes that's quite right.

-I am currently on a writing retreat in Wexford where I have been making considerable progress with the book I'm working on about WB Yeats. I really don't want to interrupt this working streak as I don't often find myself quite as fully engaged with the writing process as I have been for the last couple of weeks. So I'm only planning on coming back to Dublin in a week or so's time. I therefore thought it was appropriate for me to give you a call and to see if I could not answer some of your questions over the phone.

-Thank you very much for that. We are really interested in establishing just a few things.

-Oh yes, what are those?

-First of all, I would like to know whether or not anything of material value was taken from your apartment?

-There was little of any real value to a thief in my flat. I did not keep any money there and I had no furnishings or artwork of any real value. When my wife left me 18 months ago she kept anything that we had of any monetary value. But even then there wasn't much that a thief would be interested in. And, by the way I am fully insured.

-In that case, have you any idea why anyone would want to break-in to your home?

-Absolutely none at all.

-And what do you make of the fact that your apartment was ransacked.

-It's a complete mystery to me.

-Have you had any other break-ins in the past?

-No, none at all.

-And your neighbours?

-Not that I'm aware of. I have always felt that our block of flats was relatively safe. There are good locks on the outer doors and the street in front of the building was well lit. And as far as I know there are burglar alarms in all the different flats. There is one security firm that looks after the whole building.

-Sounds a bit like Fort Knox.

-I suppose it does, Inspector.

-So in your opinion Dr O'Toole do you think that this was just a random crime?

-I guess it was. It is really quite bizarre to me. It is not the type of thing that students would get up to. I can only think that it is some desperate and perhaps homeless person who noticed that there was no one actively coming or going from the flat, and therefore felt it was relatively safe to break in. While they were about it they rummaged through my belongings, maybe in the hope of finding some money.

-I do hope that the explanation in the end turns out to be as simple as that.

-In the meantime please do come to the station at Pearse Street and make a formal statement concerning what we have just discussed as soon as you get back to Dublin. There is no need to rush, but it's important to have the paperwork in order.

-Do you think that you will eventually catch someone for this crime?

-It's difficult to say. But as the evidence stands at the moment it does not seem to me that it is likely we will find the culprit.

-By the way Inspector Quinn, I understand that my colleague and friend, Professor Kelly, has been talking to you about our activities in Italy as well as Mullally's murder and Dr Walsh's tragic accident. Professor Kelly seems to be of the view that there is some sort of conspiracy afoot and that the murder and my burglary, and even Walsh's accident, are somehow connected.

-Yes, he has said that. However, I told him that I believe this theory to be far-fetched since there is no evidence at all to suggest that there is any connection between these events. Does your friend have paranoid tendencies?

-I was not aware of this side of his personality before.

-Professor Kelly mentioned the fact that a Mr Joe Murphy was looking to get hold of you and I think that this enquiry might be entirely innocent. So I have been encouraging Professor Kelly to be far more relaxed and not to think that there are conspiracies in every shadow that he encounters. I should also say to you, as I said to Professor Kelly, I am not interested in the activities that you and he have been engaging in in Italy. If a crime has been committed there then it is up to the Italian police to take an interest in it and we, here in Dublin, will only get involved if a formal extradition order had to be executed.

-I am so glad to hear that. I am also pleased to hear your view of Joe Murphy. Professor Kelly's anxiety was beginning to rub off a little on me. It's hard not to be influenced by your colleague and friend and thus he had begun to make me feel a little worried. Now that you mentioned it, I can see that Finn has had deep down a streak of paranoia in his personality that I had never witnessed before these events occurred. I feel much better about this whole business now that I've spoken to you.

-Good. I am making some enquiries about Mr Murphy but I suspect they will come to nothing. I will let Professor Kelly know what our findings are as soon as Europol and the FBI have reported back to me.

-Thank you very much indeed.

-Don't forget to come in and see us and make a statement at the Pearse Street station.

-Certainly. My insurance company has already asked me to do that. Maybe I will see you then. In the meantime, goodbye.

A few minutes later Mick Dooley was on the phone.

-I can't get a bloody word out of anybody about any Yank. I don't think everyone is trying to be cute with me. I'm pretty sure that none of the lads have a feckin clue. They would be on the lookout for Yanks as they usually have lots of dollars to throw around. Are you sure you got the nationality and the name right?

-Yes. It is a Yank I am interested in and the name is right but it might be a wild goose chase.

-Pity, I was looking forward to the dosh.

-Sorry. I'll buy you a few extra jars when next I see you.

Quinn reassembled the murder squad to get their feedback.

-What have we learnt?

-It would appear that we have been misled about how popular or unpopular Mullally was with some of his colleagues. He apparently had two big bust-ups with Heads of Schools in the College. With one of them he had an almighty row about admitting more overseas students. Mullally wanted to put a cap in it while the other wanted to take advantage of the demand and improve the income of his School. In addition, he was accused of not trying hard enough to find some scholarship money for a few particularly bright overseas students who wanted to complete their research at O'Connell College, but who had to leave because of shortage of funds. Mullally apparently was adamant that O'Connell College was big enough. He was obsessed with the fact that there was nowhere to expand outside of the old wall. The Principal, being relatively new in post, wasn't able to reconcile the different arguments and it was left to be returned to later, with quite hard feelings.

-The other row was similar but in this case Mullally was against starting to offer O'Connell College degrees in the Middle East, especially in the Gulf. There was considerable pressure in the College to follow the example of some of the other Irish Universities and have overseas operations. Mullally was a traditionalist and would argue that no one could say they had an O'Connell College degree if they hadn't studied on the Dublin campus. Once again this ended unsatisfactorily with very cross words being spoken.

-In fact one of the people we interviewed said that the row was vitriolic and that at one point Mullally said that O'Connell College would open an operation in the Middle East over his dead body!

-Maybe that was prophetic?

-Bloody hell. Keep jokes out of this.

-I wasn't joking.

-It seems that the Principal is being blamed for not being able to control Mullally and this has been hindering the growth of the College.

-This is all very interesting, but we have to be careful that we don't get sucked into the university gossip mill. Academics are famous for their ability to produce meaningless hot air in the form of gossip which in the end amounts to nothing.

-In any event a row like this is hardly the stuff that leads to murder.

-I hope you are right! It won't do the College any good if it comes out that one member murdered another.

-Well you know what they say, *No publicity is bad publicity.*

-But that's just not true. Is it?

-Well the feelings have been running high. Some of the academics have been saying that Mullally had no right to be involved in this type of debate. They argue that these are academic issues and that as the bursar Mullally should have kept out of it. The bursar is after all an administrator. There was a suggestion that a petition would be arranged calling for Mullally's resignation.

-That would have been embarrassing.

-Yes. I never heard of such a thing before.

-What did you find out from the tax people?

-Mullally was as clean as a whistle. There is nothing there to be excited about. In that respect he was a model citizen.

-And the Church?

-According to the minister and the verger he was hardly known there. He was a face in the background. His wife attended services more often than he did. They said that he had little interest in them and they were glad to see that he came to Church occasionally. But his life was really unknown to anyone there.

-The bridge club?

-Ah! Mullally was a star. He played in the national championships regularly. He won several medals. He was the co-author of a book on winning at bridge. They said that his ability to remember figures and cards was exceptional. He had no enemies there and no one could think of any reason why anyone would want to harm him.

-And the life assurance?

-Yep. A life policy for €250,000. In this day and age, not enough for anyone to get excited about. It goes to the widow with a clause that she has to survive for 30 days, otherwise it goes to the children.

-And the solicitor?

Yep. There is a will and the solicitor gave me the gist of it. Nearly everything goes to the wife. The children get a little and there are some small bequests to a couple of local charities. But nothing to write home about.

-His relationship with his wife?

-We haven't got much on that yet. The Mrs says it was good and there were no problems between them. But we need to talk to some others about this.

-We interviewed the son and the daughter. They had nothing to tell us of any use. They confirmed how conservative and stubborn their father was. The kids think that both parents were as dull as each other and suited each other down to a T. There is no suggestion there was any problem with their parent's relationship.

-Maybe we should make some enquiries at the school where the Mrs used to work at?

-OK.

-We are nowhere near finished going through his emails and we don't know how many other email addresses and accounts he may have had on the Web. But so far no sign of gambling or anything else worth mentioning.

-And door to door in his neighbourhood?

-We have just started that. But from the few interviews we have had he was seemingly the most boring man in the district. Some people said that he was a regular accountant both by profession and by personality. I think that was said as a sort of insult.

-Well, you will have to carry on with the door-to-door enquiries in the hope that something will turn up.

Chapter Nineteen

A few days in Dublin

Maria arrived on the Aer Lingus Flight from Rome. The flight was on time but Dublin airport was heaving with tourists making their way to the St Patrick Day celebrations. Finn had been up early making sure that his flat was clean and tidy in anticipation of his visitor. It was a big deal for Finn to have a lady visitor, especially one coming all the way from Rome.

Finn waited patiently at the arrivals area in the airport. He had anticipated that Maria would take 20 minutes to complete the immigration formalities and collect her luggage. However, this was not to be the case and after half-an-hour he became quite anxious. Fortunately, he had a mobile phone number for her and was able to establish that her luggage had been delayed which was not that unusual in the event. In due course, Maria arrived and was bundled into Finn's car and taken back to his flat in Drumcondra.

-It has taken a long time for you to get around to inviting me to Dublin.

-It certainly has. But I haven't been all that sure that you wanted to come to see my home patch. It's one thing having a friendship in your home town but it's quite another if we try to keep it going across more than 1000 miles.

-Yes. Of course, I was delighted to be invited to Dublin. It is good to get away from one's own town for a bit.

-Well, we made it at last.

-What have you put on the agenda for us for the next few days? - Today I want to take you on a tour of the principal cultural sites in Dublin, although I fear they don't have the same sort of universal attraction as the principal sights of Rome.

-Oh, please give Dublin a break. Rome is nearly 3000 years old and once upon a time it probably had the biggest empire the world had known up to that time.

-Good. If we bear that in mind then I think we have quite a lot of interesting places to visit in and around the city. After the city tour today I want to take you to a little reception being held this evening by a small charity I'm involved with. It is called The Ringsend Shelter for Abused Children and I am one of the trustees of this charity. Each year we hold a small reception for all the people who work for us as volunteers, as well as our donors and other people with whom we wish to engage. I think you'll find it interesting and it will certainly show that I'm not entirely a dusty academic.

-That sounds really great. Of course I also do want to see the wonderful institution where you work.

-We won't be able to get to all the sites in the city today so we will pick up our touring tomorrow. I've also made reservations at one of Dublin's best restaurants for us to have dinner tonight and yes I will take you around the College and show you our old buildings and squares and of course our magnificent Museum of Antiques. Then on Sunday, it being St Patrick's Day, we have the grand parade. I have managed to acquire a couple of seats in the grandstands at the General Post Office. These are as scarce as dragon teeth but I managed to pull some strings and get a couple for us. In Dublin the General Post Office, known popularly as the GPO, is like consecrated ground to Irish Nationalists. It is believed to be the true centre of the rebellion in 1916 and a lot of Irish blood was spilled there in the uprising.

-Finn, It looks like you have really planned a busy few days for us. I hope you're not going to get too tired, as being a tourist can wear one down.

-I hope not Maria. And by the way, remember that in Dublin our plans are always subject to the weather. Unlike Rome Dublin can be dreadfully wet and if we get too much rain, we will be heading off to find a spot where we can stay dry while we can at the same time wet our whistles.

Finn decided that the most effective way of taking Maria around Dublin was to use the Hop-on Hop-off bus as it went to all the important places that a visitor should see. So, that afternoon was spent climbing on and off the bus as it took them from one point of interest to the next. Time galloped by so quickly that they had hardly done a third of the tour when Finn announced it was time to suspend the sightseeing and head off for the reception at the charity's offices at Ringsend.

Ringsend is not the most fashionable end of Dublin, but the charity had the use of an old converted Georgian townhouse which acted as both its main office and centre for its clients. About a hundred people had been invited to the reception and these consisted of 15 members of staff, 6 donors, 70 volunteers and 9 other individuals with whom the charity wanted to work in the future.

The party was well on its way by the time Finn and Maria arrived. Kathleen, as the host, had laid on a range of drinks; mostly non-alcoholic, but with a small amount of beer and wine on offer as well as a reasonable selection of snacks. Even for a reception such as this, with Finn's advice, the charity was careful about expenditure. Finn immediately found Kathleen and took Maria to meet her.

-I would like to introduce you to Maria Abano who has come from Rome to visit me. I met Maria while I was working for the Roman Curia last year. Maria is the Director of Facilities for those visiting dignitaries and specialists who are at the Vatican working on projects.

-Lovely to meet you Maria.

-And Maria, Kathleen Daly is the Managing Director or Chief Executive Officer of this charity, of which I am a trustee.

-Delighted to make your acquaintance, Kathleen.

At that moment Finn's telephone rang in his pocket and he excused himself as he stepped aside to take the call.

-So Maria you met Finn in Rome when he was working for the Vatican last year?

-Yes, indeed I did. It was nice working with him and being able to facilitate the research he was doing.

-He has spoken highly of the people that he met there and he clearly really enjoyed the work that he did for that assignment.

-Yes, his work appeared to be intense. He was busy all the time.

-His trip to Italy really did a lot of good for his career at O'Connell College. The Principal and other senior members of the University were impressed by his being offered work with the Vatican.

-Yes, the Vatican is choosy about whom it selects as expert advisers.

-And we at the Shelter were impressed with the fact that during his period at the Vatican he was able to find someone who was prepared to help us out of our dire financial situation.

-Oh, I didn't know about that. Please tell me some more?

-We had a difficult situation last year when the government and one of our major donors announced that they were going to withdraw the grants they had been giving us for a number of years. We are entirely dependent on this sort of money, without which we would not be able to service the very needy community we support on a daily basis. The news that this money was going to dry up suggested to us that we would have needed to cut back our operation substantially and maybe even have to close down. This came completely out of the blue.

-That must have been terrible. What did you do?

-It certainly was terrible and it was frightening, not only for our clients but for the staff here as well. I went to Finn and asked him for advice and he told me that he would make some enquiries to see if he could find any alternative sources of funds. It was a very difficult period for us and we were delighted when Finn told us that he had found enough funding to be able to ensure our future for a number of years. Of course charities like ours are always on the lookout for funding and although our problem has been solved for the moment it has not gone away entirely.

-I'm so pleased that Finn was able to do that. And he did that while he was in Rome?

-Yes. The crisis broke while he was away. I managed to get to see him when he came home for that one-week break. I think it was Italian money that he found. Yes. I am quite sure it came from an Italian bank.

-I must ask him about this. I do know that he is acquainted with some very ritzy Italian industrialists but I didn't know that they had supplied funding for a charity in Ireland. It really sounds interesting, what he's done.

Finn returned after taking his call. It was an issue with one of his students who was panicking about his work, but Finn was able to put her mind at rest while he agreed to sort everything out for her the following week. The reception continued with Finn introducing Maria to all the staff at the charity and to the volunteers and donors with whom he was acquainted. He and Maria continued mixing with the group until he realised it was 7:30 pm and his restaurant reservation was for in half an hours' time in another part of the city. A taxi was called, they quickly bade farewell and departed.

Although not always the case, today Dublin's restaurants are as good as anywhere in the world and Finn had chosen a particularly good one for that evening. They were fussed over by the maître d' who was also Italian and was delighted to have a fellow citizen in his restaurant that night. There was a small, but good range of Italian wines and these were discussed in some depth before final selections were made. As soon as they had ordered the food and the wine, they sat back to chat.

-Finn, I've had a lovely day. The sites of Dublin were interesting. It is a rather imperial city where you are constantly reminded of the past, even though it is really rather small.

-Some Dubliners say that this city was the second city in the Empire- the British Empire, that is or should I rather say that was.

-Of course. And those are a really nice bunch of people that you introduced me to this evening.

-I'm glad you think so Maria. I find my work with the Shelter rewarding.

-What precisely do you do for the charity, Finn?

-I was invited to join as a trustee a few years ago and I am mostly concerned with helping with the resource planning, as well as to some extent advising on control systems to ensure that the organisation runs as efficiently and effectively as possible.

-So, what was Kathleen telling me about your role as a fundraiser?

-Oh that. That was an emergency situation. I don't normally have anything to do with fundraising but Kathleen came to see me when she discovered that various grants on which she relied would be withdrawn and I was able to assist them by finding some replacement funds. But this is not something that I'm involved with on a routine basis. I think I was rather lucky that I was able to find the money I did and I don't expect to be able to do that again.

-I believe you found the money in Italy? Was it the Dameris who were generous?

-Oh! No. It was nothing to do with Antonio Dameri.

-I didn't think it could have been as that family are not known for their generosity.

-I didn't know that.

-Do you mind if I ask you how you raised the money while you were down in Rome?

-No. I don't mind telling you in fact I have wanted to tell you about this for some time but I never seemed to find the moment when it really was appropriate for me to bring up the subject.

-Well now's as good as any.

-My family had an old friend who had been a neighbour 50 years ago, who had died. The grandson was clearing out the attic in the house the family had lived in for about a hundred years when they found locked up in an old chest a manuscript of an unpublished play by Oscar Wilde. There was a long and complicated story associated with this, but the short version is that my old friend's neighbour's great-grandfather worked for the Wilde family and this book had been lost, or should I say mislaid by Oscar Wilde back in the 19th century, when he left O'Connell College to take up a position he had been offered at Oxford University.

-What a story.

At a certain level Finn couldn't help feeling pleased that he had created this most plausible story. He had now told it so many times he was beginning to believe it himself. But occasionally, such as now when he was talking to Maria, he felt a pang of guilt that he was not telling her the truth. He knew well enough that it did not bode well for his relationship with Maria to repeat this elaborate fiction and this worried him.

-Well, to cut this long story short the book was presented to me and I arranged for it to be sold through the Gallery Garibaldi and the profit made on the book was given to the Ringsend Shelter. That is how I managed to find enough money to save the day for the charity. Look Maria, I haven't told Kathleen this story so please do not pass this information around. Kathleen thinks that the money she got was a generous donation from someone wanting to help the Shelter.

-Of course, I wouldn't. But please tell me a little bit more about your connection with the Gallery Garibaldi?

-Don't you remember that you helped me find the name of its director, a man called Jeremy Williamson and I went to see him?

-You never told me what that was about.

-Well I've been a little shy about this because ... well it's quite personal. I guess I can tell you but once again this has got to be in confidence. When I met Antonio Dameri he showed me an illuminated manuscript he had bought from the Gallery. This dated back to the time of Dante Alighieri and, being a mediaevalist I was interested in finding out as much about this book as possible. It transpired that Antonio Dameri had purchased the illuminated manuscript from Jeremy Williamson and so I went to see him about it. This stimulated my curiosity and it led me to having more meetings with various people concerning these valuable ancient manuscripts. Do you also remember my encounter with the Cardinal?

-Oh yes certainly, Cardinal ... I don't quite remember his name now. What was it?

-Cardinal Victor Baffasa.

-Yes Finn. Now I recall. He is one of the more enigmatic Cardinals in the College. I think I told you that. He is said to have direct access to the ear of the Holy Father himself. I am sure that you are aware that a lot of people are suspicious about how the Curia runs the business of the Vatican. The situation has deteriorated in the past few years. The concern about child abuse has spread to other issues. There have been a number of scandals about the misuse of money and about corruption of one sort or another. I suppose that you might not be aware of this but we now have something called VatiLeaks, which feeds Vatican secrets to the public through social media. Of course most of it is pure rubbish. Trivial gossip with little foundation is the sign of our times.

-No. I wasn't. I hadn't heard of VatiLeaks. Has it become that bad? The Cardinal was also interested in illuminated manuscripts and he tried to discourage my doing research into Antonio Dameri's document. I found that incident disturbing.

-Why?

-The Cardinal suggested that my interest in illuminated manuscripts could adversely affect my work with the Curia. I was very surprised.

-Wow. How come?

-He asked me how I had the time to be interested in that matter. I saw that as a threat. Anyway, that stay in Rome is now behind me and, in any event, Jeremy Williamson seems to have done a good job and Kathleen got the money she so desperately needed.

-What do you mean by seems to have done a good job?

-The book sold. And for a great price.

-And were there any repercussions?

-Well, Maria last time I was in Rome I went past the Gallery Garibaldi to look in on Jeremy Williamson and he wasn't there. Furthermore, no one seemed to know where he had gone to. He seems to have decided on short notice to retire and he packed up and moved off to another continent. It all seemed strange to me. I only wanted to ask Williamson if his client was happy with the Oscar Wilde book.

-You know Finn you've been dealing with some tough people. That Dameri family has come from nearly rags to vast riches in less than three generations. Antonio's grandfather started out life as a street pedlar in Naples. He must've been a smart man because he was able to leave to his son a chain of relatively small businesses located in the south of Italy. The old man was well-to-do but it was his son that converted the business into an international one in the space of 40 years. And Antonio has been doing pretty well, pushing the business to even greater heights.

-Maria, I had that feeling from the way Antonio spoke and how he was showing off his money; a crass capitalist through and through.

-But Finn remember that to achieve the business empire they have, the Dameris have not necessarily always been as good citizens as they could have been. Put another way it is almost certain that they have not done anything illegal, or at least they have not done anything for which there has been any evidence of any illegality. But they have been tough business people. And for tough read ruthless. The Dameris would not be considered to be part of polite society in Rome.

-I know how rough business is. I suppose I shouldn't be surprised that the Dameris are not deeply established among the Roman elite. But that hardly matters to me.

-Maybe it should.

-But why?

-The Gallery Garibaldi is generally known to be a tough, if not a rough business. I mentioned to you that there was some suspicion about them trading in stolen artefacts. I know that charges were never pressed, and I'm also aware of the saying that there is never smoke without fire. I would be extremely careful of any dealings I had with these people.

-I wish you had told me that before.

-I have the sense there is something else about this affair that you should be telling me. Is there?

-Not really. I am just a bit sad that I got involved with this Oscar Wilde business. In the end I don't think it will do me any good but I guess the money has been a great assistance to Kathleen and I should be grateful for that. I have been a bit worried by the fact that there was a murder in the College recently....

-A murder?

-Yes, the College bursar was murdered at his desk.

-Goodness gracious me. That's very horrible.

-And a day or so later one of our lecturers was found dead floating face down in the Grand Canal, not far from the College.

-You have a Grand Canal in Dublin?

-Oh yes, but not like yours in Venice.

-What is going on?

-I don't know. Our police here, we call them the Gardaí, say that these are totally unrelated events. And, I sincerely hope that they are. But it is not a good time in the College at the moment. By the way there is one thing I wanted to ask you about what happened to me in Rome. When I was called to Cardinal Baffasa he knew that I had seen Dameri's illuminated manuscript and that I was interested in learning something about its history. I have no idea how he could have known this and it has bothered me. I have been meaning to ask you about it.

-I don't know how to answer that question. I assume that you knew that when you were given your personal ID card on the day that you arrived at the Vatican your movements would, or should I say could be monitored by Vatican security from that point onwards. There is a chip in that ID card allowing them to locate you within a radius of so many kilometres from their offices. I don't know how many kilometres it is but I think the area is wide enough. If they were interested in your movements they would have known that you had been to see Antonio Dameri and then you went to the Gallery Garibaldi. The security people in the Vatican are past masters and I would not be at all surprised if they knew that Dameri had bought work from the Gallery Garibaldi and they probably knew precisely what it was. As you were a mediaevalist they could assume that it would spark your interest and maybe they were just trying to be helpful in giving you some background as to the type of work it was.

-Well I never.

-Security in the 21st century is just like that. The guardians of our freedom say that they're obliged to intrude on our privacy to make sure we stay free and thus the old Latin expression *Quis custodiet ipsos custodes?* Or, who watches the watchers, has acquired a fresh relevance.

Finn took a deep breath.

-Don't you remember Finn, I never invited you to my apartment because I knew that the powers that be could have identified where you had been and that would have had direct implications for my career? Whenever I went to your apartment, I made sure that I did not have my ID card with me. This is one of the tricks that you pick up when you've been working for the Vatican for a while.

-So, the master string-pullers in the Vatican knew exactly what I was doing and when I was doing it.

-Yes Finn, I think you can assume that's true. By the way, I meant to mention this to you before. I was at a reception at the American Embassy last week. There was an American Senator visiting Rome on some sort of cultural mission. It was to do with a type of student exchange which was being considered for language students and the function was intended to introduce him to people from the Vatican and other individuals to whom he might be interesting.

-Oh yes.

-And there I met both Jeremy Williamson and Cardinal Baffasa. They did not appear to be at the event together but I did notice that at the end of the party they were chatting in a corner. In fact, I had the impression that they might have been arguing. I remembered that you had been in touch with both of them while you were in Rome. There was a third man with them. A rather large man with a loud accented voice. I am not that good on American accents but I think it was East Coast, maybe Boston. He spoke a bit like Jack Kennedy used to.

-Wow! I certainly had dealings with Williamson and I thought that I saw Baffasa's limousine outside his office one day. I had wondered if they knew each other. Rome is not that big a place. I might also know who the third man was. I have been bothered by a man from Boston.

It was now late and Finn was too tired and too distracted with having Maria in Dublin to be able to process this new information. Tomorrow was another day. He and Maria had far more pleasurable things to do before the end of the evening.

Thus, having exhausted the topic of Rome and the Vatican Finn and Maria were able to put this behind them and they spent the rest of the evening simply enjoying each other's company and the very fine wine Finn had selected to accompany the meal.

Returning to Finn's apartment shortly before midnight they tumbled into bed leaving the worries of the world and the spies at the Vatican well outside their present world.

Chapter Twenty

Paddy's Day

The next day was the great Saint Patrick's Day Parade and Finn and Maria were up early in preparation for their busy day. There could be hundreds of thousands of people lining the streets of Dublin. The colour green would be everywhere.

-Maria, Dublin goes crazy on St Pat's Day. It's a great day to be Irish. The tradition requires Irish men and women to wear the green on that day. This used to be a matter of sporting a small sprig of shamrock on one's lapel, but increasingly people now dress up in all sorts of green outfits. The colour green plays an interesting role in the Irish psyche.

-How come?

-Wearing green was a way of showing solidarity among those opposing British rule in Ireland. There is an old ballad called *The Wearing of the Green* that has a line in it saying *"They are hanging men and women for the wearing of the green"*.

-How interesting. Did they actually ever do such a thing?

Finn looked very perplexed. He had no idea how to answer that question. He decided to treat it as a rhetorical question.

-The Great Parade in Dublin is terrific. There will be a continual stream of floats, marching bands, school groups and others parading through the streets to the delight of the crowds. It will be several hours of great fun.

Finn's seats on the main stand in front of the General Post Office were really great and he and Maria had a wonderful time watching this spectacle. When relaxed, Dubliners can be funny indeed, especially as they know how to laugh at themselves.

After the parade, they strolled down the bank of the Liffey, crossing the river at the Ha'penny Bridge before heading off to Temple Bar to find one of Finn's favourite pubs for a meal and to listen to some Irish music. It didn't take long for some of Finn's students to turn up and he and Maria were delighted to join in with the younger crowd and enjoy their carefree attitude towards the celebrations. St Patrick's Day, once owned by the Catholic Church, is no longer considered to be a holy day as such, and is often referred to as Paddy's Day, conveying the feeling for merriment, if not actual irreverence, rather than the solemnity of former times.

That evening Finn took Maria to another of his favourite restaurants. In recent years Dublin had become a culinary centre which rivalled some of the smaller cities in Europe. They were now weary from the hectic activity of the day and were inclined to be somewhat subdued even in their conversation. And as Maria was due to fly back the following day, the conversation soon turned to a discussion of relationships.

-Maria, is it feasible to keep a relationship going when we are living two and a half thousand kilometres apart?

-I don't know Finn. I think that the distance is not as far as it used to be. Not that the kilometres are any less, but flights are much more frequent and much less expensive.

-I suppose it depends on how keen we are?

-Finn, that's probably the key issue?

-Maria, how keen are you?

-That's not really a fair question. Is it? Well I don't go rushing off to spend weekends with men in strange cities every day of the week. - I'm glad to hear it.

-Asking questions like this may well be rushing things a bit, don't you think?

-You're probably right. Maybe we should wait and see how things pan out.

-Relationships either last or like old soldiers, they simply fade away.

-Let's see how we feel as time goes on. We know it's no big deal going up in an aeroplane and three hours later being in the other city.

Once again this conversation was put behind them and they returned to enjoying talking about Maria's experiences during the last two days.

Unfortunately, Maria had to be at Dublin airport early the following morning to catch a flight to Rome and they decided they would not linger in the restaurant as long as they had done the night before. The restaurant was on the north side of Dublin about a kilometre from Finn's flat, and as the evening was fine, they decided they would stroll back to his flat, hand in hand.

The following morning they were both up at 5 am. The Aer Lingus flight to Rome was at 6:40 am and although the airport was close by there were always potential delays at security to be considered and Finn wanted to be sure that Maria wouldn't miss her flight.

On the way back, Finn began to feel that he should have been more forceful about the relationship issue and that he should have suggested that they see each other regularly. But he knew that this feeling was probably only the result of the romantic feelings he was now experiencing. Finn had not been good at sustaining relationships with women and he wondered how long he and Maria would want to maintain the friendship they were now both enjoying.

Chapter Twenty One

A tragic loss

After seeing Maria off on her early flight back to Rome Finn arrived in his office at O'Connell College to find a pile of work on his desk that took all morning to clear. Two of Finn's doctoral students would soon be coming up for examination and the College had to find examiners for them. Finding quality examiners at doctoral level was always a challenge. There were not that many people who were qualified to do this job and universities around the world were very fussy about whom they would admit as an examiner. In addition, there was a tradition in academe that doctoral examiners were poorly paid, and therefore the challenge was to find someone who was qualified and acceptable to the University and who was prepared to give up a number of days of their time without any or little compensation. This task was always troubling and raised anxiety levels in supervisors who were concerned for the success of their students. Having put a lot of concentration and energy into this task, Finn decided to have a proper break from his work and to lunch in the faculty club, where he met a number of colleagues who were talking about the tragic death of Paddy Walsh. Finn wondered if it was the academic lifestyle that encouraged long periods of gossip among his colleagues, or whether it was just the nature of the particular group of people who regularly congregated in the faculty club to be so introspective about issues in the College.

-You know, Paddy's death is a great loss to the College as he was one of our true Irish originals. Yes, some people said that he had the potential to be one of Ireland's great authors. Mind you, I never quite saw that in him myself. But he indeed was a popular man. -Yes, there were others who had a different view. You know, not everyone can be a Brendan Behan. Most people need to be pretty sober when they

195

write. Paddy's love for the bottle was a bit too much, even, for an Irish author or playwright. The old priests are sometimes right and maybe the Total Abstinence Pledge is a necessity in this little country of ours! Good knows we have some drunks.

-I wouldn't go near that crowd. They are the biggest bunch of killjoys you can ever come across. Imagine a life without a jar every now and again. That's not for me.

-I guess you are right. But drink has been a curse in Ireland for many a year. That's the bare reality for you. This country has been plagued by the drink. And so we see another great writer who will be leaving behind a miserably small body of work.

-But there will always be others, new bright young faces coming up behind him who can scratch a few words out on a piece of paper and make themselves famous, I don't doubt.

-I am sure that Ireland's finest will always bubble to the top and be recognised for their contribution to our ancient literary tradition.

Finn wondered if this was so.

-It's pretty hard on us here having to cope with two funerals within a couple of weeks. Mullally's funeral was dreadful. It rained the entire time. I caught my death of cold and even the drinks afterwards didn't warm me up.

-I hear that Walsh's drinks will be held in the student pub on campus.

-That should be a good shindig.

Returning to his office Finn received a message that Inspector Quinn wanted to see him, and that he was coming over to O'Connell College in the next half hour. The message suggested that if Finn was not going to be there he should phone Pearse Street station. Finn's afternoon was relatively light and he looked forward to hearing what Quinn would have to say.

-Good afternoon Inspector Quinn. I wonder what news you have for me?

-I am afraid I have some rather disturbing news.

-Oh dear. What has happened?

-I am not quite sure how to put this Finn but I think your friend Sean O'Toole may be missing.

-What do you mean?

-Last night, as you know we had one of the worst storms recorded in Dublin in recent years, starting at about 9 o'clock. Around 10:30 two vehicles were involved in a crash down in the docks at the North Wall. One was a sedan and the other was a light delivery vehicle. Both vehicles ended up in the Liffey. There were no direct witnesses. The crash was sort of observed from the other side of the river, so it's not clear exactly how it occurred and by the time the emergency services arrived both vehicles were already at the bottom of the river for a while. A frogman was dispatched to check for bodies, but, none were found.

-So what has that got to do with Sean O'Toole?

-This sedan was registered in the name Sean O'Toole.

-Good God. What car was it?

-Finn, a large blue, five-year-old Vauxhall with an Irish tricolour on the back window.

-Yes that sounds just like Sean's car, Inspector.

-The registration checks out. It was owned by Sean O'Toole all right.

-And Sean?

-Finn, there are no bodies. The man who reported the crash, and who had only observed it at a distance said that he was under the impression that both drivers were in their vehicles when they plunged into the river. So we are now working on the assumption that the drivers tried to get out of their vehicles and were swept by the current out into Dublin Bay. Due to the storm the river was flowing faster than usual and there was also a particularly strong flood tide on its way out last night that could have dragged the bodies right out into the Irish Sea.

-Inspector, I am seldom short of words, but your news has completely dumbfounded me. I don't know what to say, and I certainly have no idea what to think. I am completely flummoxed.

-We just don't know what happened. The two vehicles will be lifted out of the river later today and hopefully that should give us some idea of how the crash occurred. What we really need is an eyewitness who was on the scene. It's particularly disturbing that there is no sign of either of the bodies.

-What is the chance of recovering them, Inspector?

- Can't say for sure, Finn. We have put out an alert to all shipping passing through Dublin Bay, especially the ferries and of course to all the sailing clubs and centres along the coast. Someone might be able to spot the bodies if they are still floating. But on the other hand they might just become crab meat.

-I didn't know when Sean intended to come back to Dublin but I'd thought it would be any day now and I was really looking forward to discussing our more general situation with him. Now that he is missing like this, I am not sure what to make of it. If it turns out that he's dead, then we will have had one murder and two extraordinary deaths in the College in the last month. That must be a record of some sort!

-We are still faced with the fact that even if he is dead, this may well be just another unusual accident. It doesn't necessarily connect in any way with the murder of Mullally, nor can we assume that this bogeyman of yours Joe Murphy has anything to do with it. We just have to wait and see how it pans out and we mustn't jump to conclusions.

-I wish I didn't think that I was personally the one who was going to be the proof of the pudding; the pudding that has been prepared by Joe Murphy.

-You have no reason to believe that. I think it's about time that you stopped being so paranoid. We don't know for sure that Sean O'Toole was in the vehicle, and that even if he was we do not know for certain that he is really dead. We're going to need a body to really be clear on this. Please remember the issue of evidence. There are a number of Gardaí and recovery people down at the docks right now. I am going down to see what the latest position is and I'll get back to you if I have any interesting news. In the meantime if for whatever reason Sean O'Toole gets in touch with you, please let me know immediately.

-There's a fat chance of that, but I certainly shall.

-Oh, by the way, when I heard that you wanted to talk to me, I thought that you had news about your enquiries into Joe Murphy and the other matters we have been discussing. Is there any news on that front?

-You know I have come to the conclusion that your concern about Murphy is driven by a deep guilt at your involvement in the Being Excellent fraud.

-No, guilt is not the issue. We did a good thing. Anyway you have some news.

-A little, I suppose, but it's not all that helpful. We did check with the immigration people at the airport and a man named Joseph Murphy has been visiting Dublin a few times over the past couple of months. It's the same man who has been coming and going. He is an American citizen living in Boston. He initially stated that he was staying at the Salbourne Hotel but after his first night there he moved out and did not leave any forwarding address. On subsequent entries into Ireland he gave an address in Rathmines which does not exist. That might have been deliberate or he might have made a mistake in filling out the form.

-What else have you found out Inspector?

-Our contacts in the FBI have made some enquiries and there is indeed a US – Irish Cultural Cooperative Society which was active in the 1960s and 1970s. It got a great boost during the years when John Kennedy was President, but today the Society is low key. It appears that the enthusiasm for US - Irish culture cooperation is at a low ebb in Boston. Some of my colleagues say that with peace in Northern Ireland, American interest in this country has declined. But I am not so sure about that. Americans certainly still come here in substantial numbers as tourists. We haven't yet been able to establish what links there are between Murphy and the US – Irish Cultural Cooperative Society, but we are working on it.

-What about the crowd in Rome?

-We've also made some enquiries with our colleagues in Europe. It would appear that Europol have nothing on Jeremy Williamson. They were able to tell us that sometime back there was some suspicion about whether Williamson and/or the Gallery Garibaldi were involved in the black market for stolen Iraqi treasures. However, the artefacts that passed through the gallery were established as being completely legitimate and so no action was taken. We also asked both Europol and the FBI if there were any cases on their books about fake artworks or other valuable artefacts coming into circulation in the last five years and they reported that there was nothing outstanding.

-That's certainly interesting. Have you found any connection between Murphy and Rome?

-No. I am not sure if that isn't too vague a suggestion to even bother.

-That's going to be the issue, isn't it? Why should you bother?

-Let me make it clear that we are concerned. Your story is interesting, but we can't conduct our investigations simply on your intuition which may just be the result of your guilty conscience.

-I have been having more dreams about Williamson and they have made me wonder if there are not other monasteries like Montebello producing, shall we say questionable, illuminated manuscripts. In fact, maybe many of the works of art recently discovered and attributed to mediaeval masters are actually made by highly skilled teams working in places like Montebello?

-Now you sound crazy, Professor.

-My intuition tells me there has to be a connection between Murphy and Williamson. I know I have no evidence of this and I was hoping that the great international police machine would be able to find some.

-Finn, even if you are right and there is a connection, and if Murphy is in Ireland to threaten you, it is not clear that we can do much about it. The forces of law and order in the civilised world are often powerless before a crime is committed. At present he is not stalking you, so all we could do is caution him.

-Inspector, I really feel so on my own.

-Once again I have to say, please don't let your imagination run away with itself. If there is any evidence out there we will find it but for the time being, I hope this information I have given you helps put your mind a little at rest. It doesn't seem that you have been dealing with an international syndicate of master criminals and it's highly improbable that you need to be frightened of the prospect of Murphy coming to get you.

-But as they say, you never know.

-That is indeed true. But the probability is very low.

-I have never heard of a policeman talking about probabilities before.

-Well now you have.

Even though he was not at all satisfied by this report and his conversation with Quinn generally, there was little more that Finn could say or do. If Murphy had been legitimate then there was nothing to be done. Maybe the College was going through an unlucky period. It has often been said that unpleasant things happen in threes, and now there had been three unanticipated deaths in the College. Maybe that would be the end of it.

On the other hand deep down Finn believed that when his story was told one day, there would be plenty of evidence that there was blood on the book he had conceptualised, and Sean had written, and the monks in Rome had "re-produced".

Although he hated it, Finn knew he just had to wait and see if the Gardaí were right. But at the same time he felt the need to talk this through with someone whom he could really trust. He racked his brains as to who that might be. He had no close family. Sean was gone. Maria was back in Rome. Finn had not been an especially religious man and so he quietly amused himself at the idea that perhaps he should go to confession where he could talk the whole thing out with the priest. And the more he thought of it the more he felt that might just work.

It was generally known to students and other academics that Father Conor O'Donnell sat late into the evening to hear confessions in the University Church on St Stephen's Green and Finn decided that he would go up there the following evening and make a confession.

Before leaving the office that evening, Finn decided to email Maria.

I have been thinking about you all day. I wish we had talked more about how we felt about each other and how our relationship might go forward from where we are at the moment. I think that I should come down to Rome. I can get away at the end of next week and spend a few days with you. I am missing you already. I am due a one-year sabbatical from O'Connell College and I should look around to see if I can find a post, maybe at the Università di Roma for the year. That would give us the time we need to find out if we really want to spend the rest of our lives together. Please do let me know right away what you think.

The following day the Dublin newspapers carried the headline *"O'Connell College lecturer's car found at the bottom of the Liffey. No body recovered – yet".* The newspapers speculated that with the flood tide the two bodies were probably swept out into the Irish Sea. The television news showed maps of river currents and sea currents and the paths of ships through them. It was pointed out that the bodies could be mutilated by the ships. It was generally thought by the group of experts the television station produced that it was likely they would never recover the bodies.

That evening Finn walked from his office over the Ha'penny Bridge, through Temple Bar, past the Bank of Ireland and up Grafton Street, past the Royal College of Surgeons and turned left at Cuffe Street to arrive at the University Church on St Stephen's Green. He now realised that he had made a great mistake getting involved with Being Excellent. He was beginning to wonder what Murphy would look like. He asked himself if he would recognise him in the street if he bumped into him. He could feel his semi-conscious streak of paranoia growing and he knew that he had to control that. He would frighten himself to death if he let that run riot. But at the same time he kept on remembering the aphorism *"Just because you're paranoid doesn't mean that they are not out to get you".*

Chapter Twenty Two

An informal review

Quinn had already had a bad day, in fact a very bad day. All his ideas about Mullally's murder were leading him nowhere. His door-to-door enquiries around Mullally's home had turned up nothing. No one in the College had any information about any aspect of Mullally's life that could be used to explain what had happened. He was not all that popular in certain quarters but his rows with colleagues were not the stuff that leads to murder. Dublin's criminal fraternity was not saying anything about it if they knew anything. He may as well have been murdered by a ghost.

Detective Sergeant Siobhan Cavanagh had worked with Quinn for a number of years during which time she had grown to respect his ability to solve cases more rapidly and more convincingly than most other Inspectors in the Garda Síochána. During this time, she also learnt how to assess his sometimes unspoken concerns and moods. It was now clear to her that Quinn was deeply worried about the Mullally case. Despite a substantial amount of thorough detective work very little progress had been made and she decided it was time for her to have a private brainstorming session with Quinn.

-Inspector before we go home this evening how about you and I having a jar and a chat about what we really know about the Mullally case. As things are not going too well I think it would do both of us a lot of good to quietly review where we are.

-Good idea Siobhan. The Chief Superintendent actually asked me to report to him tomorrow on our progress and at this stage I'm not at all sure what I'm going to be able to say to him. He needs reassurance that we're going to be able to solve this case, and solve it sooner rather than later. Let's go to that little pub I like off Aston Quay. You know, it's the one with the quiet bit at the back. My friends always refer to it as the Purple Leprechaun. A previous owner of the pub used to dress up for the tourists.

-OK. As soon as you're ready, let's go.

The two detectives made their way from Pearse Street along Westmorland Street turning left down Aston Quay before arriving at Quinn's favourite quiet pub. En route Quinn began reminiscing about how he had been introduced, when he was still a teenager, to the Purple Leprechaun by his father, who was a man Dubliners would describe as being rather fond of his drink. He told Siobhan how his father had nearly lost his job because he would stretch out his lunch hours with his friends in the pub a little longer than his boss considered appropriate. This had made Quinn quite circumspect about his intake of alcohol. Nonetheless Quinn was well known for saying that he himself was a man who really appreciated the virtues of Arthur Guinness. He appreciated the founder of the brewery for the fine black liquid that they made and which was enjoyed by so many Irish men and women. He also appreciated Arthur Guinness and his successors for being such an outstanding benefactor to the city of Dublin.

Arriving at the pub they grabbed their drinks from the bar and found a quiet corner in which to chat.

-Siobhan, how shall we do this?

-Let's go through all the major scenarios and theories one by one. We can start with the least probable first and work our way up to more likely possibilities or even probabilities.

-So Siobhan the first one is … Mullally was murdered as a result of a random break-in to O'Connell College by some person or persons unknown probably looking to burgle something from the prestigious college. Maybe they were looking for some of the artworks on the walls of some of the offices.

-Right, Inspector. But that's as unlikely as my being able to swim across the Irish Sea. I'm not even sure I would assign any probability to that scenario.

-I agree, very low probability indeed. So the second one is ... Mullally was murdered by a colleague as a result of some sort of grudge within the College which we have not yet uncovered.

-Well Inspector, that is as unlikely as me walking to Belfast to get a pint of Guinness. Its probability is slightly higher than the first suggestion that the murder was a result of a random break-in, but only a little more. We have no evidence whatsoever of there being any animosity between Mullally and any of his colleagues. In fact the general impression we received is that Mullally was quite highly thought of by all those or at least many of those, who worked with him.

-So we move on to a third scenario… Mullally was murdered by a student or by an agent of a student whom he had expelled from the University, either due to a poor academic record, or being unable to pay the fees, or some other reason.

-We have looked at that and there were very few students over the last year sent down from O'Connell College. If this murder were in some way revenge for an act like you have described I would have expected it to take place pretty promptly after the event. There was no such event in the last 12 months so I can only conclude that this scenario is not likely either.

Both detectives paused while they finished their drinks. It was clear that they needed to think more widely about this affair.

-OK Inspector, let's look at Mullally's private life … Mullally was murdered because he owed a lot of money perhaps due to gambling or some inauspicious investments and he was not able to pay it back to his creditors.

-No, that doesn't wash either. There is nothing in any of the records we have looked at to suggest this.

-Mullally was murdered because he was having an affair with someone to whom he made promises that he decided not to keep.

-No Siobhan, we have absolutely no evidence of that either. There isn't the slightest suggestion in what we know about Mullally that he led anything other than a very straightforward and uncomplicated life.

-I guess so.

-Siobhan, we must go back to basics. We have decided that this murder was not random therefore it must have been deliberate. If it was deliberate we have to be able to find a motive. All the motives we've looked at so far we can discount relatively easily. Admittedly we haven't concluded all the possible investigations we could make. We haven't analysed years of his emails. But despite this I think we can possibly come to one tentative conclusion and I say tentative, because obviously we might turn up some evidence which would disprove it. What I suggest we work on for the moment is that Mullally was murdered in order to silence him. This simply means that Mullally knew something about some nefarious activity that was going on in O'Connell College.

-But what sort of nefarious activity could a bunch of boring old academics get up to which would justify his murder?

-Well as we all know there is not always a rational justification for a murder.

-What circumstances could lead somebody to want to silence Mullally?

-Siobhan, how about this? Mullally discovered there was a drug syndicate working in or from the College.

-There was a drug problem in the College a few years ago that has largely been cleaned up. If that had started up again I think the drug squad would have known about it and we would have heard.

-Maybe. On the other hand perhaps there is a completely new set of dealers which have moved in using a different MO? Maybe the Mullally murder is the first time their activity has come up on our radar.

-Maybe. But that doesn't ring true for me at this stage.

-Siobhan here is another scenario for you. Mullally discovered that there were some scams being executed regarding the college accepting overseas students on programs which contravene the Immigration Laws. Maybe somebody was effectively using the College as a vehicle for people-smuggling. There is a huge demand for people to get even temporary residency in an EU country and I'm sure that an operation like that would be highly profitable.

-Could that really happen here?

- Of course. I'm sure. But it is unlikely. Nonetheless we can't discount that.

-The immigration people need to be contacted?

-Yes Siobhan. But there are other alternatives that we could consider. Maybe there's some deeply hidden fraud in the finances or the books of accounts of the College. The College has a budget of quite a hundred million euros a year. There are also big sums of money involved in endowments. Their capital development funds which the College have accumulated from donors to erect new buildings must be huge. Education is really big business these days. Siobhan, if we go down that route we will have to call in the white-collar team and we will need to get a bunch of forensic accountants to have a look at the figures. That would not be easy. And I'm not even sure if we would get permission to conduct such an investigation.

-Inspector, offhand I can't come up with anything else to suggest but I am now really convinced that there is something wrong in "the State of O'Connell" as Shakespeare might have said. The trouble is that it's awfully difficult to see how we are going to be able to poke around in the affairs of the College sufficiently to be able to find out what is really been going on behind those closed doors. Academics are not the most forthcoming bunch of people you can ever work with. They will fight like mad to resist our getting our hands on their financial records.

-Siobhan, maybe we can put someone in there undercover. We did after all get quite a lot of information when you spent the day with your brother talking to students.

-Sure we could do that; that is going to take a lot of time and is going to be really quite hard to find somebody who would be able to get away with it. This case might not be cracked in the near future.

It was time for another drink and Quinn brought the fresh glasses back from the bar. They had now covered all the angles they could think of and it would soon be time to go home.

-Well Inspector, has this little review achieved anything for us?

-I think it has. You have helped me clear up in my mind that we are looking for something which is seriously wrong in O'Connell College. We are wasting our time on house-to-house investigations in Mullally's neighbourhood. I think I am now convinced that we won't get anywhere by prying into Mullally's private life. We have to take a different view of the circumstances surrounding this case.

-Good.

-By the way our discussion has made me recall that Professor Finn Kelly told me a strange story about how he and a colleague were involved in a scam in Italy. As it is way out of our jurisdiction I didn't see the need to take this very seriously and I am still not sure if it has any relevance to the Mullally case. But I guess it does show that there could be all sorts of extraneous activities going on in the College which we should try to keep a watch out for, as some of them might lead us to a solution to this case.

-What you going to say to the Chief Superintendent tomorrow?

-I have to be pretty straight with him. So far our investigations have not led to any spectacular results but at least what they have done is rule out quite a lot of avenues of enquiry. I have a good feeling about what we have discussed tonight and I'm going to present this to the chief superintendent as what I believe should be the main thrust of enquiries from now on. How we're going to find out what we need to know is a different matter but I feel we have a clearer vision of where our enquiries should be going.

Chapter Twenty Three

For these and all my other sins

Finn's attention was brought back to the confessional where he was kneeling. He had not been expecting the priest to challenge him in this way and he found Father O'Donnell's remarks quite disconcerting.

-Father, you are of course right. I am guilty of a number of misdemeanours, or shall we use the expression venal sins.

-No, you still haven't got it. Whether a sin is a venal sin or a mortal sin is largely to do with the outcome of the act. So, if you tell someone a lie which you might have thought was a little white lie and that leads to some horrific consequences, then this has been a mortal sin.

-Does intention not matter?

-Don't be an eejit, of course it does, but it is not the only issue.

-What can I say? My intentions were always good?

-And you know as well as anybody else the old saying we have in Ireland declaring that, *the road to hell is paved with good intentions.*

-Yes Father, I am beginning to see my role in this whole affair in a completely different light. I agree with you that I have been quite reckless and that the roots of this recklessness were pride. I also admit that I seem to easily disconnect my account of events from the truth, and that I need to do something about this as a matter of urgency. Mea culpa, mea culpa, mea maxima culpa.

-This issue of the truth is most important, and it seems that your natural response to situations is one of denial.

-I know that's true and I feel terrible about that. I promise that I will work at that.

-And furthermore you have confused the issue of criminality and morality. God doesn't care that your involvement with the fake book does not appear to have broken the law in Ireland. He doesn't care that the fraud may have been committed in Italy or some other part of the world. God's view is not restricted by any man made political entities.

-I know. I know.

-God's jurisdiction is universal, and there is no doubt that you contributed materially to a major falsehood.

-That is true. But it did a lot of good.

-You seem to have justified your creation of this caper on what one could call the Robin Hood principle. You set it up to steal from the rich so that you could give to the poor. Is that not so?

-Yes.

-Where does it say in the holy text that such behaviour is acceptable?

-I don't know, Father.

-Nowhere. The idea of taking from the rich to give to the poor can only be done by governments who as you know are not particularly good at it. Your plan to get money for the Shelter was profoundly morally flawed. And moreover that tainted money is now being used by honest people believing that it came from a genuine and loving source. Shame on you.

-Father...

Finn was getting more and more uncomfortable. He realised that this confession was not such a good idea. Getting a tongue lashing like this did not suit Finn one little bit. He had to gracefully get out of this.

-I also wonder about your responsibility to your friend Antonio. Did you not think you should have told him that you thought his manuscript was a fake?

Finn was getting ready to be more defensive.

-And if I had, what difference would it have made.

-You would have been true to yourself and to him.

-And, if I were wrong?

-You also insinuated that the Vatican might be behind this man Murphy. Highly unlikely, I should think. We all know that the Vatican is going through a difficult time at the moment. But remember it has been in business for about 2,000 years. During that time it has had some dreadful Popes and ridiculous Cardinals and yet still it pulled through. And if you think about the scale of things, the Vatican supports a body of clergy consisting of hundreds of thousands of people. It supports many millions of the faithful who are in dire difficulties, social, medical and political troubles. To do this it deals in billions of euros. Why would they be involved in fraudulent activities for the occasional million euros? Your thinking is crazy!

-I can't say. I never thought of it like that.

-Our Holy Mother the Church is eternal.

-Yes, Father.

-I also suspect that your relationship with your lady friend from Rome is also predicated on a level of insincerity and that your intentions here are probably not all that honourable. Maybe you need to do something about that as well. I know that I am not being easy on you but it seems to me that you are in a particularly difficult situation. I agree with you that this Murphy fellow appears menacing and I am sure that whatever happens, it will be good for you to sort out where you stand morally and of course spiritually. After all your immortal soul is at stake.

-Yes Father, I now realise that.

Finn was now beginning to feel even more uncomfortable. This experience was not doing the right thing for him. It was making him feel even more jittery than he had been before. He was beginning to doubt this rational mind. Finn felt it was time to discontinue his engagement with Father O'Donnell. There is only so much truth one can take at one time and Finn had now reached that limit.

-Yes, that is true. I completely agree with you. I have made a bloody mess of this whole situation. I'll never do it again. I don't think there is much more for me to confess and all I can now sincerely say is that for these and all my other sins I am truly sorry.

Father O'Donnell paused. He knew he was there not simply to chastise the faithful. He realised he had pushed Finn quite hard and he now had to rein back.

-Let us first say a short prayer.

-Yes.

A minute later the priest continued.

-My son, you do now sound somewhat more contrite. I know your heart was in the right place. And in the light of that I can grant you absolution from your sins provided you ... you faithfully perform the penance I now ask of you. You can well imagine that your penance will have to be somewhat different from three Hail Marys.

-Yes ... Father.

There was a lengthy pause as Father O'Donnell gathered his thoughts. But Finn's anxiety level was at a peek.

- And what would that penance be Father?

-I want you to make sure that Mullally's widow does not think that his murder was anything to do with any criminal or even immoral activity of his. This is essential. You don't have to tell her the whole story but you must make sure that she does not harbour any doubts about the integrity of her husband. If you can do that then I think you will have made a minor atonement for your sins.

-Father, I can certainly do that. I'll go and see her myself. I'll do it right away.

-And just for completeness say three Our Fathers and three Hail Mary's as well.

-Yes, Father.

Finn got up off his knees and stepped outside the confessional. He thought to himself, Thank Goodness that was over. He would never go to confession again! The church was empty and was largely dark except for the candles that were burning next to the confessional and he knew that Father O'Donnell would not stay much longer that evening. Deep down, despite his discomfort, he was relieved that he had been able to say a few things to the old priest he knew he could not tell to anyone else.

Finn walked slowly out of the main body of the church, down the vestibule which led to the front door of the church, his eyes pinned to the floor. As he arrived at the entrance he was aware of something or someone standing deep in the shadow a few yards inside the door.

Finn began to make out the shape of a man.

-Professor Kelly

The Boston accent was unmistakable.

-Murphy! In the Church?

-Yes, Professor Kelly.

Finn was transfixed like a rabbit in the headlights of a car. Murphy raised his right hand in which he was holding a small gun with a substantial silencer on the end of it.

-Why Murphy? Why are you doing this?

-Professor, surely a smart man like you must know the answer to that question. Come now it's obvious. It is the view of my boss, Mr Williamson that we can't afford to have any loose ends. You and O'Toole are like a couple of old sieves. You are leaking all over. O'Toole has been giving talks about how to write like the great masters. He has let it slip that he has already written something like this. He is out to make every penny he can from this business of imitating famous authors.

-But….

- If you two had kept your mouth shut and laid low for a few years things might have been different but O'Toole is a loose cannon and you are quite dangerous to us. It was just as well that O'Toole wrote himself off in the Docks the other night.

Finn remained speechless.

-Our client has paid many million dollars for that book and we can't have him disappointed by learning that it was, shall I say, a counterfeit. You are smart enough to see that.

Murphy pulled the trigger and Finn slumped to the floor. It was all over in a second. The silencer was most effective and Finn's body did not make much noise as it reached the stone floor. It was a life cut short in one of the cruellest of ways in that Finn did not have the slightest chance to come to terms with his impending death. But Murphy who had done this type of thing many times before wanted it that way. *No talking to your target* was his lifelong motto. Even saying the man's name before he pulled the trigger was more than

Murphy normally allowed himself. He realised he had just broken his rules and he thought to himself that he must be more careful in future. The rules he had made for himself about the way he assassinated his targets had been made to maximise his efficiency and he wanted to do nothing to jeopardise that.

Murphy stepped over the body and walked back into the church towards the confessional. The old priest was still there trying to make up his mind whether he should give up and go home for a mug of cocoa or stick it out for another half hour in the hope of being available for more sinners that night. Murphy opened the door and pointed the gun at the priest head.

-Sorry Father. You are just another loose end that we have to tidy away. Nothing personal, of course, Father.

The old priest did not realise what was happening to him. He died without the last rites and with a cup of hot cocoa on his mind.

Murphy placed the gun in his pocket in such a way that there was no obvious bulge, squared off his jacket and turned his back on his victim.

The assassin moved slowly out of the church once again stepping around Finn's body now lying in a pool of blood with a mutilated face. He turned left and walked 50 yards down the pavement where a large white car was waiting for him. The driver was dressed in a chauffeur's uniform and looked like he was waiting for an official from the government department on that side of St Stephen's Green. Murphy quietly slipped into the front seat and whispered to the driver.

-As they say in the classics, Home, James, and don't spare the horses.

The car slowly drove away with no sense of urgency heading towards the north side of the city.

Murphy felt completely at ease with himself. His mission has been accomplished. He would call his bosses later and his money would be transferred to the appropriate bank account. He would now take a break before accepting another job. He felt two weeks in Acapulco would do the trick.

Murphy carefully disassembled the gun and the silencer and left them on the floor of the car. He took out of his inside pocket a large white envelope containing a bundle of €100 notes.

-As agreed this is the second half of your fee. I assume the hardware will go back into your armoury and the lettuce will be passed onto your superiors.

The driver simply nodded.

Murphy amused himself by reflecting on the fact that his slang word "lettuce" for the €100 notes was understood by the driver.

-By the way will you take me to the airport tomorrow morning?

-Certainly, Sir.

For Murphy this had been a scrappy job. He had been away from his base for too long. But now it was done. He would be travelling home soon. The next flight to Boston was at 11.40 am the following morning. He would be glad to leave Dublin and its miserable weather behind.

Chapter Twenty Four

Catch-as-catch-can

Quinn decided to call in at his office in Pearse Street as it was on the way home from the Purple Leprechaun. He had just walked through the door when his mobile phone rang. It was the Duty Officer at the Gardaí Control Centre.

-Inspector Quinn, we are rather pressed here at the moment with a lot of unusual activity and we have received another call from a squad car up on St Stephen's Green. It appears that two bodies have been found in the University Church. Could you please get up there as quickly as possible?

-Certainly, I'm on my way.

Quinn had been to the University Church a couple of times. It was a very unusual place. From the outside it looked tiny. It was squashed in between very important buildings on the highly prestigious square which surrounded St Stephen's Green. The Church was located there to support the congregation of Ireland's first Catholic University but the University had moved to a big campus out of town and so the little church often looked lonely if not virtually abandoned.

Quinn immediately phoned Siobhan Cavanagh who was still walking home a few blocks away and they both rushed to the Gardaí car pool to pick up a car, and were at the University Church within minutes. The church had already been cordoned off and the Garda on duty walked up to Quinn, handing him a wallet.

-Inspector, there are two bodies here. There is a man at the front door and there is an old priest in a confessional inside the church. I took this wallet from the jacket of the man at the door.

Quinn opened the wallet. He stood there staring at it for a good minute. He could hardly believe his eyes. Could this be a sick joke? There was a driving licence together with a bunch of credit cards in the name of Professor Finn Kelly. He walked across to the body and although the face had been severely disfigured by a bullet in the forehead there was no doubt that these were the remains of O'Connell College's Professor of Mediaeval studies.

Quinn was struck dumb but in his mind he kept repeating to himself *"Holy mother of God"*.

Quinn felt sick to the core. He wasn't sure if his stomach was going to be able to keep down the pint of beer he had recently consumed. As he tried to make sense of what he could see in front of them his brain felt as though it had been mashed by a herd of stampeding buffalo.

He kept on saying to himself in a semi-audible voice, how could this happen? What is going on? This doesn't make any sense at all. Then the name Murphy occurred to him. Quinn told Siobhan Cavanagh to take over at the scene of the crime as he was going back to his office. Siobhan Cavanagh was highly competent and was pleased to take over.

Back at Pearse Street Quinn put out an all points message that Mr Joseph Murphy travelling on a US passport was to be stopped and held for questioning. When encountered, Murphy was to be told that his papers were not in order and that an inspector would need to talk to him before he continued with his journey. Quinn said that it was thought that Murphy might have important information relating to murders that had just been committed in Dublin but no suggestion was made that he might be the murderer. This was sent to all airports and harbours in the Republic. Quinn also got in touch with his counterpart in Belfast and asked him to arrange for the same request to be sent to all Northern Ireland's exit points.

With a bit of luck, Quinn said to himself, Murphy won't know that we are on to him.

In due course Siobhan Cavanagh returned to Pearse Street.

-Siobhan I'm sorry to have left you on your own earlier but it was really important for me to get back to the office as I'm pretty sure I know who the murderer is and why these people were killed.

-Really?

-Oh Jaysus, I am in an awful state. I never quite felt like this before. I feel profoundly sickened by the sight of Kelly's body. I can't get my mind off it. Much more so than I've ever been before. You see, Kelly had told me several times that he thought his life might be in danger and I had pooh-poohed this suggestion. In fact, I had told him to stop being so paranoid.

-Oh, dear.

Siobhan realised that Quinn was not at his articulate best.

-Until an hour ago Finn Kelly was just a pain in the neck. A self-obsessed man with an over active imagination. A paranoid with too much time on his hands for thinking about monsters under the bed. I guess I've changed my mind.

-Yes, I remember. I did a bit of snooping around O'Connell College for you a few weeks ago. One of the people you wanted to know more about was Professor Kelly.

-Yes, and now he's the late Professor Kelly and maybe we could have stopped that from happening. Damn it. This shouldn't have happened. Damn it, I should have listened to Finn. But he had no evidence at all. Only premonitions and his dreams. No evidence. - Seamus, you know that we can't control everything. Even if you had believed him, we couldn't have given him a police nanny. And he wouldn't have wanted one either. This was completely outside of your control.

-Of course you're right, but the shock of seeing him dead there at the front door of the church this evening was quite overpowering. And having got to know Finn a bit I can't help but feel some responsibility.

-The bodies are now on the way to the morgue and the crime scene is secure. We will have the forensic lads down there tomorrow morning. By the way the media were at the church. Both RTE and Sky had camera teams there and they were desperately trying to find someone to interview. I think that they would have broadcast just about any old rubbish from just about anybody who would talk to them. I told them that I was pretty confident that a statement would be made late tomorrow morning and that would probably be from Pearse Street station. I didn't commit to anything.

-There is nothing left for us to do tonight. Let's call it quits. And we'll start bright and early tomorrow morning. I have the feeling that we are going to have a couple of challenging days ahead of us.

By 8 o'clock Quinn and Siobhan were in the office. They had both picked up newspapers on the way to work with the headlines *Two bodies found in the little Newman Church on St Stephen's Green.* The story was presented as a complete mystery and there was no suggestion as to who the bodies were or of any motive, and no detail of how the murders were committed except that both victims were shot.

Quinn sent a team to Professor Kelly's office at O'Connell College and to his flat in Drumcondra. Both teams went through his possessions with a fine-toothed comb. At his office Moira Flannigan was as helpful as she could be. She knew his password for his email and she allowed the officers to peruse his correspondence. There was a mountain of material from students and from other researchers with whom Finn had collaborated and all this was copied to be analysed further. But they were able to find nothing that they believed had any direct bearing on the case. However, whilst looking on Finn's computer they did find one email just arrived from Maria.

I felt quite similar after I left you in Dublin. What a wonderful suggestion. I will take time off work. I am sure you will find an interesting post here in one of the universities or even in the Vatican. Maybe we can think about where we might live! Let me know as soon as you can when you intend to arrive. There is so much for us to talk about. I will be at the airport.

Back at Pearse Street it was now a waiting game to see if Murphy would be picked up. Quinn, whose general propensity was for action, found this most difficult, but he kept a cool exterior as he wanted Murphy brought in without alerting him to what the Gardai knew. It was unlikely that he was already out of the country and he had no reason to believe that the police were looking for him.

Quinn and Siobhan began to work on what they would tell the press conference at midday.

-There will be one hell of a hullabaloo if we don't come clean on the identity of the victims. It will have to come out eventually and we will be accused of hiding it. The media don't pull any punches these days.

-But we will be hiding it for good cause. If for any reason Murphy isn't planning on leaving the country today we want to make sure that nothing in the media spooks him into going to ground and hiding out.

-The first flight to Boston is Aer Lingus at 11:30 and so we should know soon whether Murphy presents himself for travel then.

At 10:15 the telephone rang on Quinn's desk.

-Murphy checked in. As cool as a cucumber. Just another visitor to the Emerald Isle on his way home.

-So you have him in custody.

-Yes, as you suggested after he presented himself for travel on the early Aer Lingus flight to Boston this morning, we informed him that his travel documents were not in order and that he would have to be seen by the authorities before he could leave the country. We also asked him as a matter of routine to turn out his pockets and we looked in his brief case.

-Did you find anything interesting?

-A pile of cash.

-How much?

-Around ten thousand euros and dollars and sterling.

-Wow. That's enough to detain him anyway, in case there was some money laundering going on.

-It sure is. What do you want me to do with him now?

-As calmly as possible bring him to Pearse Street but don't give the impression that he is under suspicion for anything, other than maybe money laundering. Officially his passport is the main issue and the boys in town want to talk to him about it.

-Okay he'll be on his way within the next 10 minutes.

Quinn sat nervously in the interview room awaiting the arrival of Murphy. This was not going to be easy. There was no evidence to place Murphy at the scene of the crime. There was in fact precious little evidence at all other than Professor Finn Kelly's intuition that Murphy was up to no good. Maybe Murphy would say something that would give the game away but on the other hand if he was a professional assassin this was unlikely.

Murphy arrived escorted by two uniformed officers and was led into the interview room. He was a tall slim man, aged about 55 years. He was already significantly grey at the temples but other than that he had a fair amount of brown hair. He was dressed in a business suit and he sported a golden tie pin and some expensive looking cufflinks. He looked like a professional businessman who was on his way to meet an important client.

He sat down as he was instructed to and in a loud Boston accent he exclaimed.

-I understand you are Inspector Quinn and I believe there is something wrong with my passport.

-Yes that's correct, Mr Murphy. The US State Department informed us a short while ago that a number of passports had been stolen and the number of the passport you presented to our immigration officials this morning coincides with one of the stolen numbers. So I am afraid we can't allow you to travel on that document.

-Isn't that amazing? I have been travelling in and out of the USA for some months on that passport and I've been in and out of Ireland a few times, and this is the first occasion anything has been said.

-Often the law grinds slowly, Mr Murphy, but like the mills of God, the law can grind exceedingly fine. We need to get a statement from you concerning the precise circumstances, in which you obtained your passport, and then you will need to acquire another document from the US Consul here in Dublin, and you will need a new passport if you wish to travel out of this country.

-I suppose I need to speak to the American Consulate as soon as possible.

-They have been informed and they tell us that they will send someone over here before the end of the afternoon. I'm going to have one of my sergeants take a statement from you and after that I would like to speak to you again myself.

Quinn retreated to his office to brainstorm the situation with his team. Siobhan was expecting Quinn to be elated by the success in picking up Murphy but he was far from it.

-The moment we start questioning him about O'Connell College or about the murders last night he will know that we are onto him and he'll close up like a clam. We're going to have to find another way of getting to the truth about what has been going on.

-Yes, but how.

-What have the forensic lads come up with?

-Nothing. The place is as clean as a whistle. There will be a report on the gun and the bodies later today.

-You can see by just looking at him how professional he is.

-Yes.

-It seems to me that Murphy hasn't been acting on his own. He must've had help from some element of the criminal classes in Ireland. He must've got the gun from somewhere, and he hasn't been staying in a hotel so he'd have to have had some lodgings in or near Dublin. I wonder if we can't get somebody in his network to break ranks and tell us something about what is going on.

-What do you mean, put out a notice for a reward?

-No, I don't think a reward is going to do this one.

-What else then?

-This is the first time I can think of that a priest has been murdered in a confessional in Ireland. There may be honour among thieves but I suspect these murders might be a bridge too far. I think that even the criminal classes in Ireland are going to find this shocking. I also think that there may be a strong reaction to the idea of one of our own homebred scholars being needlessly gunned down. Maybe we should play those cards at the press conference and see if any information is forthcoming.

-You know you might well be right.

-It's worth a try. Let's prepare something for the media along those lines.

Chapter Twenty Five

The press conference

The following morning Pearse Street Gardaí station was like a mad house. No one, at least in living memory, could remember a priest being murdered in a church like this before. The TV, the radio and the newspapers were saying that this was not only a crime but an affront to the nation and of course to God himself. The death of the professor, bad as it was, was overtaken by the priest's.

At 12:45 PM the press conference began with the following statement.

-*Last night at about 9:30 pm there was a double murder in the University Church on St Stephen's Green. Father Conor O'Donnell who had served in the church as Parish priest for 30 years was shot in the head at close quarters. At approximately the same time Professor Finn Kelly was murdered in a similar way. At this point in time there is no clear view as to what the motive for these murders was. We can only speculate and our current thinking is leading us in the direction of suggesting that Father Conor O'Donnell was executed because of what he may have heard in his role as confessor. We think that Professor Finn Kelly was collateral damage. He was an internationally renowned mediaevalist working at O'Connell College who had recently been working on an assignment with the Vatican. We are awaiting our forensic team to give us more information about the type of gun used and any other evidence the murderer or murderers may have left behind. Of course, we are exploring other avenues of enquiries as well and we appeal to the public to come forward with any information they may have which might help us in our enquiries. Before finishing I would like to add that this is the first occasion I am aware of where a priest has been murdered in a confessional in Ireland and as such it is an outrage not only against the individual concerned but against everyone in the Republic who has the slightest concern for maintaining the Irish way of life. Anyone who has any information may contact me directly. As I have no further information at this time there will be no questions and we will call another press conference as soon as we have more information to provide the public. In the meantime, the public are requested to contact Inspector Shamus Quinn of the murder squad with any information they might have.*

Quinn was pretty happy with this statement and he thought it would produce the reaction that he was hoping for.

The media corps were clearly disappointed with this short statement but they knew that for present they would get no more so they rushed to get what they had in print and on to the television and radio and up on the Web.

The early afternoon newspapers produced the headline, *Priest and Professor Slaughtered in Chapel on the Green.* RTE and Sky started to research the murders of priests and professors. Many priests have been murdered over the years but these were for the most part for political reasons. The media couldn't find much on murdered professors. The media began interviewing anyone who had an opinion on these types of crimes. Both TV stations were going to make the most of this story.

By 4 pm that afternoon the US consulate sent an official to speak to Mr Murphy. The message was that it is true that a substantial number of passports were recently stolen in the USA. The consulate had sent a message off to the State Department and the FBI to enquire whether Murphy's passport number was amongst those reported but they had not yet received a reply. The official wanted to know if Murphy had been charged, or whether it was the intention of the Garda Síochána to charge him.

-No decision has yet been made. We don't know whether Mr Murphy is simply a victim or whether he is more deeply involved with the improper use of stolen property from the US government.

-Inspector Quinn, how long can you hold him for?

-Initially for 48 hours, and after that it'll depend on what evidence is required. We will have to wait and see. He will be comfortable enough here in the cells at Pearse Street station until we can sort this out.

-I don't think he is going to see it quite that way himself.

-That's up to him.

Quinn knew that he had to get more information from the FBI and so he spent the next couple of hours on the phone to various acquaintances in the US trying to get more information about Murphy and what he might have been up to on the other side of the Atlantic. His various contacts were most enthusiastic about being helpful but also emphasised the fact that they had little information to go on, and that there were thousands if not tens of thousands of Murphys in the US. Anyway they promised to do their best and to get back to Quinn as soon as possible.

As the afternoon came to an end, Quinn realised that he hadn't yet received the full report from his forensic team so he called up the Chief of the forensic squad.

-What news have you got for me about last night's murders?

-Well we don't have a full autopsy completed yet but I can give you a quick overview.

-Right. Let's have it.

-Both men were shot with the same 9 mm Beretta at what we would regard as close to point-blank range, that is, less than 6 feet between the gun and the target. That weapon would make a great mess with flying blood, flesh and bone. The murderer would have been covered by it.

-Yes.

-There is no sign of any struggle. There is no question that the deaths were instantaneous. The murderer left no trace behind. There are no fingerprints. There is no residual DNA. This has been a most professional job by a top professional assassin.

-So can you not help us at all?

-I'm afraid not. By the way, the old priest was dying of cancer and he didn't have long to go, so maybe his killing was a mercy. But that's not for me to judge.

-Okay thanks for the information. Let me know if anything else interesting crops up from your side.

-I almost forgot to tell you. Remember the Mullally case from a few weeks back?

-Yes. What about it?

-It was the same gun that killed Kelly and Mullally. So the Mullally murder is down to Murphy too. As O'Toole's name was on the computer screen in the dead man's office, we won't be out by a country mile if we say that Murphy killed Mullally to cover up his trail after he found out where O'Toole lived.

A visible sigh of relief emanated from Quinn.

-Oh, thank god for that. That's great news. There isn't a second manic out there in Dublin killing academics or academic administrators.

There was nothing else to be done that night, so the team went home for some needed rest.

The following morning Quinn was at his desk bright and early. He had told the others that there was no need to come in at the same time. It was now a waiting game to see whether Quinn's fishing exercise was going to produce any results.

At 10:30 the phone rang. It was the Gardaí traffic control office informing Finn that they just received an anonymous call to say that there was a gun in an airline travel bag on the number 48A bus leaving Dun Laoghaire in two minutes' time, and that it might be of interest to Inspector Seamus Quinn. The Garda who took this call believed that it was not a hoax but a genuine lead intended to be helpful to the Inspector. That was the sort of break that Quinn was looking for.

An unmarked squad car was urgently despatched from the Dun Laoghaire Gardaí Station to catch the bus as it was moving down the high street. The Garda caught up with the bus on George's Street Lower, and retrieved the bag and raced it back to Pearse Street.

The airline travel bag contained a Beretta 9 mm.

The forensic team was waiting.

-We will have a result back to you within the hour.

True to their word, by midday Quinn knew that this was the gun that had been used to murder Father O'Donnell, Professor Kelly and Mullally, but he had an extra bonus coming to him that he had not anticipated. There was a fingerprint on the gun.

Quinn could hardly believe his luck.

-That's sloppy for a professional. I wonder how he slipped up like that. But now he's banjaxed and that's all that counts.

-Yes, Inspector you've got him now.

-The good guys have got to get lucky some of the time. It's a pity that we have to rely on luck!

-Shall we ask Murphy for his fingerprints?

-I guess we could do that but on the other hand he has been handling glasses of water and cups of tea and coffee for nearly a day and a half now. We could pick up his fingerprints without having to let him know that we are going down that road.

-OK. Let's do that.

The fingerprints were obtained and by the end of the afternoon Quinn was able to confirm that one of Murphy's finger prints was on the gun. They could connect him to the crimes. Quinn immediately instructed Murphy's finger prints to be despatched to his contacts in the FBI and Europol.

Quinn was very pleased with this development and shared his feeling with his sergeant.

-Siobhan, it is surprising just how much the criminal justice system relies on the help of the criminal classes. It puts the expression *Set a thief to catch a thief* into perspective.

Siobhan did not answer immediately but slowly gave Quinn a wry smile.

-It is a pity, Inspector, we are not dealing with a thief.

It was now 30 hours since Murphy had been detained and Quinn's time was running out. It was urgent that they decide what their strategy was going to be. They now had firm evidence that Murphy was connected with the murders through the fingerprint on the weapon but that didn't place him at the scene of the crime. It might not be easy to do that as he was likely to have sewn up an alibi. Nor did having the gun throw any light on the motive. Finn had believed that Murphy was threatening because of the book but Quinn actually had no evidence that there had ever been a book. Maybe Finn was a fantasist? Maybe the book was a figment of his imagination. If there was a book there was certainly blood on it.

But there were now three unexplained murders in Dublin, two from the College and an elderly priest who had all the signs of being simple collateral damage.

Quinn wondered how he was going to be able to put a case together. Would he ever get enough evidence? Quinn wasn't sure. But he instinctively knew that Murphy was his man and he would nail him.

Chapter Twenty Six

Meeting the Commissioner

Quinn was still reluctant to confront Murphy with an accusation of the murders. He felt that his case wasn't strong enough and he now began to worry about the wider political ramifications of what had been going on at O'Connell College with the creation of the "lost" Oscar Wilde book.

Quinn asked Chief Superintendent Clancy, the man in charge of Pearse Street, if he could arrange for them to meet with Ireland's top cop the Commissioner, in order to discuss this case. Quinn was aware that this was an unusual request and he justified it by saying that there were a number of significant people involved, as well as the US Consulate, the FBI and Europol. The request was granted and the three men met within the hour.

-I'm sorry to trouble you with this matter but we're getting to a critical point in a case which has potentially disturbing political implications and I think it's much better for you to hear about it from me rather than read about it in the press or hear it on RTE.

Over the next half hour Quinn spelt out as best he could the detail of how the fake Oscar Wilde had been created, and how it had been sold for a king's ransom and how this had triggered the dispatch of a professional assassin to Ireland to eliminate the people who could alert the world to the fraud that had been perpetrated. And Quinn did not hold back on the guilt he felt about Finn's death.

The implications of this whole catastrophic situation were not lost on the Commissioner.

-Inspector, if this story gets out it'll bring the good name of O'Connell College into disrepute. It will also have severe implications for the status of Irish education in general. We have thousands and thousands of overseas students coming to Ireland every year. Also our universities have branches or centres abroad and the news of a fake like this will make people wonder whether they can still trust the quality of the education produced in this country. This is a serious matter.

-And there is more.

-What?

-If this gets out who is going to tell the Pope what has been happening in one, or maybe even more of his monasteries? We may trigger a diplomatic incident with the Holy See.

-This is potentially the worst situation we have had for twenty years.

-That's why I asked for this meeting. I am not entirely sure we will be able to bring Murphy to trial. As it stands, our evidence looks shaky. If he tries to produce an alibi for the time of the murders maybe his Irish friends will let him down. But maybe they won't. Money talks or prevents talk. So, we may end up with having a weapon and not an opportunity.

-So Inspector, you're worried about the motive for the murders.

-Exactly. We won't get a conviction unless we have a satisfying motive. We can hardly say the man is a raving lunatic and went around murdering a priest and a professor for fun. We could concoct a story about drugs or some sort of gang warfare, but I don't think for a minute that it would hold up under any serious scrutiny.

-My goodness Inspector. You're not proposing that we let him go.

-Oh no, far from it Commissioner. I want this man to spend a very long time behind bars in a penitentiary, somewhere.

-Well Australia has closed their doors to convicts so that's out of the question. What you have in mind?

-This man is not a newcomer to the assassination game. If you met him you would see that he is a most polished individual who thinks that he is really in control of the situation. He must have a long list of previous crimes. I have been in touch several times with the FBI and with Europol but I was only able to give them his fingerprints today. I am sure they are going to come up with something that he is wanted for.

-So Inspector, you're proposing that we forget about the murders in Dublin and ship him out to serve time in another jurisdiction. That's unusual isn't it? Don't you want crimes committed in Ireland to be punished in Ireland?

-Yes Commissioner, that has been our traditional stance and it's one about which I have always had strong reservations. If we put him in jail here for 20 years we have to look after his welfare, his health requirements, we have to feed him and entertain him at the Irish taxpayer's expense. Why should we do that Commissioner? Would we not be better off just making sure that someone else is going to lock him up and hopefully throw away the key?

-But Inspector, what you are asking me to consent to could be regarded as a cover-up. I personally don't see it quite that way, although I could argue that there are good cover ups and bad ones. I propose that for the moment we are going to have a complete news blackout on anything to do with Murphy and these murders and we will wait and see. I wonder if we should privately tell O'Connell College? Give the O'Connell College's Principal a briefing?

-Good God, no. Absolutely not.

-Inspector, I am not sure that what we are proposing is a politically correct view, in fact come to think of it, I know it's not, but I can certainly see the logic in it. But such a decision is above the pay grade of even a Commissioner. That decision will have to go to the Minister or even the Taoiseach. The best case for your suggested course of action is the lack of conclusive evidence.

-OK, Commissioner.

-What are we going to say about the people behind the professional assassin, whoever they might be?

-We have to be realistic. We won't be able to touch them from here. And although I am scared of an Irish scandal, I really shudder at the trouble we will generate if it gets out that an Order of holy monks is implicated in this. And there is the suggestion that there might be a Cardinal involved. There will be the greatest shite storm you have ever seen. Please excuse the local idiom.

-Yes. I see your point. So, tell me, where are we at the moment and what have we to do?

-The standard 48 hours' detention will expire tomorrow morning at approximately 10:30. If we don't have an extradition request by then we would technically have to release him. On the other hand, if we argue that the passport irregularity - and by the way we haven't finally confirmed that his passport is valid, and I suspect that it may not be - is linked to some terrorist activity we will be able to hold him for a considerably longer period of time.

-Terrorism?

-Well let's not forget that Ireland was a hotbed of terrorists for many years. You hardly need reminding that Michael Collins, our great Irish patriot, invented terrorism. Today there is still the odd loony who thinks that the Good Friday Agreement was a sell-out of the rights of Northern Irish Catholics. And remember that for a long time the Irish diaspora were active in sending guns to this country with the help of contacts in Boston. So it is not such a big leap to think that Murphy might be involved in something like that. -Inspector, I really like your way of thinking. We will keep Murphy here for a bit longer and will see what we can do to arrange for him to spend some time at the pleasure of someone else's government and taxpayers' expense. I'll inform the Minister of your plan and ask him to make sure that there will not be any other political ramifications.

On the way back to Pearse Street station Quinn was in a pensive mood.

-Inspector, you did a grand job in convincing the Commissioner to see the situation your way. I congratulate you. I am sure you have a long way to go in the Garda Síochána. If ever you need it, I will be a helping hand.

-Thank you very much Chief Superintendent Clancy. We are still some way from sorting this whole matter out and of course, I know how difficult it will be to convince my team of the argument I made for the Commissioner. I know ... I know that's not going to be easy.

Quinn was right.

-Inspector, I want to see this guy do serious time right here in Ireland where he committed the atrocities. We can nail him on the murder of the priest, and Kelly and with a bit of luck on Mullally and maybe even Walsh. O'Toole is still missing so we don't know what the hell has happened to him. I'd say that it was a racing certainty that Murphy was involved in that as well. You can't be serious to suggest that we are going to turn our backs on this list of crimes.

-First of all, remember that we only have the evidence of a fingerprint on a gun. A smart lawyer could take that to pieces. We think we might be able to find evidence that puts Murphy in a position to have committed the other crimes but I suspect that he is too smart a cookie for us to do that easily.

-But what about Kelly's evidence?

-At the end of the day, Kelly had nothing. It was pure intuition that led him to suspect Murphy, and you know how far that's going to get us in a court of law.

-Dammit. I am sure Murphy is guilty.

-So am I. But in the criminal justice system that is worth as much as a slap in the belly with a cold fish.

-If we hand this guy over to the FBI, what do we say to the public about the Dublin murders?

-I'll have to work on that.

-They will accuse us of being sloppy, or incompetent, or both.

-No. I won't let that happen.

-Oh. Yes.

-Well gentlemen what if I concoct the story that we have discovered that Kelly was a paranoid schizophrenic who murdered Mullally and who then confessed and then regretted it and murdered the priest and then committed suicide.

-You won't get away with that cock and bull story.

-Of course I won't. I'm not that much of an eejit. But I will come up with something much more convincing given a little time. If nothing else, we Irish are great story tellers. And be absolutely sure that this guy is not getting out of here before we are convinced that he is going to spend the rest of his life in circumstances that he is going to deeply regret. For now, we will hand him over to the terrorist lads and they will keep him safely for us until we know exactly how we will play this.

The following morning Murphy was brought before the Dublin Central Magistrates' Courts and the Public Prosecutor applied for the extension of his custody on the grounds that there was concern that he was involved in the smuggling of arms into the Republic of Ireland. No date was specified for his release.

Murphy protested loudly, threatening to sue the Irish criminal justice system for false arrest.

By that afternoon replies had been received from both the FBI and from Europol. According to the FBI, the fingerprint was not associated with the name of Joseph Murphy, but rather with a man called Victor Bachman. Victor Bachman had been arrested, charged and convicted of multiple homicides and had been serving several life sentences when he escaped from Sing Sing. In USA terms he was going to be in jail for at least a hundred and fifty years, or at least for the rest of his life.

The FBI had applied for urgent extradition papers which they believed could be processed rapidly with the cooperation of the Irish authorities. Someone in the FBI actually made a rather flippant suggestion that they could ask their friends in the CIA or the NSA if arrangements could be made for the private transfer of Murphy back to the good old USA, but Quinn who was not in the slightest bit amused immediately barked back that it was essential that full process of law be complied with.

His associates in Europol informed Quinn that the fingerprint was known to belong to Paul Silver who was also wanted by the police in several different countries. Silver was known to have had multiple aliases that included names like George Thompson, Brian Smith, Tommy Long and Freddie Lovejoy. It seemed to Quinn that the US had a priority call on Mr Murphy, or should one call him Mr Bachman or whatever.

In the meantime, Murphy was safely ensconced in Dublin jail and was not likely to move from there before he was taken to the airport for a ride home to Boston.

Quinn thought about the work that had gone into the Mullally murder and how they had been barking up the wrong tree. They couldn't admit that to anyone. He wondered what he would now do. He couldn't just close the Mullally file. It had to remain a mystery. He would have to leave it open for a while. But he would move his murder squad onto other matters.

The murder case or more correctly the murder cases were now out of Quinn's hands.

Chapter Twenty Seven
Where else can you go?

When Quinn's team was told about Murphy serving a hundred and
fifty-year sentence in Sing Sing they were less upset by the idea of
shipping him back to the US. It was generally agreed that the
resources of the Irish penal system were needed to help rehabilitate
Irish men and women who had strayed, and there was no point in
holding foreigners in Irish jails unnecessarily. It was also made clear
that this was not an official view of the Garda Síochána. Quinn made
sure that everyone in his team was aware that what had really
happened at the University Church and St Stephen's Green had to be
kept secret. The statement was made to the effect that Father Conor
O'Donnell had been a victim of drug gang warfare because he had
been known to have made sympathetic comments about members of
one of the gangs. Professor Finn Kelly's death was ascribed to
collateral damage. This poor man had been in the wrong place at the
wrong time. Nothing more and nothing less. The Mullally case was
an entirely different matter and was for the time being to remain
unsolved.

The O'Connell College's Oscar Wilde affair was satisfactorily swept
under the carpet.

Quinn had been told about the email from Maria and he was
struggling as to how to deal with it. Maria was not Finn's next of kin
so there was no reason for the Gardaí to say anything. That did not
rest well with Quinn as he worked out what to do.

Later that morning Quinn was called by the duty sergeant to the
reception desk at Pearse Street.

-Dr Sean O'Toole is here to see you.

-What?

-Dr Sean O'Toole. He says he is from O'Connell College and that you asked him to come in and make a statement.

Quinn was down to the reception desk in a flash.

-What the hell! Where have you been? We've all been looking for you.

-I was working on my latest book and I'm pleased to say it is now finished. My cousins, that is my mother's brother's children have a cottage in Ballyfitzbegbie in Wexford. It's a wonderful place to work. It is up in the hills, right in the middle of some dense woodland. It is a 3-mile walk to the nearest village. There is electricity there but no Internet. I do get a signal on my mobile phone, but it isn't a good one and it's often intermittent. I said I'd come and see you as soon as I got back to Dublin. So here I am.

-But what about your car?

-What car?

-The five-year-old blue Vauxhall.

Oh that old thing. I haven't used that for ages. It's been standing in the field behind my mother's house for the past year. I've been meaning to sell it, but I've been far too busy doing other things. What happened to it?

-it was involved in a terrible accident and we think the driver was killed?

-When did that happen?

-Nearly a week ago.

-Well Inspector, that's nothing to do with me. I have been far away in Ballyfitzbegbie. It must have been stolen. It was hardly my mother as I have just spoken to her.

-Feckin joy-riders again. And we thought that it was you who ended up in the Liffey. It was probably some stupid drunken kid.

-I hate the word joy-rider. I don't have any sympathy for car thieves.

-So, Dr O'Toole you haven't been keeping up with the news?

-No. Anything interesting been happening?

-Yes. I think that you had better come and sit down.

Quinn took Sean into the interview room and over the next 15 minutes explained to him what had been happening during the course of the previous few days. Finn was not only dead, but he had been murdered in a brutal way.

Sean was completely devastated. He was sad beyond description. His lifelong pal was no longer with them. This was a monumental loss to him. He was also hopeful that one day Finn would ask him to write another Oscar Wilde play and give him €100,000 for his trouble.

-What can I do, inspector, what happens now?

-I don't know. Finn's body is in the morgue and will be available to be released in the next day or two. I don't know if any of us know who his next-of-kin is.

-Finn's mother died a long time ago and his father passed away a few years back now. He had no brothers or sisters. I think there was an uncle and aunt but I have a feeling that they went to live in England more than 10 years ago now. So there may not be next-of-kin nearby. It is possible that the College has a next-of-kin on record. -We will ask the College but in the meantime, I wonder if you would look after the funeral arrangements.

-I don't think that it would be appropriate to have his body unclaimed, do you. Please let the relevant authorities know that when the body is released, I will have some undertakers come and pick it up. I expect that there will be money in his estate to cover the funeral expenses. I am sure that members of the College and some of his students will want to attend his funeral service?

-OK

-I suppose I'm going to have to find somewhere to bury him?

-I have a feeling that this is going to be all up to you … Sean, I think it is also important for you to know that although we have taken Mr Murphy out of circulation, it is perfectly possible that there will be other Mr Murphys who may come to finish the job that this one didn't complete.

-What do you mean?

-I would bet that Murphy thought you had died in the accident in the docks. For now that suits both you and the Gardaí, and we don't want to go informing the people behind Murphy that you are still around. I think your book the Soul of the Author and your lectures on the topic of understanding the inner workings of particular writers attracted the attention of these gangsters. I suggest that you take a low profile for some time to come.

-But what exactly does that mean?

-I don't mean that you necessarily have to go into hiding, but I suggest you give up your public speaking engagements and get rid of any suggestion that you are able to teach people how to imitate the great authors of the past.

-That will be a substantial reduction in my income as I was doing rather well out of fees I earned doing that.

-The fees won't be much use to you if you are not around to collect or spend them.

-You may know inspector that I have been casting my eye around for a new position at another university and just before I went off on my writing retreat in Wexford, I received an invitation to an interview

with a university in Australia. I never really wanted to go to
Australia, but I have a feeling that, under the circumstances a few
years in the Antipodes might be a good thing for me.

-You know I think that is a splendid idea.

Quinn thought to himself, but he was too polite to say, that he'd be
lucky to get into Australia considering the mischief he'd been up to
in the past couple of years. Of course he hoped that Sean would, as it
would allow the Australian police to look after his problems.

-If you go to Australia make sure you don't leave any of the debts
you owe to the bookies at Fairyhouse behind you. You don't want
writs or bailiffs from the Irish courts following you out there.

-Of course not. What a horrible suggestion that is! I always pay my
debts!

-By the way Sean, Finn was becoming quite attached to a lady he
met in the Vatican called Maria. Finn was planning to take his
sabbatical in Rome to be near her. She emailed him yesterday and
clearly she does not know that he is dead. I think that you should
intervene on your friend's behalf and break the news to her. Maybe
she will want to come to the funeral?

-Oh dear. Oh dear. That's terrible.

-If you really don't want to do it I will. But it is probably better
coming from a friend. Did you ever meet her?

-No. I will look after it. It is the least I can do.

Sean went back to the College and Moira Flannigan produced
Maria's email address.

*I am a very long-standing friend of Finn Kelly's. We have known
each other since schooldays. He was my closest friend.*

I am very sad to have to tell you that Finn died the day before yesterday. He was murdered in a church on St Stephen's Green near O'Connell College. I will send you some more details later when the police confirm what actually happened.

I will also let you know about the funeral arrangements as soon as I know them. I think that there will be a memorial service at O'Connell College. If you wish to come, I will meet you at the airport and take you to the funeral.

Please send me your telephone number and address.

The next day funeral arrangements were made and circulated on the grapevine in College. Sean had made some enquiries about the funding of this event and was told that Finn's estate would pay the bill. He was not unhappy to spend Finn's money. He thought that Finn might have died intestate and if that was the case, in Sean's view the money would be wasted. So, he proposed to make a big splash. Finn was an important professor and there were many people who were genuinely fond of him. It was decided that there would be a memorial service for Finn conducted by the College Chaplin. The Principal agreed to say a few words. And then, a swanky reception. The date was settled for the following Friday afternoon and Sean contacted Maria who decided to come to the funeral.

Maria arrived on the early flight from Rome and was picked up at the Airport by Sean who was standing at arrivals holding a board with her name on it. She had no luggage other than a small overnight bag, so she came through quickly. She intended to spend one night in Dublin and she had booked herself into the big hotel near Finn's old office.

Sean felt obliged to tell Maria some of the detail about Finn's death but he did not tell her about the anxiety he had been going through over his telephone encounters with Mr Murphy. Sean felt that would be an issue the Gardaí should address if they felt the need to.

In any event she was too upset to hold much of a conversation with him and he gave her time to be alone in the O'Connell College library until the funeral service began. They were not in the mood for lunch that day.

An hour later Sean returned to the library.

-Maria, I will take you down to the chapel were we are having the memorial service. It is on the other side of the campus.

-Thank you.

As they walked Sean began to talk to Maria.

-You know Finn and I were very old friends. We had gone to school together.

-I don't think that he mentioned you to me.

-And neither did he tell me about you. How long had you known Finn?

- I met him as soon as he arrived to work for the Curia.

-And how long had you two been involved?

-Well we started to see each other socially a few months after he arrived in Rome. But I would not say we were involved until a month or two ago. We had only just started talking about the possibility of a future together. Finn had thought that he might do his next sabbatical in Rome. It wasn't all that easy to get close to Finn.

-Yes. I know how remote he sometimes was.

-Well, we had been able to start to break that down.

-This whole business must be a terrible shock to you.

-I was stunned and I still am stunned.

-I can see that.

-Over the years I have been very unlucky with men and I was beginning to think that my luck was changing. But clearly it was not.

-Sorry to hear that.

-Although I was shocked by the news of Finn's murder there was something deeply ingrained in the back of my mind which said to me that I should not be too surprised. It was a very funny feeling I had. You see Finn had obviously been mixing with some very racy people in Rome. The Dameri family are known to be pushy capitalists and I have heard through my family connection with the Carabinieri that they were being considered for prosecution a few times. That was just not a good scene for Finn.

-On what charges were they think of prosecuting them?

-I was never interested enough to ask or find out. And I knew that there had been plenty of rumours about the Gallery Garibaldi dealing in prohibited artworks. I was never comfortable when I thought of Finn dealing with these people.

-Didn't you ask Finn about these things? And what did he say?

-I sort of did but it was obvious that he didn't want to talk too much about them and I did not feel that it was my place to be too nosey. I felt I had to play it cool as they say in America.

-Maybe you should have been a bit noseier.

-Yes. Indeed. But I am not sure if that would have discouraged Finn in any way except perhaps discourage his interest in our relationship.

-That could be true. Finn did have an obstinate streak.

-I just need to get through today and then get home tomorrow. I am glad you are here to be with me.

-And then what?

- Fortunately I have a very busy job which I generally like. The bosses in the Curia don't know about Finn and I and I can't tell them. They are very disapproving of relationships between anyone who works with or for them. I am going to take some of my annual leave and I am going back to my parent's home for a week. They live on the coast and it is a good place to get away from it all.

-And then?

-I'll just have to see.

As they arrived at the chapel Quinn was already standing there waiting. He was a man who was never, well hardly ever, late and that usually meant that he usually arrived early for appointments.

Quinn was still feeling quite bad about this whole affair and he had decided that the least he could do was to attend the funeral. He would represent the Garda Síochána and would come dressed in uniform. He was also beginning to suffer from some self-doubt about his decision not to try to catch the men behind Murphy. Letting them get away scot-free was creating a bitter taste in his mouth. But he just didn't know where to start the hunt for these villains.

Sean introduced Quinn to Maria and he presented his condolences. They did not discuss the investigation of the murders. The three of them sat together. They were as close as Finn had to family. There were at least 300 people at the service. A few of these were students. The Principal spoke admiringly about Finn's achievements and especially about how highly he was regarded in the Vatican.

Kathleen Daly gave an account of his work with the Shelter and how he had been able to raise so much money for such a good cause. Finn was going to be sorely missed in that quarter. There was a suggestion that a plaque would be put on the wall next to the door of the Shelter commemorating Finn.

Quinn wondered what the service would have been like if the story of Being Excellent had come out and if Finn's role in it was known. He reflected that the consequences of the easy money that Finn found for the Shelter may not yet be fully accounted for. He knew that if the whole truth came out, including the fact that Italian monks had a hand in re-producing the book there would be shocking consequences. And he wondered if O'Connell College has seen the last of its members murdered for this book. There was certainly blood on this book.

A few hymns were sung and there were some readings from the Holy Books. It was all rather flat. People were going through the motions required when someone significant dies.

The service was over in thirty minutes. Everyone shuffled out of the church. There would be cocktails and canapés in the Senior Common room after the burial. The funeral cortege made its way slowly through the Dublin traffic to Mount Jerome where a plot had been hurriedly acquired for Finn. It was understood that he had some distant family members buried there some years before, but no one knew who they were or where their graves could be found.

The Dublin weather obliged with a fine rain and mist which produced an extra gloomy feel to the occasion.

The hearse managed to get within 20 metres of the grave side.

There were about 30 people standing around the grave as the coffin was lowered by four strong grave-diggers. Sean, Maria and Quinn stood together by the side of the grave while the priest muttered the rite of committal and a few last words over the coffin.

Maria bravely held back the tears she could feel building up at the back of her eyes.

Standing at the graveside Quinn could not help but remember his disastrous words to Finn. *Don't make Murphy a bogeyman.* Oh! How that now seemed to be such a completely inadequate and inappropriate thing to say. He asked himself what had he really been thinking? Quinn had real difficulty in coming to terms with how this case had turned out. He had grown used to success as one of Dublin's most accomplished detectives. He had put plenty of villains behind bars. He saw the cutting short of Finn's life as his failure and the taste of that was bitter. But then there was a streak in him which popped up and said, *if only* Finn had some evidence. Almost any evidence would have helped. Quinn knew the futility of indulging in fantasy thinking based on words like *if only*. If only was a dead end thought. Waste of time. He must avoid that. He promised himself that he would never make a mistake like this again.

At first Sean O'Toole's thoughts were firmly fixed on the issue of how sad it was to lose his old friend. He asked himself how many decades had he known Finn? Three or four? Maybe three and a bit. But then he thought of Paddy Walsh as well. A newer acquaintance. Walsh had not been as great a friend as Finn but he had been one of O'Toole's best students and they had both really enjoyed working with each other. The book they co-authored was good. O'Toole's mind drifted to Oscar Wilde's quip, "to lose one parent may be regarded as a misfortune; to lose both looks like carelessness". Should this apply to friends as well as parents? Wilde's wit just wasn't appropriate and such a thought was too frivolous for this sombre occasion. O'Toole chastised himself silently. He knew that he must keep focusing on the event. But that was hard. The real question now was what would he do next? Would he give up Dublin in search of a new life in a faraway place or at his age was he too accustomed to his comfortable way of living in Ireland? He worked for a good university. He had increasing publication opportunities. But then there was the issue of whether someone might come looking for him in the way that Murphy had come for Finn. This thought seriously disturbed him. No that wasn't the way to describe it. It really frightened him. What could he do? He just didn't know but he did know that this was neither the time nor the place to spend too much energy on his thoughts. He had to focus on the funeral.

Maria's thoughts were much less complicated as she watched the final stages of Finn's funeral. This was not the first funeral of a man in her life. Giorgio had died some years back. It had taken quite some time to get over that tragedy. Two men who had been important in her life had died young. She wondered whether she had been cursed but she was too rational to believe in hocus-pocus like that. Or was she? On the other hand, it was clear to her that she had been very unlucky and maybe that alone was a sort of curse. Maria wondered about the limits of luck and whatever the opposite of luck was; she wasn't sure what word to use for this. Was it misfortune, she wondered? But dwelling on the past was problematic. Maria wanted to leave the past behind but she wasn't sure if she knew how. She was just too sad to think about the future. So she had to keep her mind on the present. She remembered that years ago she had believed in the afterlife. There had been a time when she believed that Finn or some part of him would now be looking down on her and the others. But this was no longer the case. She had given up such fanciful thoughts. Finn was simply gone. The funeral was the thing to focus on. She was sorry that things had not turned out better and she knew that she would remember Finn fondly for a very long time.

Maria looked up and to her surprise she noticed a face among the people standing on the other side. He was wearing a black trilby with an oversized bow on the side. She felt the face was familiar but as it was raining and the men's hats were drawn down over their foreheads and Maria's eyes were full of tears, she did not immediately recognise him.

Who was that she wondered? It had to be someone from Rome. Was it an official from the Vatican? Had the Catholic Church sent a representative to Finn's funeral? That would be a very nice tribute to Finn. But it would also be most unusual. No the man did not look like he was associated with the Catholic Church. It slowly dawned on her. She had seen him recently at one of these receptions in Rome. Yes. It was in the American Embassy. He had been talking to the

Cardinal. Which Cardinal was it? She was scratching around in her head for a name. It was the one that Finn had seen. She couldn't remember the Cardinal's name. But she did recall the name of the man across the way from her. It was Jeremy Williamson from the Gallery Garibaldi. What was he doing here?

Maria turned her head towards Quinn.

-Inspector, I think that man over there with the hat pulled down over his eyes is Jeremy Williamson who used to or maybe still owns the Gallery Garibaldi in Rome. Finn had quite a lot to do with him when he was working for the Vatican. I think that they may have done some business together. Maybe you might like to talk to him about Finn?